THE DEAD

DON'T CARE

JONATHAN LATIMER

NO EXIT PRESS

1987

No Exit Press
18 Coleswood Road
Harpenden, Herts AL5 1EQ

British Library Cataloguing in Publication Data

Latimer, Jonathan
   The Dead Don't Care
   I. Title
   813'.52 [F]   PS3525.A75/
   ISBN 0 948353 07 4
   ISBN 0 948353 08 2 (pb)

            9 8 7 6 5 4 3 2 1

First published in the USA by Doubleday, Doran & Co Inc, 1938

Printed by Guernsey Press, C.I.

CHAPTER ONE

SUNSET splashed gold paint on the windows of the
white marble house, brought out apricots and pinks
and salmons in the flowering azaleas. The sports
roadster turned left round the freshly scrubbed trunk
of a royal palm, gravel crunching under its tyres; then
right round a fountain, and came to a halt below a
marquee of iron and amber glass.

Thomas O'Rourke, awe on his long, dark, tanned
face, ran grey eyes over the massive front of the house,
allowed his breath to pass his lips in a half-whistle of
admiration.

'Not bad,' he said.

His companion shut off the roadster's engine. His
name was William Crane and he was looking at the brass
knocker on the great ebony door with perplexity.
'Are you supposed to pound that thing?' he demanded.
A partially recovered black eye, his left, gave him a
humorously reckless appearance.

'Why not?' O'Rourke asked. 'We got invitations.'

'All right.' Crane slid off the leather seat on to the
gravel. He mounted the three crescent-shaped steps,
was about to raise the knocker, when a noise from the
drive made him turn his head.

Two pink flamingos slowly approached the roadster
from the fountain. They walked with rheumatic
dignity, moving their stilt-like legs deliberately, carrying
their heads at an inquiring angle. Their eyes were like
highly polished waistcoat buttons.

'For the love of Mike!' said Crane.

'I'm glad you see 'em too,' O'Rourke said from the roadster. 'For a minute I thought I had the horrors again. What in hell are they?'

The flamingos halted ten feet from him. They looked, with their patrician beaks, their politely inquiring heads, their bright, unblinking eyes, like two elderly savants. They looked as though they were wondering what in hell O'Rourke was.

'They're kind of birds,' said Crane vaguely, turning back to the knocker.

O'Rourke, apprehensive of flamingos, slid under the roadster's wheel and followed Crane. As he neared the ebony door it opened, disclosing a dour man with black hair and thin lips. Years of repressions had made a mask of his face. He was the butler.

'Mr. O'Rourke?' he asked. 'And Mr. Crane?'

He wore patent leather shoes, dark trousers, a Dubonnet-red cummerbund, and a white drill coat tailored like a mess jacket.

'Mr. Crane,' Crane said, 'and Mr. O'Rourke.'

'Beg your pardon, sir.' The man left the ebony door open, came out on to the first crescent-shaped step. 'Mr. Essex is expecting you. Shall I bring in your luggage?'

Crane gave him the roadster's keys. 'In the dickey.'

He started to follow the butler down the steps, but O'Rourke's elbow nudged his ribs. 'Take a look at the window above the door.'

Casually Crane's eyes roved over the grounds, the house. He saw the arched back of the fountain, the green expanse of lawn, the dusk-subdued azaleas, the palms, the white wall of the house, the window above the door. . . .

His eyes went on to the roadster, to the butler tugging at the dickey seat, but his mind retained a photographic impression of the window. A man was seated in the

recess, his face shadowed by a hat pulled over his eyes.
He was peering down at them.   He looked sinister.

The butler had the dickey seat open.   He put one
foot on the chromium bumper and reached down for
the large pigskin suit-case.   His drill jacket slid up
his back, disclosing a small blue pistol, possibly a .25
calibre Colt, tucked under his cummerbund.

For a divided second Crane's and O'Rourke's eyes met.

One hand on the knob of the door to Crane's bedroom,
the butler said: 'I shall try to locate Mr. Essex, sir.'

'Thank you,' said Crane.

The butler's eyes were small and black and unblinking.   He stared into the room until the door, apparently
closing of its own volition, swung shut with a thud.

O'Rourke was seated on the arm of an easy chair.
'Nice looking guy,' he observed.

'Like a wildcat.'   Crane flung open the french windows
on the side of the room opposite the door, stepped
out on a Spanish balcony.   'Hello!   The ocean!'

Below him was a very large patio, luxuriant with
small palms, clumps of tropical flowers, gaily coloured
umbrellas, and metal tables and chairs painted a
brilliant orange.   At the open end of the patio was a
white swimming-pool and behind that was a magnificent
beach of ash-blond sand.   Rollers from the Atlantic,
moving ponderously, cast themselves on the beach,
making silver lines in the dusk.

Moving to the french window O'Rourke dispassion-
ately regarded the scene.   'What's the set-up here?' he
asked.   Speaking made the cigarette dangling from
his lips glow angrily.

Crane shrugged his shoulders.   He was enchanted
by the perfection of the view, by the serenity of the
verdant patio, by the languid beat of the surf, by the
soft warm wind on his face; a wind heavy with the
perfume of flowers.   He could almost taste that wind.

'Well, we should worry,' said O'Rourke, 'as long as the food is good.'

Crane lit a cigarette and contentedly filled his lungs with smoke. The food would be good, and the liquor. And the beds. He was very tired after the long drive from Charleston and he thought with pleasure of the double bed in his room. He always slept well with the noise of the sea in his ears. It was pleasant, too, to be sent from rain-swept New York into the languorous perfection of Miami in March, or rather the perfection of Key Largo, fifty miles south of Miami.

Moreover, he approved of what he had seen of the Essex house, of the Essex estate. He always preferred to pursue his occupation as a detective in luxurious surroundings among rich, congenial people. One of the troubles with crime was its prevalence among criminals.

O'Rourke said: 'I could do with a bottle of beer.'

Crane leaned one elbow on the balcony rail. 'Ring up old lynx-eyes and tell him to fetch you one,' he suggested. He peered out at the ocean; navy blue now that the sun had set.

'Good idea,' said O'Rourke.

Left alone, Crane wondered what had happened to the young Essexs. It couldn't have been very serious or he'd have read about it in the newspapers. They were always in the newspapers. The boy, Penn, twenty-five years old, had a penchant for fast automobiles, chorus girls and breach of promise suits, in the order named. The girl, Camelia, twenty-three years old, had most recently been forcibly taken from a liner as she was about to elope to Peru with a gentleman styling himself Count Paul di Gregario of the Holy Roman Empire. The removal had been accomplished by attorneys for the Union Trust Company, trustee of the Essex fortune and guardian of the Essex children, which had discovered there was no longer a Holy Roman

Empire and therefore di Gregario was no count. He was also, it developed, already married.

Crane hoped that O'Rourke would be thoughtful enough to order two bottles of beer. He decided to go in and make certain of the second bottle. He flipped his cigarette into the air, paused to watch the arc of the descending glow. His eyes caught sight of the figure of a man on another balcony over the left wing of the house, at right angles to his balcony. He felt the hair rise on the back of his neck and resisted an impulse to dive through the french window to his room. The man might have been a statue, so motion-less did he hold himself. There was the same sinister intentness, the same poise, the same down-pulled hat that had characterized the man in the front window, but Crane did not think this was the same man. This man seemed smaller, but he looked very unpleasant.

Once inside his room, Crane wiped his forehead with a linen handkerchief. 'Whew!' he said. He opened the cupboard door and looked inside, then peered under the bed.

O'Rourke watched him from the bathroom door. 'Lost something?'

'I thought maybe they had a guy tucked in here too.' Crane told him of the man on the balcony and added: 'The house is full of guys.'

'Maybe the Seminoles have risen,' suggested O'Rourke.

Crane was about to say, 'Nuts', when there was a knock on the door. Instead he said, 'Maybe it's the beer,' then, louder: 'Come in.'

A hollow-chested young man in a white linen suit came into the room. He had a thin face, blond hair and a pointed chin. He didn't look well. He looked very much like his newspaper pictures.

He smiled at them, said: 'I'm Penn Essex.' Carefully he closed and bolted the door. 'I'm certainly glad to see you,' he said.

Crane introduced O'Rourke and himself, then asked: 'What's the trouble? Colonel Black didn't have time to tell us.' He sat down on a bedspread the colour of guava jelly, rested an arm on the carved headpiece.

Essex sat in the larger of the two easy chairs. His face was mostly eyes. He began, 'It started . . .' then abruptly turned toward Crane, anger in his voice. 'I suppose I'm a fool to be in a funk over this; it's so damn silly. But I am. And you'll laugh. . . .'

'No, we won't,' said Crane. 'Start at the beginning.'

'Well, anyway, you know about these things . . . Whether they're real or not.' He paused and they could hear the deep noise of the surf. 'It's notes.'

'Notes?'

'Here.' Essex uncoiled from his chair, thrust three sheets of paper into Crane's hand. 'Read them.' He turned to O'Rourke, leaning against the hall door, and said: 'Probably somebody's idea of a practical joke.' His voice didn't sound convincing.

Crane examined the first note. It was crudely printed in red ink on a diagonally torn sheet of white paper. It read:

'MISTER ESSEX,

'You come clean, or else . . . Follow instructions when they come. . . . Don't try to escape because I am watching every move you make. . . .

'THE EYE.'

'Well, well, well,' said Crane in a pleased tone of voice. He laid the note face down on the bed and picked up the second between his thumb and forefinger.

It read:

'MISTER ESSEX,

'Hire more guards if you like. . . . They will do you no good. . . . Your instructions are to get fifty thousand dollars ($50,000) in unmarked bills . . . keep them handy. . . .

'THE EYE.'

This sheet of paper had also been torn diagonally from a larger piece. Crane picked up the first piece and placed the two together. They matched. The ink on both, too, was red. The paper seemed to be of excellent texture and Crane held first one note, then the other, to the light, but there was no water-mark.

Essex was pacing back and forth in front of O'Rourke. His feet were noisy on the absinthe-green tile floor, silent on the red and black and white Mexican saddle rug. His eyes kept coming back to Crane.

The third sheet was torn like the others and the ink was red. Crane held it to his nose and drew a long, slow breath. There was no odour. He read:

'ESSEX,
        'The time nears when you must pay your debt. . . . You have a choice. . . . Fifty thousand in small, unmarked bills . . . or your life! Instructions follow. . . . Don't try to escape. . . .

'THE EYE.'

Crane blinked his eyes, laid the sheet on the bed, and said: 'The fellow's getting familiar; he didn't call you mister in the last note.'

'Familiar?' Essex's eyes were wide. 'You don't know how familiar he is.'

'What do you mean?'

'The way he gets the notes to me.' Abruptly, Essex halted, one foot ahead of the other, in the middle of a step. 'I find one in my wallet, another. . . .'

'Wait.' Rays from the indirect lamp in the corner shadowed Crane's eyes, made both of them appear to have been blackened. 'Better tell us in chronological order. When did you get the first note?'

Essex returned to his chair, sat with elbows on knees, chin on fists. 'The first note came just a month ago, on the twenty-seventh of February. It was the damnedest thing. . . . I had some rooms at the Waldorf, in New York, and I woke up in the morning with something scratching my chin. It was the note, pinned to the pillow.' He smiled at Crane. 'I never came out of a hang-over so quickly in my whole life.'

Crane, who was also troubled with hang-overs, felt a bond of sympathy between them. He smiled, too, and asked: 'Any idea how it got there?'

Essex shook his head.

'Anybody staying with you?'

After a pause so slight that Crane could not be sure it was a pause, Essex replied: 'Nobody but Brown, my man.'

'Your valet?'

'Not exactly a valet. Sort of a combination valet and body-guard. He used to be a top-flight welterweight.'

From the door, O'Rourke spoke. 'Buster Brown?'

'Yes. That was his ring name. His real name's Chester.'

'I saw him fight Tony Capezzio in Pittsburgh,' said O'Rourke. 'He hung his Sunday punch on the Wop in the fourth round.'

'Did you come home alone that night, Mr. Essex?' inquired Crane.

'Yes. I went to a party and I guess I got a little tight, but I certainly would have known if anybody came home with me.'

O'Rourke said: 'He would've been a great fighter if he hadn't had such big feet. He carried dynamite in both hands.'

'He still does,' said Essex.

Crane asked: 'And you don't think he could have put the note on your pillow?'

'He could have, all right, but I don't think he did. Especially in view of the others.'

'Yes, you better tell us about the others.'

'Well, the next note (the one about the fifty thousand dollars) came the day after I got down here. That was ten days ago. I found it in my wallet.'

'So?'

Essex's grin failed to conceal his anxiety. 'I can't even imagine how it got there. The Eye must be handy at magic. I put five hundred dollars in the wallet and drove up to Miami for a fling at the Blue Castle; that's Roland Tortoni's place, y'know.' Crane bobbed his head and Essex continued: 'The note wasn't there when I put the five hundred in the wallet, but when I opened it to buy some chips for the roulette game it fell out. I can tell you it gave me a start.'

'I can see how it might,' said Crane.

'And a funny thing was that two of the five one-hundred dollar bills had disappeared.'

O'Rourke said: 'That wouldn't be funny to me.' He was resting one arm on the door-knob, his silver-streaked head against the upper panel. His grey-blue eyes rested on Crane's brown eyes. 'A dip?'

'Might be.' Crane explained to Essex: 'Mr. O'Rourke suggests some one might have picked your pocket, removed the two hundred dollars, inserted the note and then replaced the wallet.'

'That's barely possible,' agreed Essex, 'but it seems to me a very risky way for The Eye to get the note to me.'

Crane asked: 'Where was Brown that evening?'

'Somewhere between New York and Miami, driving the Bugatti down. That's why I've eliminated him.'

Crane frowned. 'And the third note?'

'It came four days ago, in the morni . . .'

With a liquid movement, O'Rourke unlocked the door, turned the knob, flung the door open. A man in a white monkey coat regarded them with a startled expression on his face. He carried a tray on which there were two glasses and four bottles of imported Holland beer. He had black hair, big brown eyes, a small, round face.

'I believe you desired beer? . . .'

'Bring it in,' said Crane.

The man put the tray on the small table beside the bed, fumbled in his pocket.

'Never mind,' said Crane. 'We'll open them.' He shook his head in response to the question in O'Rourke's eyes.

O'Rourke stepped out of the doorway, let the servant depart, and closed and bolted the door. 'I think the guy was doing some listening,' he said.

Essex's face was pale. 'I hope not; I'd hate to have everybody know about the notes or that you are detectives.' He brushed by Crane's knees, picked up the French phone by the bed, spun the dial once. 'Craig,' he said, 'how long ago did you send Carlos up to Mr. Crane's room with the beer?'

The phone spluttered.

'Thanks.' Essex turned to Crane. 'Five minutes.'

O'Rourke said: 'Let's get the guy and find out what his idea is.'

'We'd better wait,' said Crane. 'We don't want to tip our hand yet.' He took one of the dark green bottles, tossed it to O'Rourke. 'You've got an opener, haven't you, Tom?'

O'Rourke opened the bottle, exchanged it for an unopened one. Essex said he didn't believe he cared for any beer. O'Rourke drank his beer from the bottle, Crane from a glass. It tasted fine. It was smoother, less carbonated than American beer.

After a second drink, Crane asked: 'And the third note?'

'That one really scared me. I . . .'

'I don't blame you for being scared,' said Crane in a sympathetic tone. 'Fifty thousand or your life. . . .'

'That wasn't what did it. I've received lots of nasty letters.' He moved nervously in his chair. 'But never one like this.' He made a feeble attempt to laugh. 'It was in my hand when I woke up—in my hand!'

'Gosh!' Crane's brown eyes were wide. 'How do you figure it got there?'

'I suppose somebody came in through my window—the door to the bedroom was locked—and put it there.' He ran fingers through his blond hair. 'That's what I don't like; the idea of somebody prowling around my room.'

Crane said: 'It's curious that two of the notes should have come to you in bed. You're sure you weren't'—he coughed delicately to show he meant no offence—'ahem—with some one?'

Surprisingly, Essex smiled. His face became younger; he looked, with his white skin, like an unhealthy boy. 'You've been reading about me in the newspapers,' he said. 'I assure you they exaggerate; I sleep alone.' He detected an expression of doubt on Crane's face, added: 'This would be no time to lie, anyway, with possibly my life at stake.'

'Or fifty thousand dollars?'

'Much more likely my life. I haven't an idea where I'd get fifty thousand dollars.'

In the following silence, the leisurely beat of the surf, like the delayed *tempo* of a tango, came to them. Out at sea some birds called hoarsely. The air was oppressive.

Essex said: 'I'm not joking. Dad left everything tied up in trust for me and Camelia. We get an allowance, but mine goes a lot faster than it comes.'

'And you couldn't get extra money if it meant your life?' asked Crane.

'Oh, sure, if the trustees thought my life was *really* in danger. But they wouldn't be apt to pay fifty thousand dollars to anybody who threatened me.'

'Would you pay it on the strength of these notes if you had it?'

'Hell, no.' Essex's pointed jaw was set stubbornly. 'I'm worried, but I'm not that scared.'

'How much is your allowance?'

'Camelia and I each get two thousand a month.'

'That's not so much,' said Crane calmly, 'when you consider the upkeep of this place and the Long Island estate.'

'Oh, no. All that's paid by the trust company. Even the food and the servants. The allowance is for our personal use.'

O'Rourke, still leaning against the door, let his breath run through his teeth. 'A fellow could struggle along on that.'

'Not this fellow.' Essex's expression was petulant. 'I keep just one jump ahead of the bill collectors. It's terribly annoying. Yet the trust company won't listen to any hints that my allowance should be increased.' His voice was bitter. 'You'd think it was their money, the way they hoard it.'

Crane was looking at the third note. He read: 'The time nears when you must pay your debt.' He glanced at Essex. 'Do you owe somebody?'

Essex's voice didn't sound convincing. 'No. No, I don't. Nothing but small debts . . . clothes, and hotel bills, and liquor bills. I don't suppose any of them run over a couple of thousand.'

'You don't know what the note means by "your debt"?'

'No. Unless, of course, the fellow thinks because I inherited money I owe a debt to society. There are some people who think like that, you know.'

'So I've heard.' Crane put one of the unopened

beer bottles between his knees, jerked off the top with
the metal opener. 'Have you any enemies?'

'I suppose there are lots of people who don't like
me, but I'm sure none of them is gunning for me.'

'No people with shot-guns?' demanded Crane.

Essex's head jerked upward. 'What do you mean?
What have you heard?'

Crane deliberately poured the pale beer into his
glass, allowing it to foam. 'What am I supposed to
have heard?'

'Nothing.' Essex fastened angry eyes on the beer.
'Nothing. The trouble is there's always so much
gossip about me. It gets under my skin. I thought
maybe you'd heard some of it.'

'No,' said Crane.

O'Rourke said: 'Open a bottle for me, too.'

As Crane tugged at the cap, Essex said: 'I think
somebody's trying to scare me into paying him fifty
thousand dollars. Probably some racketeer. If he
knew me, he'd know I couldn't get my hands on any
such sum.'

'I don't know that "somebody" would have much
chance to stick notes in your hand while you're asleep,'
said Crane.

'That's so. Unless he had an accomplice in the
house. Do you think? . . .'

'I don't know, but it could be possible.' Crane took
a long drink of the beer. 'Is that the whole story?'

Essex nodded.

'No more notes?'

'No.'

'No attacks made on you?'

Essex's face expressed mild alarm. 'No.'

'And you're sure you can't think of a reason for
the notes?'

They could hear the ocean again.

'Yes.'

'Well, what do you want us to do?'

'Oh, I suppose the usual thing.' Essex relaxed in
his chair, allowing his chin to sag towards his chest.
'It wasn't so much my idea bringing you down here
as it was old Hastings's.' He caught the inquiry in
Crane's eyes. 'He's president of Union Trust and an
old friend of dad. He was worried about my safety,
thought the fellow might be a crank.'

'We're not bodyguards,' said Crane. 'We're
detectives.'

'I don't expect you to guard me; I've provided for
that. You're to see about The Eye . . . collar him
if you can.'

Crane complacently drank his beer. 'I wouldn't
worry much about anybody who signs himself The
Eye.'

'He sounds like he's been reading bad detective
stories,' O'Rourke said.

In three jerky motions, arms raising his body, legs
taking the weight over, arms shoving him into a balanc-
ing position, Essex came out of his chair. 'I can take
care of myself.' His face was angry. 'You get The
Eye, whoever he is.'

As he neared the door, Crane asked him: 'What are
we supposed to be?   Friends of yours?'

'Yes.   Only Camelia and the trust company repre-
sentative know you are detectives.'

Crane asked: 'Is that the fellow who sent us a wire
telling us to be here yesterday or we'd be fired?'

'Yes. Major Eastcomb. He's still furious over
your telegram in answer.'

'I only said "Nuts",' Crane said innocently.

'Well, you *are* a day late.' He opened the door
with his left hand. 'I'll tell everybody I met you both
in New York and invited you down here. That's
all right because Camelia's giving a sort of house
party.'

Crane let the last of the beer slide down his throat.
'I accept with pleasure.'

O'Rourke said: 'Me, too.'

CHAPTER TWO

'IT looks nice,' Crane said, padding across the beach
after O'Rourke.

They waded through green and silver breakers, digging
their feet in the sand against each impact, and swam
in the darker water beyond. The water was luke-cold;
the morning sun was warm. Where it was deep there
was no surf and the waves came like great wrinkles in
a bedspread, gently lifting them on rounded crests,
then lowering them into hollows.

'It is nice,' O'Rourke said.

In either direction, as far as they could see, ran a
wide beach the colour of Camembert cheese. Oases
of palms, leaning away from the ocean, made bright
green breaks in the shore-line, but inland the colour
was dull; grey-green where mangrove jungles covered
swamps, brown where the tundra of the Everglades
began.

O'Rourke dog-paddled toward Crane. 'What do
you think about this business?' he asked. 'Some of
the servants trying to knock off a piece of dough?'

'I don't know.' The sun warmed Crane's face. 'I
don't think our employer's telling all he knows.'

'He's scared, though. Damned scared.'

'Threatening letters scare most people.'

'I wouldn't know.' O'Rourke sank under the
water, then emerged vertically, like a Japanese bob-
bing toy. 'I never got any threatening letters,' he

said. 'They just come and take a swing when they're mad at me. They don't bother to write.'

Crane said: 'You must have very informal friends.'

O'Rourke made a noise with sea water and his cupped hands, then said: 'That Eye guy wouldn't scare me.'

'Nor me,' said Crane, turning toward shore. 'He sounds like a guy in a melodrama. He sounds phoney.'

They half swam, half coasted in on foam-smeared waves until their feet touched the sand bottom. The undertow pulled at their ankles, making a sucking noise and picking up milky clouds of fine sand. On their chests and shoulders the sun had already evaporated some of the moisture.

As they reached the strand of damp, brown, firmly packed sand at the water's edge, a flamingo ran round the left-hand corner of the house and came toward them. Behind the bird was a blonde in a tight, white Lastex bathing suit, running like a boy. Her legs were slim and brown and her hair, cut in short curls, was bleached the shade of pine shavings.

'Head him off,' the girl called, still running. 'Send him back this way.'

Crane obligingly ran toward the patio, but the flamingo suddenly cut loose with a burst of speed, lifting its feet off the ground with quick thrusts of his wings, passed him by a good three feet and vanished round the other side of the house.

'Oh, too bad,' cried the girl, coming to a halt. She turned to face a tall young man in blue wool trunks who had just rounded the first corner. 'No use, Tony,' she called to him, 'Abelard went through tackle for a touchdown.'

Crane examined her while she waited for Tony to come up. She was a small girl, not much over five feet tall, but she was not as young as he had first thought. At least she was well developed. Her hips were curved

and her breasts were round under the white suit.   Under
her arms, in the V between her breasts, on the circles
of her thighs where the suit had been pulled up by running, her skin was perfectly white, contrasting with the
golden tan of her legs and arms.

O'Rourke coming to a halt beside Crane, said in his
ear: 'I'm beginning to be glad I came.'

The girl and her companion came toward them.
'Thanks for the gallant effort,' she said to Crane, her
teeth white behind red lips.   Her eyes matched the sky.

'I'm just as glad I was too late,' said Crane.   'I've
never tackled a flamingo.'

She said: 'Nobody ever has.   We've been trying for
years.'

Her companion had short-cut black hair.   He was
very tall and thin, and his long face was quite handsome.
Crane did not think he liked him, but he realized that
this was possibly due to the fact that he did not care for
the name Tony.   The name always suggested a smooth
guy to him; a sort of cocktail-hour gigolo.

The girl said: 'I'm Camelia Essex.   You're Penn's
friends, aren't you?'

'I'm William Crane,' said Crane, 'and this is Thomas
O'Rourke.'

'And this is Tony Lamphier.'

The young man's expression was glassy.   'H'lo,' he
said.   He looked over their heads, suddenly thrust out a
hand at O'Rourke and shook hands with him.   'Enjoyed
your party very much, sir,' he declared.   Abruptly he
started for the ocean.

Miss Essex laughed, uttering a sort of flute-like giggle
which made Crane regard her closely.   'He's a little
tight,' she said.

'So early in the morning?' asked Crane in astonishment.

'Oh, no.   We're just rounding out the evening.'

'You must have had some evening.'

'Oh, yes. We went to Tortoni's.' Her eyes turned from Tony Lamphier, struggling with the breakers, to Crane. 'You're the detectives, aren't you?'

'Yes.'

Her face serious, she looked up into O'Rourke's eyes. 'You can help Penn, can't you? I'm really frightened.'

'Sure,' said O'Rourke. 'Don't worry at all.'

She put a hand on Crane's arm. Her fingers were hot. 'This may be the only chance I'll have to speak to you alone.' Her words were hurried. 'Penn's lost a lot of money gambling . . . twenty-five thousand dollars. . . . Tortoni holds his I O Us and has been trying to collect. He's a dangerous man.'

'Cam! Oh, Cam!' Tony Lamphier was shouting from a point fifty yards out at sea. 'Come and see the sharks.'

'Coming, dear.' She tightened her fingers on Crane's arm. 'Penn doesn't know I know about it, but I thought you ought to be told. He doesn't intend to pay the debt, says Tortoni's wheel is crooked.' She took her hand from Crane's arm.

'Wait a second,' said Crane. 'How did you find out about this?'

'I overheard Tortoni threatening Penn in New York . . .'

From the ocean came a petulant shout. 'Caam!'

'You mustn't tell Penn how you found this out.' Crane nodded his head and she ran toward the surf. 'Here I come, Tony.' Breast deep in water, she faced the shore for an instant. 'See you this afternoon.'

Crane shouted: 'It's a date,' and watched her dive through a comber and swim vigorously toward Lamphier.

'Well, that gives us something to think about,' said O'Rourke.

'In what way?'

O'Rourke glared at him in mock disgust. 'You have a low mind.'

'Perhaps I have, thank God,' said Crane.

They went up to their rooms and turned on the water in the green-tiled shower. The connecting bathroom was a large one, gay with chromium, bright tile and highly coloured tropical fish painted on the walls, and Crane shaved while O'Rourke took his shower. Thick sunlight, reflecting from the branch of a coco-nut palm, cast a greenish-yellow scar along his jaw-bone.

'How's your black eye?' asked O'Rourke, turning off the shower and seizing a green-trimmed bath-towel. 'Better?'

Crane cocked his head, said: 'It's beautiful. Sort of Kelly green, like mildewed pork.' His razor made a sandpaper noise against his chin. 'We better go out to-night and see if this Tortoni's wheel is really crooked.'

'What will we use for money?'

Crane doused warm water on his face. 'Maybe we could write I O Us.' He buried his face in a towel, spoke with a muffled voice. 'But we don't have to. We got dough.' Marching into his room, he returned with a pigskin wallet. 'The colonel gave us a grand for expenses. Look!' His right hand drew out the contents of the wallet. 'Well, for God's sake!' he said.

Amid the lettuce-green hundred-dollar bills was a folded sheet of paper. He opened it, noted the red ink, read aloud:

'MESSRS FLATFEET:
          'You got till 12 noon to-day to get out of here. ... This is no joke. ... Get out or the 'gators back in the swamps will be fatter. ... You get the idea? ...
                                        'THE EYE.'

Crane's voice died away. The wind in the dry palm leaves sounded as though some one were trying to fold a newspaper. Water in the shower fell in an ever-slowing *tempo*: drip-drip ... drip-drip ... drip.

O'Rourke said: 'The Eye's some little letter writer.'

'I bet he's the guy who wrote *Nellie, the Beautiful Cloak Model*,' Crane said.

He went into his room and compared the new note with those he had received from Essex. The ink was the same shade of red and the angle at which the sheet had been torn was identical. He proudly waved the sheet under O'Rourke's nose. 'A genuine Eye,' he said. 'An authentic, genuine Eye. Mr. O'Rourke, we are fortunate indeed to possess such an example of this craftsman's art.'

O'Rourke pulled a ribbed silk underwear top over his head, thrust one lean leg, then the other, into a pair of Nile-green shorts. 'We better scram downstairs and get some breakfast,' he said. 'He gives us only three hours to go.'

'The master's autograph,' said Crane, still examining the note with admiration.

'I wonder what we should eat.' O'Rourke, a frown making wrinkles on the skin between his eyes, buttoned his shirt. 'Eggs? Bacon? Pancakes? Cereal? What do you think an alligator would like?'

'I don't think an alligator cares.' Crane put all four notes in his wallet, took a white linen suit from the cupboard. 'Just as long as we eat a big breakfast.'

When they finished dressing, Crane looked at his wrist-watch. It was ten minutes past nine. He thought, but he could not remember, when he had been up so early, excepting, of course, the times he had stayed up all night.

'I suppose we ought to look up Essex,' O'Rourke said. 'The Eye may be about to throw him to the alligators.'

'The Eye's a phoney,' Crane said.

There was a faint noise of laughter outside and they went out on the balcony in time to see Camelia Essex and Tony Lamphier cross the patio and enter the house. The girl's pretty face was gay and she half walked, half skipped, her left hand in the young man's right. He walked rapidly, but unsteadily.

'She doesn't act a hell of a lot worried about her brother,' said O'Rourke.

'No, she doesn't,' said Crane. 'Let's have breakfast.'

They went down the curved marble stairs with the wrought-iron balustrade into a tile-floored hall. A serving-man in white came toward them. 'Good morning,' he said. 'If you like, breakfast will be served in the patio.'

A stocky, red-faced man in grey flannel slacks and a black-and-white checked sports coat was reading the *Miami Herald* at a round table by the side of the swimming-pool. His hair was flecked with grey; there was a white line on his neck at the point where his collar halted; he was eating liver and bacon.

He didn't bother to get up. 'The energetic detectives?' he said. His voice was hoarse and vigorous, and his accent might have come from England or from Boston's Back Bay.

'Major Eastcomb? . . .' Crane inquired.

The man nodded. 'Time you got here.' His face was brick-red, sullen. 'Past time.'

'I'm sorry about that wire,' Crane said. 'I didn't know who you were.'

'You might have been more civil.'

O'Rourke spoke to the approaching serving-man. 'Scrambled eggs.'

'The same,' said Crane, 'and a Scotch and soda.'

'Make it two,' O'Rourke said.

The major grunted. Crane leaned confidentially toward him. 'We drink because our lives are forfeit.'

The major blinked bloodshot eyes at Crane. 'You got one of those damned notes?'

'The Eye gives us until noon to get out of here.'

O'Rourke was drinking iced tomato juice. 'Or else we are trun to the alligators.'

Major Eastcomb demanded: 'How did the fellow know you were detectives?'

The serving-man appeared with a bottle of whisky, a silver bowl of ice cubes, a siphon and three glasses. Crane raised his shoulder toward his ears, shook his head. The serving-man started to pour whisky into the glasses, but Major Eastcomb took the bottle from him.

'I'll manage, Pedro.'

He mixed a drink in one glass, set the bottle on the table. The detectives stared at him in surprise. 'In a way,' he said, 'you are under my orders. Any payments to your agency must have my approval.'

O'Rourke looked at him blankly. 'What about our drinks?" he asked.

Crane said: 'I don't believe we want any liquor.'

'That's better,' said the major. 'You men are on a job, not a drinking bout.' Crane saw that his eyes, in addition to being flecked with blood, were very small. 'I've heard stories of your alcoholic tendencies.' Crane thought the small eyes made him look like a pig.

'That's the way we work,' O'Rourke objected. 'We always combine pleasure with business.'

'While you're working for the Essex estate you'll stick to business.'

'O.K.' Crane looked away from the whisky-bottle. 'No pleasure.'

The major's eyes gleamed in triumph. 'Now I'll tell you about young Essex. . . .'

While the whisky diminished in his glass, he recounted the more important episodes in Essex's life—the Ruby Carstairs breach of promise case ('Devilish fortunate to settle for ten thousand'); his deportation from Japan for booing the Mikado; the Lido Club row in which a Broadway columnist was blinded by a thrown bottle; his arrest for doing one hundred and three miles an hour on the Boston Pike; his expulsions from Groton, St. Paul's, Phillips Exeter, Valley Ranch.

Deftly the serving-man laid silver and linen on the table, took the ice-surrounded glasses of tomato juice from Crane and O'Rourke, departed.

'There's more . . . a wild lad if ever . . .' The major tossed the remainder of his drink down his throat. 'But you've an idea. Only pertinent thing is his debts. Yes, his debts. Especially a bloody big one to Tortoni, the gambler.'

Crane's eyebrows lifted. 'So?'

'Don't know how much it is,' confided the major. 'Penn denies it altogether. But Tortoni tried to collect from me in New York. Cheeky beggar! Had him shown out of the office.'

'You think Tortoni's behind the notes?'

The major attempted to quote from the second note. '"The time has come to pay your debt . . ."'

'The walrus said,' Crane said.

'How's that?'

'Skip it,' Crane said. 'Would the estate pay it if his life was actually in danger?'

'Absolutely.' The major's face looked angry. 'But simply because some fellow has written a few notes.' He glared at Crane as though he was contemplating homicide. 'Supposing I ask you a question. What do you propose to do?'

Crane said: 'Keep our eyes open.'

They sat in silence while the serving-man put plates before them, ladled out eggs and bacon from a silver-covered platter, passed thin slices of dry toast, poured coffee, helped them to cream and sugar. The eggs were as Crane liked them, very soft, and the coffee was marvellous, at once bitter and sweet.

When the man had gone, O'Rourke asked the major: 'You got any ideas for us?'

The major ignored him. 'I understand your office's keeping tab on that fake count of Camelia's,' he said to Crane.

'Count Paul di Gregario? Yes, I guess they are.'

'Waste of time. They're washed up.'

'Maybe,' said Crane.

The major glared at him.

Craig, the butler, entered the patio from a door in the left wing of the house, half-circled the steel supports of the swimming-pool's diving-board, walked up to Major Eastcomb. 'Good morning, sir,' he said, ignoring Crane and O'Rourke.

The major grunted: ''Morning.'

Usually, Crane thought, butlers looked pompous, ponderous; Craig looked alert and nasty. Under heavy talcum his beard glistened, blue-black, and his eyebrows met over his nose. His eyes were beady. 'I have the accounts ready for you, Major,' he said.

'I'll be along in five minutes.'

'Very good, sir.' The butler turned from the table, his small eyes passing over Crane and O'Rourke without a change in their expression. Crane said: 'Craig!' The butler abruptly halted. 'Will you have my roadster brought round? Mr. O'Rourke and I are going into Miami.'

The butler's eyes gleamed. 'Shall I pack your bags, sir?'

The major was absolutely motionless. Crane demanded. 'What makes you think I want my bags packed?'

'I thought possibly you were leaving.'

'Craig'—Crane leaned across the table towards the butler—'when we decide to leave you shall be the first to know it.'

The butler left them. The major grunted, said: 'No one, except Penn and I, knows that you are detectives. I suggest an improvement in your manners.' He grunted again. 'A trifle more dignity would aid the deception. You're supposed to be gentlemen, y'know.'

O'Rourke scowled, allowed a damp piece of toast to

halt midway between the coffee-cup and his mouth. Crane said: 'And we thought our disguise was perfect!'

'Another thing.' Rising, the major grasped the bottle of whisky, tucked it under his arm. 'I want to warn you again about drinking. I won't tolerate it. Remember.' He went towards the same door the butler had used.

Crane lifted the silver cover of the platter, but there weren't any more eggs. He sighed.

Making a circle of his thumb and forefinger, O'Rourke held it to his left eye, monocle-fashion. 'Pleasant beggar!' he observed.

Crane asked: 'You know how I spell beggar?'

CHAPTER THREE

MIAMI'S sidewalks dazzlingly reflected sunlight on south and west sides of streets, bore crowds of deliberate, shirt-sleeved tourists on shady north and east sides. The roadster passed a yellow building with a sign, 'Five Course Dinner—25c,' swung into a parking place. 'Back after lunch,' Crane told the Negro attendant.

They walked over to Flagler Street, elbowing their way through the crowds, and turned right toward the bay. Two blondes in halters and white shorts, saunter- ing arm in arm, smiled at O'Rourke, but Crane said: 'Hey! None of that.' He looked over his shoulder. 'Besides, we can do better.'

They passed a stand selling orange juice, a stand selling pineapple juice, a drug store, a clothing store bearing a banner marked END OF SEASON SALE—FIFTY

OFF, a stand selling a mixture of milk and pineapple juice. A policeman warned them not to jaywalk. From a loud-speaker over a leather goods store came a sticky Wayne King waltz. They both began to sweat.

'The town's lousy with dames,' observed O'Rourke.

They turned into a book store and Crane asked the elderly lady clerk for a *Bartlett's Familiar Quotations*.

Behind the tortoise-shell glasses her eyes seemed about to shed tears. 'The only one we have is second-hand.' Her face was thin.

'That's all right. How much?'

He gave her two dollar bills and a fifty-cent piece, said, 'You needn't wrap it,' and handed the heavy book to O'Rourke. 'That's for you.'

'What do I want with it?' asked O'Rourke surprised.

Crane was looking from one side of the street to the other, up and down side streets as they walked. 'I'll tell you soon as I find some beer.'

A block to the left they found the New York Bar. It was cool inside and there was a lovely odour of Scotch whisky, limes, Cuban rum and beer in the air. They sank into leather chairs on opposite sides of a black composition table.

'Two beers,' Crane told the waiter.

O'Rourke pretended astonishment. 'What'll the major say?'

'Wait!' Crane called to the waiter. 'Cancel the order. Two Scotch and sodas instead.'

'Make 'em triple Scotches,' said O'Rourke.

His expression dazed, the waiter hurried away.

Crane felt perfectly justified in disregarding the major's orders about liquor. He belonged to the pleasure school of detection. He never found that a little relaxation hindered him in his work. His best ideas came while he was relaxed. However, it was hard to make a client see this. Clients were often stupid. That's why they had to hire detectives.

'Give me a chit,' he said to O'Rourke. 'I'll make that phone call we came in for.'

When he returned, he was smiling. 'Doc Williams and Eddie Burns are in town.'

O'Rourke looked up from his half-finished drink. 'So that phoney plate of spaghetti did get here after all!'

'Yeah, the count's over at the Miami-Plaza. Burns is with him on the beach and Doc's trying to make up some sleep.' Crane raised his glass above his head. 'Here's to the major.'

They drank and ordered another and O'Rourke asked: 'What about this book?'

'Oh, yeah,' said Crane. 'That's culture. That's what you need, a little culture.'

'What is it, a book on etiquette?'

'No. Look. You look all right; you dress all right; most of the time you act all right.'

'Hell, I act all right all the time.'

'O.K., you act all right all the time. But sometimes you don't say the right thing.' Crane took a long drink. 'That's good. A good bar. But here's how the book'll help you.'

'How?'

'You're a strong, silent guy at the Essex's house, see? Most of the time you don't say anything but yes and no and thank you. But every once in a while, to show you got culture, you spout one of the quotations in this book; whatever'll fit the occasion.'

'You mean I gotta learn everything in this whole book?'

'No. Just a half dozen or so quotations. Look up the ones on women and liquor and love; those'll fit in easiest.'

O'Rourke thumbed through the book. He halted somewhere in the centre. 'You mean like this?' He read:

'I'd be a butterfly born in a bower,
Where roses and lilies and violets meet.'

Crane said: 'Why, *Mister* O'Rourke!'

'Well, damn it,' said O'Rourke. 'That's in here.'

'You have to use judgment,' said Crane. 'Or some big strong man will elope with you.'

Ice clinked against the bottom of O'Rourke's glass as he set it down. 'O.K. I'll drip culture all over the place. Now what about another drink?'

'I think we ought to have a sandwich.'

'What! No drink? No toast to the major?'

'Oh, sure. But I think we ought to have a sandwich. Waiter, two triple Scotches and two roast beef sandwiches.'

'Two triple roast beef sandwiches,' said O'Rourke.

'That reminds me,' said Crane. 'The word trun. You do not use trun.'

'No?'

'No. You do not use trun. We are not going to be trun to the alligators.'

'You're tellin' me!'

'If you have to use trun, use it this way: he fell like a trun of bicks.'

'You mean a trun of bricks.'

'Or a one-trun tuck.'

'You seem to be confused,' said O'Rourke. 'Perhaps a sip of this harmless beverage . . .?'

On the curving stairs inside the Essex house they met the serving-man who had brought them beer on the previous night. 'Mr. Essex has been inquiring about you, sir,' he told Crane. 'Every one is having cocktails by the swimming-pool.'

They climbed the stairs, and Crane went to the balcony and peered down at the patio. In the box-like swimming-pool the water looked like lime pop; in the ocean it was royal blue. Under a gay red and yellow and green sunshade, in the place where breakfast had been served, was a long table covered by bottles, glasses, ice, hors-d'œuvres. A servant in white was flourishing a cocktail shaker.

Crane said: 'O'Rourke! Babes!'

One of the women by the pool didn't count. She was past fifty and her figure had lost most of its shape. There were three others who did count, however. One of these Crane recognized as Camelia Essex. She was about to dive into the pool, and her figure was supple under a French blue brassiere-and-trunks suit. Another woman, English-looking, athletic, slightly horsey in the better sense of the word, stood talking to Tony Lamphier and another man. Her hair was brown; her face was aristocratic; her legs were long and slender; her breasts were firm; her hips narrow under the silver-grey swim-suit.

But the third woman held their eyes. Even from the balcony they could see the golden sheen of her tanned arms and legs. She was an egg-yolk blonde, and O'Rourke described her by saying: 'Look out, Mae West!' She was talking with the major and Penn Essex. Her breasts pushed so strongly against her white silk suit that the dip of the fabric into her flat stomach was entirely without wrinkles. Her shoulders were rounded gracefully, and her hips had a curve neither soft nor muscular.

O'Rourke spoke in Crane's ear. 'Am I glad I came! Where're our suits?'

Essex, when they entered the patio, saw they were given planter's punches and took them around to the others. The woman with Tony Lamphier had nice teeth and her name was Eve Boucher and she was about thirty years old. She said: 'How d'you do.' The man with them was Gregory Boucher. Black hair grew in patches on his chest, on his arms, on the backs of his hands. His face, with a large curved nose, was French, almost Semitic; he looked cunning and unreliable. He was over forty, and Crane wondered how Mrs. Boucher happened to marry him.

Sybil Langley was the name of the older woman.

She was seated by herself in a cushioned deck-chair and she held in her hand what looked to Crane like half a glass of straight whisky. Her face was white and tragic, long, with huge violet eyes. 'So glad,' she said in a deep, glowing voice. She was wrapped in a purple beach-robe.

When they left her, Essex said: 'She's an aunt of ours—was a top-flight actress once.'

Crane asked: 'Peter Langley, out in Hollywood, her brother?'

Essex said: 'Yes.' He said: 'Dawn, this is Mr. Crane . . . and Mr. O'Rourke.' He turned to them. 'Dawn Day.'

Miss Day was even more appealing at close range. Her eyes, baby blue, passed over Crane's wiry body, lingeringly appraised O'Rourke's beautifully muscled shoulders, his prize-fighter's waist. 'I'm pleased to meet you, Mr. O'Rourke,' she said. 'Real pleased.' She sounded as though she meant it. 'And you too, Mr. Crane.'

Her voice made Crane think of Minsky's.

Major Eastcomb was scowling at the glasses in their hands. 'Have a good time in Miami?' he asked.

Crane said: 'I had a good time, but it was awfully hot.' He added: 'We hurried back.'

Essex was interested. 'What time did you make?'

'Forty-seven minutes.'

'Not bad, but I've made it in an even forty in the Bugatti.'

Crane was genuinely surprised. 'That's better than seventy-five an hour average.' He didn't believe Essex, but he didn't say so. 'You must have pushed her.'

'I had her up to a hundred and ten twice.'

Miss Day said: 'You boys and your cars.' She smiled at Essex. 'You won't mind if Mr. O'Rourke gives me a swimming lesson? I just know he's a wonderful

swimmer.' She rolled her eyes up to Mr. O'Rourke.
'Don't you think it would be fun?'

O'Rourke replied enthusiastically that he thought it
would be fun. 'Let's go to the shallow end of the
pool,' he said.

'Oh, no.' Her tone was a caress. 'Let's try the
ocean. It's so much bigger.'

This was obviously true and she and O'Rourke started
for the beach. Crane gazed after them with envy.
Miss Day's back, a glistening brown to a point inches
above the base of her spine, was perfect. He'd like to
teach her to swim.

Major Eastcomb said: 'What d'you find in Miami?'

Crane started to say, 'A damned good bar,' but he
thought better of it. Instead, he said: 'I ran across the
trail of a friend of Miss Essex.'

'Who?'

'Count Paul di Gregario.'

Anger made the major's face tomato red. 'What's
that impostor doing here?'

'Probably up to no good,' said Essex.

Crane said: 'I don't know, but we have a couple of
men watching him. They came down with him from
New York by plane. Eddie Burns and Doc Williams.'

Major Eastcomb's teeth were clenched so tightly his
jaw muscles showed white. 'I'll teach him to follow
Camelia down here. Where's he staying?'

'At the Miami-Plaza.'

A noise somewhere between a squeal and scream
carried to them from the ocean. O'Rourke's arms
under her back, Miss Day was floating on the surface
of the water, her kicking feet sending up a column of
white spray. The surf had subsided; small waves licked
the shore daintily, like kittens' tongues after cream.

'I'll teach him,' said the major.

Essex's eyes were on the sea. He said: 'What are
you going to do about the note you got?'

'I told him,' said the major. 'I warned him to keep away.'

'What can I do?' asked Crane. 'Except wait. I *am* going around to see Roland Tortoni to-night.'

Essex's pale, youthfully dissipated face was surprised.

Crane asked impatiently: 'He *has* twenty-five thousand dollars worth of your I O Us, hasn't he?'

'Yes, but I'm not going to pay him. He's crooked . . . his wheels are crooked. He can't collect.'

'Hasn't it occurred to you he might be using the notes to make you pay?'

Essex clenched his hands. 'He wouldn't dare.' He frowned. 'Besides, we're friends.' He's given up trying to collect.'

They could hear Miss Day's laughter, high and piercing.

Crane said: 'I never heard of anybody giving up twenty-five thousand dollars.'

Essex's hand pressed Crane's arm. 'I'll see you a little later.' He hadn't heard what Crane said. He went off in the direction of O'Rourke and Miss Day.

'Look here,' said Major Eastcomb fiercely, 'this won't do.'

'What won't do?'

The major gestured toward Miss Day and the Atlantic Ocean. 'You're hired to work; not to sop up liquor and go running after women.'

'Why not mention it to O'Rourke?'

'I'll do that.' The major flattened his eyebrows in a scowl. 'But the important thing is to keep an eye on Essex. One of you should have stayed here.'

'You really think he's in danger?'

'I wouldn't have asked Mr. Hastings to hire detectives if I didn't.'

The major left him. Crane went over to the big table and had the serving-man make another planter's punch. He ate five caviare canapes. He felt better. He still wanted to punch the major on the nose, but he now felt he could control this impulse. He took a drink and put his glass on the cement ridge of the swimming-pool and dived in the lime-coloured water. It was cooler than he had expected. He was glad he had sent the major the nasty telegram.

At the other end of the pool he encountered Camelia Essex and Tony Lamphier. They seemed glad to see him.

She asked: 'How was Miami?'

Crane said: 'Miami was wonderful.'

She said: 'Aren't the tourists splendid?'

'I am a sailfish,' said Tony Lamphier, writhing about on the surface of the water. He seemed to be drunk, too.

'Your friend sort of goes for Penn's girl, doesn't he?' she said.

'She wanted to learn to swim.'

'She always wants to learn to swim.'

'I am a fish,' stated Tony Lamphier.

Crane noticed a girl, in black Chinese pyjamas, coming across the patio.

Camelia Essex said: 'At least you drink like a fish, darling.'

'I can stop,' Lamphier said. 'Any time you will.'

'Fishes can't stop, Tony.'

'I can stop, darling.'

Even from a distance Crane could see that the girl was different from any he had ever before seen. She had black hair and a white face and she walked with short, gliding steps, as though her feet were bound.

'Don't stop, dear,' said Camelia Essex to Lamphier. 'You're so much more fun this way.'

'Who's that girl?' asked Crane.

'What girl? Oh. That's our mystery woman. She's a dancer . . . a friend of Penn. Her name's Imago Paraguay.'

'She's exotic,' said Tony Lamphier. 'Don't you think she's exotic?'

'Would you like to meet her?' Camelia Essex asked Crane.

'Why not?' said Crane.

Miss Essex put her chin over the side of the pool and called: 'Imago, this is Mr. Crane.'

She had halted by Sybil Langley. Her figure, small, sharply breasted, slender as a lotus plant, was virginal. 'How do you do,' she said in a soft flat voice.

'She's exotic,' said Tony Lamphier. 'Don't you think so?'

Crane swam the length of the pool and climbed over the edge. He picked up his drink and went over to the table where the two women were now sitting. 'May I get you something to drink, Miss Paraguay?' he asked.

'Tha-ank you.' Her voice was lazy. 'A sherry, please.'

Miss Langley's violet eyes, large, heavily mascaraed, blank as a sleep-walker's, were fixed on him. 'I think perhaps I will,' she said. 'My nerves . . . I become so tired . . . so terribly tired.'

Crane took her glass. 'What are you drinking?'

'Oh, nothing but Scotch. I feel that to mix it impairs its medicinal value.' She swayed a little to the left, as though she were going to topple from her chair, but caught herself. Her face did not change expression. 'Just a little, Mr. Crane. Do not fill the glass more than half-way. . . .'

Crane poured half of a pinch bottle of whisky in her glass. A dipsomaniac, he thought. What a lovely household! A drunken old actress, a prize fighter (where in the hell did Brown keep himself, anyway?) a super-sex strip queen right out of Minsky's, a dancer who looked more Chinese than South American, an exceptionally sinister butler, guards. He felt the disadvantages of being rich almost outweighed the advantages.

'Have you some sherry?' he asked the serving-man.

The serving-man poured a glass of sherry and Crane went back to the table. Miss Langley was sitting very close to the dancer. She accepted the glass of whisky, said: 'Oh, you filled it *so* full.'

'Would you like me to get a smaller one?'

'Oh, no. Don't bother. I shall drink what I can.' She was being very brave. 'I'm so tired.' She put a hand on the dancer's arm. 'So terribly tired.' She smiled mistily at the dancer.

Uninvited, Crane sat down. He felt an extraordinary interest in Imago Paraguay. 'The sherry all right?' he asked.

She smiled just a little. Her face was like an ivory temple-mask; calm, bland, contemptuous; delicately dusted with rice powder, tinted under the eyes with blue, slashed with scarlet at the lips. The thin arch of her jet black brows might have been made with a bamboo brush.

'Tha-ank you, yes,' she said.

One hand clasped by Essex, the other by O'Rourke, Miss Day ran by the swimming-pool. She was laughing loudly. She called to Crane: 'When are you going to give me a lesson?' Her big blue eyes said that nothing would give her such a thrill as a lesson from him. So tight was her white suit that her breasts hardly moved when she ran.

'Any time,' said Crane.

The three went on to the serving-man, ordered him to make Bacardis. Without turning her face in his direction, Imago Paraguay asked: 'The tall man?'

'A friend of mine,' said Crane. 'His name's O'Rourke.'

He felt her oblique eyes upon him. 'He is ha-and-some.' There was lazy malice in her tone. 'No?'

'Oh, yes,' said Crane. 'Very handsome.'

'And the Miss Day, señor? She is beautiful?'

'Well,' said Crane, 'she has a certain appeal.'

'I thi-ink so also.'

He glanced at her suspiciously, but her slant-browed face was serene.

Miss Langley's hand was resting on the dancer's knee. 'That woman,' she said, looking at Miss Day's bare back. 'To think . . .' As if conscious of their eyes, Miss Day looked round at them smiled warmly at Crane. He was aware of a sudden tension in Imago Paraguay's expression. Miss Langley dramatically put a hand on her forehead. 'Oh, I feel unwell,' she said throatily. 'Imago, come for a walk beside the sea.' She rose unsteadily.

For an instant Imago Paraguay's hand was in Crane's; her sloe eyes on his. He felt his nerves suddenly become tense. 'Go-ood-bye, señor,' she said, her voice flat.

'Come, Imago,' said Miss Langley.

'I am co-oming.' Her Asiatic face was without expression.

They walked toward the sea, Miss Langley leaning on the dancer's arm. Because he would have liked to talk to Imago Paraguay, Crane felt a sudden anger and abruptly drained his glass. He would have drained Miss Langley's glass, too, only it was empty.

CHAPTER FOUR

WILLIAM CRANE was slipping a silk handkerchief in the breast pocket of his white shawl collar dinner-jacket when O'Rourke came through the bathroom from his room. The Irishman looked fine in a Burma shade dinner-jacket, black trousers, a white silk

shirt with a dark green bow tie, a dark green cummerbund and dark green silk hose. His black hair, flecked
with grey, was parted at the side.

Crane whistled. 'Boy! You'll slay 'em to-night.'

'I thought I'd get dressed up for Miss Day. She's
gonna show me some dance steps in return for the
swimmin' lesson.'

'That isn't all she'll show you,' said Crane darkly.

'Aw, you needn't be jealous,' said O'Rourke. 'She
thinks you're cute.'

'I am,' said Crane. 'Real cute.' He adjusted his
black tie. 'Did you know she was Essex's girl friend?'

O'Rourke's broad shoulders moved forward, upward.
'That's his look-out, not mine.' He grinned at Crane.
'Besides, I found out a lot of stuff from her.'

'What?' asked Crane suspiciously. 'That she doesn't
wear corsets?'

'No. Seriously, she gave me an earful. She says,
for one thing, that the major's after Camelia . . . wants
to marry her.'

'Who wouldn't with all that dough?'

'Well, Camelia's really considerin' him, Dawn says.
She has it figured out this way: Camelia don't like the
major, being still soft over that count. But if she gets
married a part of the estate comes to her, a couple of
million, Dawn says. Then with this dough, she can
divorce the major and marry the count.'

'So,' said Crane.

'And Dawn says Camelia talked with di Gregario over
the phone to-day. They're going to meet somewhere
to-night.'

'Let her,' said Crane.

O'Rourke grinned. 'Dawn says Tony Lamphier's
soft about Camelia. He's got dough, too, so it ain't
that he's after.'

'What about the Bouchers? What've they got to
grind?'

'Dawn don't know. As far as she can make out they're just friends of Camelia's.'

'How'd you get all this out of the dame, anyway?'

'She likes to talk . . . to the right guy.'

'Yeah?' asked Crane. 'For two bits I'd go after that babe myself and cut both you and Essex out. I'll show you who'll get her to talk.'

'You better stick to that Chinese dame you were talkin' with,' said O'Rourke. 'She's the mystery lady in this joint.'

'I'm good at mysteries. What's the one about her?'

'Well, Dawn says nobody knows what she's doin' here. She's been here a week and hasn't opened her mouth to anybody. She's supposed to be Penn's friend, but he don't pay any attention to her.'

'Maybe he liked her when he invited her here.'

'No. Dawn says he's afraid of her. He's always wanting to get away from where she is.'

'So, he's afraid of her.' Crane frowned thoughtfully. 'That's just fine. You may make a detective some day, O'Rourke.'

O'Rourke said: 'I get more information in an hour than you do in a day, and that's all the thanks I get.'

'That's all you get when you can play around with a gal like Miss Day in getting it.'

'You're jealous, that's what.'

'I'm hungry.'

'Jealous of your old pal? Tsk. Especially when there's champagne and plenty of liquor waiting for you downstairs.'

'And food.' Crane brightened. 'I'll bet they even have food for dinner.'

Everybody except Miss Langley was very gay after dinner. Miss Langley had a dizzy spell and had to be carried up to bed. Miss Day whispered to Crane: 'I don't know what's come over her. She don't usually

pass out until ten o'clock.' Crane had made a considerable play for Miss Day at dinner, and both O'Rourke
and Essex were watching him. O'Rourke, however,
was amused.

They had a smooth Spanish brandy in the patio, and
Crane suggested they go to Roland Tortoni's Blue Castle.
Everybody except Camelia Essex thought this would be
fine. 'D'y'know,' said Mrs. Boucher, 'I feel disgustingly
lucky.' Crane thought she looked English. She was
handsome in that lean, athletic way only Englishwomen
can achieve without becoming masculine. Her long
figure, in a black evening gown, had interesting curves.
She would look well, Crane thought, on an Irish hunter,
in tweeds on the King's course at Gleneagles, on an
African *safari*, or at breakfast in pyjamas.

Camelia spoke in Crane's ear. 'Do you think Penn
will be safe there?'

'If Tortoni's after him,' Crane assured her, 'it's the
safest place in the world for him.'

'Aw, come on, Camelia,' called Miss Day, moving her
torso slowly from side to side. 'I'd like to do a little
truckin'.'

That settled it.

Crane and O'Rourke went up to their rooms while the
cars were being sent round. Taking five one-hundred
dollar bills from his wallet, Crane gave them to O'Rourke.
'Let's both of us watch Tortoni's wheel,' he said. 'It's
not much to work with, but maybe one of us will see
something crooked.'

They discovered two cars in the driveway. Penn
Essex was at the wheel of a black and chromium Bugatti
sports touring model, and Dawn Day sat beside him.
He called to Crane: 'You and O'Rourke take Miss
Paraguay in the Lincoln with the Bouchers.' He raced
the motor, sending smoke from the exhaust. 'Cam and
Tony and the major are coming with me.' With a
deep-throated roar the car rolled away, and a chauffeur

brought up the Lincoln sedan. 'Would you care to
have me drive?' he asked.

'I'll manage,' said Boucher.

Moving in that short-paced glide of hers, Imago
Paraguay came toward them from the door. Crane
felt her curious attraction. She was wearing a bolero
for a dinner-jacket, of black *crêpe*. Her skirt, split
eight inches up the side, was of black *crêpe*, but her
blouse was red. Snug round her thin waist was a red
sash, the bright tassel of which hung down in front to
her feet, splitting her skirt in two. On her left hand she
wore an enormous ruby, cut in the shape of a rectangle.

'I am sor-ry to have made you wait,' she said.

'The evening's young,' Crane said, helping her into
the sedan. Her hand, against his, was cool.

'So are we,' said O'Rourke, closing the door. 'Let
'er go.' He probably would have yelled 'Yippee!' but
for Crane's elbow in his ribs.

They went toward Miami at a comfortable fifty-five
miles an hour. Mrs. Boucher seemed to be interested
in Imago Paraguay. She lit a cigarette and asked:

'You like gambling, Miss Paraguay?'

'Oh, yes. I ha-ave gamble very much.' She might
have been a cat talking, so miaowlish was her voice.
'One time, in Ha-abana, I win thirty thousand do-lars
in a night.'

'What did you do with them?' asked Boucher.
'Buy a house?'

'Oh, no. I lo-ose them another night.'

O'Rourke said:

> 'Gold! Gold! Gold! Gold!
> Bright and yellow, hard and cold,
> Spurn'd by the young, but hugg'd by the old
> To the very verge of the churchyard mould.'

Crane gaped at him in utter amazement.

Mrs. Boucher said: 'That's a pretty compliment to

Miss Paraguay's youth, Mr. O'Rourke.' Her voice sounded amused.

'But I do not spurn the gold,' said Imago Paraguay in her flat voice. 'Oh, no.'

Boucher and O'Rourke got into a discussion of the coming baseball season, O'Rourke liking the Yankees and Boucher liking Detroit, and soon they were entering Miami on Brickwell Avenue. Imago Paraguay slipped a cold hand in Crane's, let it remain there. Crane experienced a mingled sensation of desire and repulsion. He had never felt that way before. They went over to Biscayne Boulevard, past the tall stucco hotels overlooking Bay Front Park, and turned right over the Venetian Way.

Both women craned at expensive frocks in the brilliantly illuminated shops on Lincoln Road. They turned right again on Collins Avenue, then ran on to Ocean Drive. The traffic was heavy; they moved slowly, in their noses the damp, salt smell of the sea; in their ears the pounding of the surf.

They turned right again; then, two blocks farther, to the left into a lighted drive, and came to a halt in front of a large blue stucco house. The Negro door-man's brass buttons gleamed in the light. 'Good evenin'.' His square teeth were white against suede skin. 'Good evenin'.' He pulled open the doors of the Lincoln.

Crane got out, reached an arm up for Imago Paraguay. She uncrossed her knees and came towards him. He had a glimpse of a white thigh, of red silk, of bright, needle-sharp metal. For an instant, before she stepped on the ground, she leaned against his chest. Her perfume was like the heavy odour of sandalwood.

He stiffened his arm, held her away from him. 'The butterfly has a stinger,' he said.

Her face was calm. 'At times.' She walked alone, ahead of the rest of them, into the house. Penn Essex, Tony Lamphier and the major met them in front of the booth occupied by the blonde hat-check girl. 'The gals will be along in a second,' Penn Essex said, turning to Crane. 'We've got a table . . . thought we'd dance a little first.'

The hat-check girl said nasally: 'Check, Mister?'

O'Rourke handed her his Panama. 'Double check, baby,' he said, looking into her eyes. He leaned an elbow on the counter.

'Nix,' said Crane.

The other four men had moved a little farther along the hall, were talking. As if muffled by heavy draperies, music came softly to their ears.

'I'm wondering . . .' said Crane. 'You know that Imago dame? . . .'

'Do I?' O'Rourke ostentatiously adjusted his dark green bow tie. 'Didn't she hold my hand all the way from Essex's house to here?'

'Did she? She held mine, too. But she didn't fall in your arms when you helped her out of the car.'

'I didn't help her out of the car,' said O'Rourke. 'That's why.'

'Anyway,' said Crane, 'she's carrying a dagger tied to her leg with red ribbon.'

O'Rourke bit his lower lip in mock dismay. 'That makes two.'

'Two?'

'The major's luggin' a pistol the size of a French seventy-five.'

'How d'you know?'

'I saw it under his coat.'

There was a sound of women's voices. Crane turned and saw Miss Day walking towards the group with Essex. She had the most provocative walk he had ever seen, or the most provocative hips. He didn't know which. They were connected in a way, but not in the usual way hips are connected with walking. Her hips were sheathed in silk the colour of flame, pulled so taut

that light rippled over the fabric when she moved.
They flowed under the dress like heavy and seductive
liquid, like molten metal. They gave her the appearance of a big jungle cat, graceful, stealthy, dangerous.

The other women came from behind the purple door.
With Mrs. Boucher walked Imago Paraguay. Her eyes,
under the slanting brows, sought Crane. There was a
suggestion of amusement, of malice, in them. He felt
goose-pimples rise in his body.

Their table was beside the dance floor. 'Champagne,'
Essex told the head waiter. 'Six bottles . . . to start.'
O'Rourke gazed at him with approval.

Almost as luxuriant as a tropical jungle was the room
around the black composition dance floor. Out of the
floor, out of blue boxes, grew banana trees with broad
green leaves and clusters of green bananas. Vines
clung to the trunks of the trees, bearing fragile blossoms;
pink, orange, bronze, henna and cream-white. Half
the room had no roof and overhead there were
stars.

O'Rourke was seated across the table, between
Camelia Essex and Mrs. Boucher. Miss Day looked at
him, then leaned towards Crane. 'I think your friend's
kinda cute,' she said.

'You do?'

'Well, he says the cutest things.' She leaned toward
Crane, and his senses reeled under the impact of about
four dollars' worth of Essence Imperiale Russe ('The
essence that quickened the pulse of kings'). 'J'know
what he said to me?'

Crane said he didn't know.

'Well, I asked him what I oughta wear to-night, my
black dress or this? And he said . . .' She giggled a
little. 'He said: "A lovely lady is garmented in light
from her own beauty."'

'You should have slapped his face,' said Crane.

'Oh, Mr. Crane! He didn't mean for me to come

nak . . . nude. He just meant it didn't make any difference what I wore.'

'You should have slapped him, anyway.'

The orchestra leader raised his arms, made a one-two movement with the baton. Drum and violins carried the melody for a minute; then out of the trumpets rolled muted notes like balls of quicksilver, round and smooth.

'Come on, Penn,' cried Miss Day. 'Let's go.'

Crane turned to Imago Paraguay. Her jet eyes watched the dancers on the floor.

'Would you care? . . .' he asked.

'If you wish.'

He imagined her body would be soft, but the back muscles were firm against his arm. She was taller than he thought and she danced beautifully. Her face was exquisite, like a painted ivory mask, but her hair was the remarkable thing about her. As black, as dull, as coarse as soot, it skull-capped her head and bunched in an ebony knot at the nape of her neck. Its distinction was its lack of lustre. It seemed to pocket the rays from the lamps. It might have been dead.

The floor was not crowded and he pivoted a few times, ending up near the orchestra. A man in a green gabardine suit scowled at him from beside the stand. Before he danced away he noticed the lobe of the man's ear was missing.

Imago Paraguay said: 'You da-ance quite well.'

They had made three circuits of the floor when the music stopped. They went back to the table and found a tall, dark man with a moustache talking to Camelia Essex. He was handsome and his brown eyes were lively.

'Paul, I'd like to have you meet these people,' said Miss Essex. Her voice was excited. 'Miss Paraguay, this is Count Paul di Gregario.'

The smile fled from the count's face. He drew back a step from the dancer. His skin was the colour of a peeled banana.

'We ha-ave met before,' said Imago Paraguay in her soft, flat voice.

The count bent over the dancer's hand. Imago's face was serene. Crane nodded to the count when he was introduced, made no offer to shake hands with him.

With the sush-sush of birdshot in a gourd, the orchestra started a tango. The count nodded to Tony Lamphier and took Camelia Essex on to the floor. Crane would have danced again with Imago but for the fact that the waiter was pouring the champagne. Boucher took her instead.

The major was off somewhere with Mrs. Boucher and that left only three of them at the table. The waiter started to put the champagne bottle back in the bucket, but O'Rourke said: 'Wait.' He drained his glass and held it toward the waiter. The waiter filled it and Crane, holding out his emptied glass, said: 'Me, too.'

Between them the quart vanished. 'Have another, Mr. O'Rourke?' asked Crane. 'Why, yes,' said O'Rourke. 'Another,' said Crane to the waiter.

Tony Lamphier was watching them. 'Do you mind if I join you?' he asked. 'It looks like fun.'

They didn't mind at all.

Lamphier rose to his feet. 'Gentlemen, I propose a toast.'

'To the queen . . .' said Crane.

'Yes, to Camelia Essex.'

They drank that toast. They drank a toast to the United States of America. They drank to the Army and Navy. They drank to 'the Stuarts o'er the sea.'

People at the neighbouring tables began to eye them.

'Now, gentlemen,' said Crane, 'I give you the finest toast of all. . . .'

They waited attentively.

'I give you our regiment . . .   The Seventh Hussars.

They drank the toast.

Tony Lamphier said: 'Now I want to give a confusion.'

O'Rourke was surprised. 'A confusion?'

'Yes. I drink to the confusion of Count Paul di Gregario.'

'Good,' said Crane.

'May he take the count,' added O'Rourke.

'That's very good,' said Crane. 'Don't you think that's very good, Tony?'

'Yes. I think that's very good.'

'I wish I had said that,' said Crane.

As they were drinking the orchestra stopped. Crane walked away from the table, skirted the dance floor, and came out into the hall leading to the front door. He saw the blonde hat-check girl and went over to her.

'Madam . . .' he began.

'To the left,' she said. 'Down that hall.'

Doc Williams and a Negro attendant were in the washroom. Doc Williams's Christian name was Orville and he was employed by the same detective agency as Crane. He was slapping eau de Cologne on his face. 'Hi,' he said. He was a dapper man with a waxed moustache and pouches under his eyes. He was wearing a green gabardine suit with a sports back, a tan silk shirt, a maroon necktie; and there was a streak of perfectly white hair over his left temple. Chorus girls always thought he looked 'distinguished.'

'Hi,' said Crane. 'What's the word?'

Williams glanced warningly at the attendant, who was rubbing his patent leather shoes. 'Our guy's here.'

'I saw him.'

'He's got three pals with him, too.'

'So,' Crane said.

The attendant finished the shoes, pushed the dirty towel through the swinging opening of a green metal container.

'Another thing.' Williams flipped the attendant a

quarter. 'A guy I used t'know in New York told me ...'
He looked at the attendant, said: 'You don't mind if
we go off in the corner and whisper?'

The Negro rolled his eyes: 'No, saar.'

In the corner Williams said: 'Tortoni's in a jam,
and is plannin' on leaving in a couple of days.'

'A money jam?'

'Not exactly. That is, it doesn't have to be. He's
been cuttin' in on the slot-machine racket, accordin'
to my friend, and some people are kinda mad.'

'How mad?'

'A week ago they knocked off Tony Ghenna, Tortoni's
muscle man.'

'That's pretty mad,' said Crane.

Major Eastcomb came into the wash-room. His face
was flushed from drinking, his bloodshot eyes were
angry, his jaw was set. His shoulders were bulky under
his black dinner-jacket.

'I can't possibly make it,' Crane said to Williams.
'I haven't time for golf. I'm down here on business.'

'It's a darned good course.'

'So I've heard. But nothing doing. I'll try to look
you up some afternoon, though, Doc.'

They shook hands and Williams departed. The
major scowled at Crane. 'Who's that?'

'A fellow I used to know in New York.'

The coloured man filled a bowl full of warm water
and laid a face towel beside it. Crane washed his hands
and face and dried them. On a glass shelf in front of
the long mirror was a large assortment of perfumes,
pomades and powders in fancy bottles, jars and cans.
Fascinated, he stared at them, inwardly struggling
against a desire to try them on himself.

Through the mirror he saw Count di Gregario come
into the room. He saw the count was really handsome
in a Latin way. That is, handsome and pretty. He
was tall, almost as tall as O'Rourke, but his figure was

slender. His double-breasted dinner-jacket, of heavy linen, was tailored in the Cuban style, padded and squared at the shoulders, pulled tight at the waist. Long, curling lashes shaded his brown eyes, and his skin, cream-rose, was as smooth as a girl's.

Major Eastcomb saw him a second later. He swung round and said: 'Ha!' He looked ferocious.

The count halted abruptly.

'So you're around again,' said the major.

The coloured attendant bent down and began to wipe off Crane's shoes.

Count di Gregario began: 'I assure you . . .'

'You bloody scoundrel.' The major mumbled his words as though he were talking with his mouth full. 'I told you to keep away from that girl.'

The attendant got down on one knee, turned his face so he could look at the two men. Crane could see the whites of his eyes.

Count di Gregario laughed. 'Since when must I obey your orders, Major Eastcomb?'

The major was shaking his head from side to side. 'You be out of town to-morrow or . . .'

Count di Gregario smiled and turned to leave the room. The major caught his arm, swung him round, hit him a solid blow on the chest. Count di Gregario came back at him. 'You pig!' he cried. He got a hand on the major's face, shoved. The major stepped backward; his buttocks striking a porcelain wash-bowl, his head the mirror, cracking it vertically. A piece of soap skidded across the tile floor.

Hands fluttering, the count followed. 'Aah!' he said. The major rolled off the wash-bowl; jerked an Army automatic from under his coat, thrust it at di Gregario.

The coloured boy at Crane's feet moaned: 'Lawd Jesus!' and slithered under the row of wash-basins. His skin was the colour of coffee with cream in it.

Cat quick, di Gregario snatched the pistol, struck the major across the face, across the bridge of his nose with the butt. Blood stained the major's white dress shirt, splattered on the lapels of his dress suit; his knees folded under him; his head hit the wash-bowl. There was a silvery bong, like the strike of a distant clock.

Di Gregario stood over him. 'Pig!' he said. 'Murderer!' He wiped the automatic with a towel, thrust it in his pocket. He turned to Crane. 'I do not think your *amigo* will bother me again.'

Crane looked at the major. 'I don't think he'll bother anybody for a while.' The major was making a feeble effort to get to his feet. Blood was still running from his nose.

'Señor, it is not well for any one to bother me,' said di Gregario. 'I wish you to speak of this to others.'

'I will,' said Crane.

'Thank you. *Adios, señor.*'

'*Adios.*'

Cold towels quickly cleared the major's head, helped to staunch the flow of blood. There were red bruises on his forehead and cheeks, and his left eye was going to be black, but Crane did not think his nose was broken. The coloured boy, induced to come out from under the wash-basins, found some cleaning fluid and they got most of the blood off the dinner-jacket.

'There,' said Crane at last. 'I guess you'll do.' He saw another spot, reached for it with his cloth.

'That's enough,' said Major Eastcomb. 'That's enough.' He pushed Crane away.

'I've paid money to see worse fights,' said Crane.

The major scowled at Crane. 'You're a fine coward.'

Crane's eyebrows lifted in surprise.

Anger made the blood ooze again from the major's nose. 'You stand there and let that dago beat me up.' He daubed at the blood with his handkerchief. 'You're through.' He waved the handkerchief at Crane.

'Through! You get out of the house by to-morrow morning'—he shouldered past Crane—'or I'll have you thrown out.' The door slammed behind him.

His eyes big as halves of hard-boiled eggs, the coloured boy turned to Crane. 'You work for him, boss?'

'I guess not,' said Crane.

CHAPTER FIVE

WILLIAM CRANE went back to the table, but there was no one there. He examined the bottles beside the table, found one with champagne in it, filled his glass. He put the bottle back in the bucket and sat down at the table. There were many dancers on the floor now, but he didn't see anybody he knew.

He had finished his glass and was reaching for the bottle when a crowd of people at a neighbouring table got up to leave. A pretty red-head in a green gown detached herself from the crowd, ran over and threw her arms round Crane's neck.

'Don't let 'em take me home,' she begged.

This created quite a sensation. 'Look out, Janey!' cried a girl in the crowd. The others giggled, halted. Two men, one of them quite drunk, came over to him. Vainly, they tried to pry the girl's arms from his neck.

'I like you,' the girl said, rubbing her cheek against the back of Crane's head.

'You . . .' said the drunker of the two men to Crane. 'Try to steal my girl, willya?'

'Now you wait a minute, Jake,' the other said. 'I'll handle this guy.'

'I like you,' the girl said. 'Don't let 'em take me.' Most recently she had been drinking *crème de menthe*.

The drunken man assumed a fighting pose. 'Steal my girl, willya?'

'Wait a minute, Jake,' the other said. 'Janey, don't you want to go home with Jake?'

She cuddled closer to Crane. 'No!'

'But, Janey . . .'

The drunken man asked: 'Ya wanna fight or not?'

'Now, Jake, I'll handle this guy. . . .'

The drunken man said: 'Nobuddy's gonna steal *my* girl.' He waved his left arm in front of him.

The other man attempted to drag the girl from Crane. He was afraid the drunken man would hit him when she was pulled away, so he held her tightly. The other man tugged at her. 'Don't be a damn fool, Janey. . . .'

Suddenly the girl released her hold and slapped Crane's face. 'You held me,' she accused him. She ran and threw her arms round the drunken man's neck. 'Oh, Jake, he wooden lemme go,' she wailed.

The other man began: 'Brother, you better watch your . . .' when the head waiter and two assistants arrived. 'What's the matter here?' The other man eagerly told him, finishing, '. . . and it took two of us to get the little lady away from him.'

The two assistants moved toward Crane.

'Take him to Mr. Tortoni,' said the head waiter.

They pushed their way through the large crowd surrounding the table, crossed a corner of the dance floor, and mounted two flights of heavily carpeted stairs. They went down a long corridor and passed an open door. Crane saw men and women clustered about a roulette wheel and piles of ivory counters behind the barred cage of the cashier. Among the men he saw O'Rourke.

'Look,' he said, 'this is insane . . .'

'Shut up,' said one of the assistants.

They went through a small room with a black marble

floor and chairs covered with white leather, and halted
in front of a door. One of the assistants knocked.
There was a buzzing noise and the assistant pushed
open the door. The other man took Crane's left hand
and twisted him into the room. Behind a desk on
which sat two French phones and a square electric
clock was a thick-jowled man in a cream suit of silk
pongee. Bushy above small eyes, his black brows met
over his nose. He had on a violet silk shirt and a maroon
tie with a spot near the knot.

'What's the matter?' he asked the first assistant.

Behind Tortoni, half in shadow, a woman smoked a
cigarette through a jade holder. Crane saw it was Imago
Paraguay.

'This guy tried t' grab a dame from tha party at table
eleven,' said the first assistant. 'Damndest thing I
ever seen . . . he was tryin' to hold tha dame on his lap
and fight two guys at the same time.'

'A stew,' supplemented the other assistant.

Crane had difficulty repressing a giggle.

Imago spoke in her flat, feline voice. 'A sudden
pa-ssion, Mr. Crane?' Smoke floated from her red
mouth as she talked. 'This is Mr. Tortoni, Mr.
Cra-ane.'

'Who's Mr. Crane?' demanded Tortoni.

'Mr. Cra-ane is with the Essex party.'

Tortoni's scowl faded. 'Pleased t'meet ya, Mr.
Crane.' He reached a broad hand over the table.
'Now what's the trouble?'

Crane ignored the hand. He pretended to be angry.
'This is a swell sort of a place . . . where your thugs can
pick out some innocent person and . . .'

Tortoni looked startled. 'Some mistake?'

'All right. All right. Put it this way. I saw a
girl with auburn hair.' He leaned over Tortoni, fixed
him with his eyes. 'Do you know what happens to
me when I see a girl with auburn hair?'

'No, Mr. Crane,' said Tortoni.

'I see red,' said Crane triumphantly.

Imago Paraguay explained: 'Mr. Cra-ane makes a joke. He has mu-uch humour.'

Tortoni grunted. Puffy cheeks and bushy brows made his small eyes look like animals peering out of caves. He moistened his lips.

The dancer continued: 'I shall be responsible for Mr. Cra-ane. I think I can prevent his seeing red again.' She removed the cigarette from the jade holder, squeezed it out in a brass tray on the desk. 'Now, Mr. Tortoni, if you will just cash my che-eque, we will bother you no longer.'

Tortoni fumbled in a drawer of his desk, produced a metal box. 'It was for five . . .'

'One thousand do-lars, Mr. Tortoni.'

His stubby hands counted out ten one-hundred dollar bills.

'Tha-ank you,' she said. 'Shall we go, Mr. Cra-ane?'

Once in the hall on the other side of the room with the white leather chairs Crane experienced a strong sensation of relief. He realized he had been frightened, but he was unable to determine exactly why. What could Tortoni do to him?

He felt the dancer's hand on his arm. 'Thanks,' he said.

'It was nothing,' she said.

'Yes, but he could have . . .'

'It was nothing,' she said. They reached the roulette room. 'Shall we gamble, señor?'

Crane blinked in the brightly lit room. He saw most of the Essex party at the end of the roulette table. The major had a piece of court plaster on the bridge of his nose. Tony Lamphier, standing behind Camelia Essex's blonde head, waved at them. The others were intent on the wheel.

Imago Paraguay, to Crane's surprise, bought a

thousand dollars' worth of counters.   He had intended
to spend a hundred dollars, but instead he gave the man
five hundred.   He put the counters in his pocket,
followed the dancer to the table and found a place for
her.   Some one touched his shoulder.   It was O'Rourke.
He drew Crane aside.

'Doc and Eddie have lost track of the count.'

'Yeah?'

'He and the three Cuban torpedoes with him must
have got out through a back door.   Eddie's been
watching out in front all the time.'

'Cubans?'

'They look like Cubans.'

Crane thought for a minute.   'Well, we're supposed
to be fired, but there's no use quitting until we make
sure.   Tell Doc and Eddie to go back to the count's
hotel.   Maybe they can pick him up.'

'Who fired us?'

'The major.

O'Rourke grinned.   'So you were the guy that slugged
him.'

'I didn't, but I might just as well have.'   Crane told
him of the fight between the count and the major. . . .
'So we're out in the cold now.'

'It's not so cold,' said O'Rourke.   'I've knocked
down a couple of C-notes on the wheel.'

'You think it's straight?'

'I'm two C's ahead, ain't I?'

'Don't let Miss Day find out.'   Crane winked at
O'Rourke and went back to Imago Paraguay.   She
said: 'You must bring me luck, Mr. Cra-ane.'   She had
only four hundred dollars' worth of counters in front of
her.

'Make your bets, please,' the croupier whispered.

Crane leaned between Imago and a large woman
glittering with diamonds and put a hundred on
red.   With a lean hand, the croupier spun the wheel,

whispered: 'No more, please.' His brilliant black eyes were on Imago.

The ball halted on red and odd. At the end of the table Essex said petulantly: 'Damn!' The croupier pushed chips at Crane. He let them stay on red. Imago also put two hundred on red, saying: 'We will go down together.'

Red came a second time. 'Let it ride,' said Crane.

Red came again, and again. People began to look at them. A hard-faced man in a tuxedo took up a position behind the croupier, watched them through cold blue eyes. Crane let thirty-two hundred ride on red.

The hard-faced man pushed two hundred dollars' worth of the counters back. 'Three thousand limit,' he said.

'Oh, I see,' Crane said. 'Penny ante, hey?'

There was silence as the ivory pea bumbled about the wheel. The cold eyes of the hard-faced man were riveted on Crane. The large woman with the jewels was breathing heavily. The rattle of the ball ceased.

'Red and odd.'

Crane accepted the pile of counters. 'We can't bet them,' he said to Imago Paraguay. 'What will we do with them?'

Her sloe eyes were glittering. 'This way,' she said. She let the three thousand remain on red. The other three thousand she put on odd.

Crane took the remaining two hundred dollars and put them on 33. 'Swing it,' he said to the croupier.

It seemed to Crane the wheel spun for hours. He noticed the eyes of the hard-faced man were almost the colour of ice. He noticed Miss Day looking at him with admiration. He felt Imago Paraguay's cool hand on his wrist.

'Thirty-three, red and uneven,' whispered the croupier.

The hard-faced man said: 'The wheel is closed for the night.'

'Yow!' shouted Tony Lamphier from the end of the table. 'A toast to the man who broke the bank at Monte Carlo.'

Miss Day, breathless, leaned over Crane. 'Wasn't that marvellous?' Waves of perfume floated from her.

The lady with the jewels said: 'May I ask what your system is?'

'I start with one hundred dollars,' said Crane, 'and stop when the bank is broken.'

Imago Paraguay said: 'Shall we cash in, Mr. Cra-ane?'

Their counters came to nineteen thousand, six hundred dollars—nineteen thousand in winnings, and the four hundred Crane had left of his original purchase and the two hundred Imago had left of hers. He gave her nine thousand, seven hundred dollars and put the rest in his wallet.

'I think we can afford a glass of champagne,' he said.

The entire party went down to their table and drank the champagne Crane bought. Crane danced once with Camelia Essex.

'I wish you'd keep a closer watch on Penn,' she said. 'I'm worried about him.'

'He'll be all right,' Crane said.

Miss Day didn't think the orchestra was hot enough. She wanted to go to the Club Paris. 'They really swing it over there,' she said.

'Let's do go over there,' said Essex. 'It's only two o'clock.' He got the bill.

They waited for the women in front of the check-room. Tony Lamphier was admiring the hat-check blonde.

'Isn't she a lovely thing?' he said.

'I think she's a blonde,' said Crane.

The hat-check girl simpered.

'She's lovely,' said Tony Lamphier. 'Isn't she lovely?'

'Where *are* those women?' asked Boucher.

'Where is my hat?' asked Crane.

'Dincha have a check?' asked the girl.

'Isn't she lovely?' said Tony Lamphier.

'I gotta have a check,' said the girl.

'No hat, no check,' said O'Rourke.

'I'm going out for some air,' said Major Eastcomb. He went out through the front door.

'Has nobody a check?' Crane repeated. 'This lovely little lady has gotta have a check.'

'She *is* a lovely thing,' said Tony Lamphier.

'They have a lovely wheel here, too,' Crane said.

'It's honest,' O'Rourke said.

'It's lovely and honest,' Crane said.

Mrs. Boucher came up to him. 'Imago's been telling us of your . . . adventure.' She linked her arm with him. 'Tell me, are you only affected by red-heads?' She smelled the nicest of any of the women. She smelled of English lavender.

Miss Day appeared with Imago Paraguay. For a second the dancer's eyes were on Crane. Miss Day said: 'Come on, let's go. This joint's stuffy.'

Essex and O'Rourke both went to escort Miss Day to the door. Boucher seemed pleased to get Miss Paraguay.

'I like you,' said Crane to Mrs. Boucher.

'And you a rich man,' said Mrs. Boucher.

They started to follow Tony Lamphier and Camelia Essex to the door.

'Doncha want yer hat?' asked the hat-check girl.

'No,' said Crane. 'Keep it as a memento.'

'You *are* having a fine time,' said Mrs. Boucher.

The Bugatti, black and low, was in front of the door. Essex was standing beside it with his sister and Tony Lamphier. 'Where's the major?' he asked.

Crane was noticing that the doorman was a white man now, not a Negro, when two men with handkerchiefs tied over the lower portions of their faces came round the back of the Bugatti. They both carried automatic pistols.

One of them said: 'This is a stick-up. Put 'em up.'

Miss Day started to scream and the other man snarled: 'Can it, sister.' He shoved his pistol at O'Rourke, beside her.

The first man took hold of Camelia Essex's arm, jerked her toward him, saying: 'Come along, baby.' For an instant he was in the path of light from the door and Crane saw the lobe of his ear was missing.

Tony Lamphier moved to help Camelia and the first man slugged him with the barrel of his pistol. He crumpled against the Bugatti, slid down to the gravel drive. Essex moved forward and the man hit him, too. Camelia screamed as her brother staggered backward.

Crane tried to reach the man covering O'Rourke, but the doorman hit him on the cheek-bone, sent him spinning into Boucher. When he got his balance, Camelia, the man with the lobeless ear and the doorman had disappeared. The second masked man, his body crouched, was backing round the Bugatti 'Move, you dudes, move,' he jeered. 'See what happens.' He swung his pistol in front of him, like a man using a garden hose.

There was the beep of a horn. 'O.K.,' said the man. He scuttled behind the Bugatti and an instant later a black sedan roared down the drive. Miss Day screamed. Crazily, the sedan twisted into the street. In the back seat two men fought with Camelia Essex; in the front, beside the driver, the doorman was ripping off his uniform.

Essex scrambled into the Bugatti, pressed the starter. 'Come on,' he yelled. His pale face was wild.

Tony Lamphier was trying to get off the ground.

Crane pulled him into the back seat of the Bugatti, fell with him against the leather cushion as the car got under way with a roar. O'Rourke was already in the front seat.

Far down the street, as they came out of the drive, they could see the tail-light of the sedan. It was steady for several seconds; then it curved to the right. An instant later they heard the scream of its tyres. 'He's taking the County Causeway,' Crane shouted.

Essex nodded and braked for the turn. The Bugatti's tyres wailed, too, and alarmed householders switched on lights in bedrooms, telephoned police. On the causeway the Bugatti leaped like a greyhound, raced past a sleek roadster. The sedan was still far ahead.

Tony Lamphier moaned and made a gagging noise in his throat.

After a minute Crane asked: 'Feel better?'

Tony Lamphier nodded and asked: 'They got her?'

O'Rourke yelled over the noise of the wind and motor: 'A turn!'

Essex, braking, said: 'I see it,' and in an instant they were on Biscayne Boulevarde, heading for town.

'They got her?' Lamphier asked again.

'Yeah,' said Crane.

They neared the row of big hotels opposite Bay Front Park, gained a little on the sedan, and O'Rourke leaned out of the tonneau. Three times his revolver flashed, deafened their ears. The sedan swung to the right.

O'Rourke looked back at Crane. 'That ought to bring out the cops,' he shouted.

It did, but too late. They had turned right, past part of the business section of Miami, and were turning left toward the bridge over the river when a squad car came out of a side street and joined in the chase. Its spot-light flashed through their rear window: its siren was ululant, but it soon dropped far behind.

'Too bad,' said Crane.

'We'll catch 'em ourselves,' shouted O'Rourke. 'We're on a straight road.'

Behind them the police siren howled plaintively.

'How are we going to handle them?' asked Tony Lamphier. 'They had guns, hadn't they?'

The Bugatti was now travelling very fast. Hard and tangible, the wind rushed in the open sides of the tonneau, pressed them back against the seat. The cement road, white in the glare of their head-lights, swept under them. The whine of the engine, the tyres, the wind, rose shriller and shriller, piercing their ears.

Essex, jack-knifed over the wheel, spoke to O'Rourke who repeated to Crane: 'There's a revolver in the pocket on the left-hand door.'

Crane found it, flicked open the chamber. There were five cartridges in it. 'Got it,' he told O'Rourke.

The Bugatti's light picked up the black bulk of the sedan, outlined the swaying top. They were steadily gaining.

'You better get on the floor,' Crane told Lamphier. 'The fireworks are about due.'

'I'm not scared,' Lamphier replied, and then asked: 'Isn't there danger of hitting Camelia?'

'They'll keep her down.'

'It'd be awful . . .'

With a breath-taking swerve that sent Crane flying against Lamphier, the Bugatti angled toward the ditch on the left side of the cement, then, as sheerly as crazily as before, it yawed to the right. Crane ducked his head, held his breath for the crash. . . .

Instead, the Bugatti straightened out, less sickeningly this time, and slackened speed. Cautiously Crane raised his head. O'Rourke was leaning across the seat, his hands on the wheel, but Essex was not in sight.

'Oh, my God!' said Crane. 'Did he fall out?'

'How do you stop this thing?' asked O'Rourke.

'Great Joseph!' Crane yelled. *'Did he fall out?'*

'Naw,' said O'Rourke calmly. 'He's on the floor. Where in hell's the hand-brake?'

Crane sank back on the seat and rubbed his forehead with the back of his hand. He was surprised to find he was sweating. 'What happened?' asked Tony Lamphier.

The Bugatti was coming to a stop. Crane said: 'God knows,' and opened the door and stepped out on to the cement. O'Rourke lifted Essex from the floor. 'Cold as a haddock,' he observed.

'We better get him to a doctor,' said Crane.

'Are you going to let Camelia go?' asked Tony Lamphier.

'Essex may be dying,' said Crane.

'He's breathing,' volunteered O'Rourke.

'But Camelia . . .?' Tony Lamphier's voice was anguished. 'Those men . . . what will they do to her? We *have* to go on.'

'What can we do now?' Crane looked down the road. 'They're out of sight. Besides, the police will block all roads.'

'Oh, God!' Lamphier sat on the Bugatti's front fender, hid his face in his hands. 'I love her so.'

'I think our guy's coming to,' said O'Rourke.

While a soft, fragrant breeze fingered their faces, they watched Essex, listened to his laboured breathing. There was an odour of jasmine in the air. It was funny to be smelling jasmine, Crane thought. He saw that it was only two-thirty-four by the clock on the Bugatti's dashboard. He felt surprised that so much could have happened in such a short time.

'You're all right now, pal,' said O'Rourke.

Essex sat up on the seat, looked blankly around him. 'Cam! . . . Cam!' His eyes became normal. 'What happened?'

'You passed out,' said O'Rourke.

'While I was driving? How did you stop the car?'

'I don't know myself,' said O'Rourke. 'You slumped over and there I was at the wheel.'

'And the sedan?'

'It kept on,' said O'Rourke.

The thought of the Bugatti's swerve made Crane's stomach turn over. 'How fast were we going?' he asked.

'A hundred and five,' said O'Rourke.

'That fast?' Crane found he couldn't swallow. 'I need a drink.'

'There's some port in the dashboard compartment,' said Essex. 'I'm afraid it's Californian port, though.

'Any port in a storm,' said Crane.

CHAPTER SIX

SUNSHINE as liquid, as thick, as golden as pancake syrup laved the bed, warmed his face. Through the French windows came the soft frou-frou of the surf, like a woman moving about in a satin gown; the whisper of wind in the palms; the buzz of insects. The air was sticky hot. He hid his face under a pillow.

'Go away,' he muttered. 'I am unwell.'

O'Rourke shook him again. 'Come on, dope,' he said, 'it's almost ten.'

Crane opened one eye, peeked out from under the pillow. He saw O'Rourke was dressed in a freshly-pressed tan gabardine suit. He closed the eye.

'The cops are here,' said O'Rourke. 'They'll be wanting to see you.'

'Hold the bed still,' said Crane, 'and I'll see if I can sit up.'

He sat up, pressing the sides of his head with his palms.

'Try this.' O'Rourke thrust out a glass half filled with a milky liquid. 'A hair of the St. Bernard that bit you.'

'Oh, no. I'll never drink anything again. What is it?'

'Pernod.'

'I can't feel any worse.' Crane took the glass, gulped the contents, fell back on the bed.

His pallor alarmed O'Rourke. 'You gonna be sick?'

'I don't know.'

He didn't, either. There was considerable agitation, almost an earthquake, in his stomach, and he closed his eyes and waited. Presently he felt better.

'Ha!' said O'Rourke.

Crane sat up, pushed the Nile-green sheet from him. 'I may live,' he said, 'but I'll never be a well man again.'

'They found the sedan at a place called Matecumbe,' said O'Rourke. 'There was blood on the back seat.'

'Sleep no more!' said Crane. 'O'Rourke does murder sleep!'

'They figure they took her on a boat,' said O'Rourke. 'The sedan was right by the water. The whole state's looking for her—police, militia, coast-guard, everything. Biggest search in history.'

'"Innocent sleep,"' said Crane, '"sleep that knits up the ravell'd sleeve of care."'

'Doc Williams telephoned, too.'

Crane was massaging his sore jaw. '"The death of each day's life . . ."'

'He said the count didn't get in until six this morning.'

'Huh?' Crane's eyes focussed on O'Rourke. 'Not until six?'

'And the three torpedoes with him have disappeared.'

'That's very interesting.' Crane swung his feet over the side of the bed. 'How's Essex?'

'He's all right, I guess. Oh, yeah, he got another note.'

'From Old Bright Eye?'

'Yeah, it was pinned to his pillow. He found it when he woke up. He gave it to the cops, but I made a copy of it. Here.'

Crane took the piece of paper. It read:

'ESSEX,

'If you want your sister back alive get ready to pay the fifty thousand . . . in small bills. . . . I will let you know when and how.

'THE EYE.'

Crane gave the note back to O'Rourke. 'That's not as pretty as the one I got,' he said, taking a folded piece of paper from under the pillow. 'Would you care to see it?'

This note read:

'FLATFOOT,

'The alligators in the swamp are hungry for your flesh . . . and they shall have it. . . . I rarely warn twice. . . . Did you enjoy your winnings? . . . Ha, ha, ha!

'THE EYE.'

Crane held out his foot in the beam of light from the window. 'O'Rourke, would you call that a flat foot?'

O'Rourke asked: 'What's he mean about your winnings, ha, ha, ha?'

'He got my wallet.' Crane straightened his leg. 'I really think I have a nice arch.'

'He got all nine grand?' O'Rourke sounded as though he were about to weep.

'No, Uncle Willy was too smart for that,' said Crane. 'Uncle Willy left about seven hundred dollars in his wallet and hid the rest.'

'Where?' asked O'Rourke. Crane pointed and O'Rourke said: 'Well, for God's sake!'

Mixed with a crumpled *Miami Herald*, some torn brown wrapping paper, a piece of string, a black silk sock with a hole in the foot and a shirt cardboard, all in a green metal waste-basket, were nine one-thousand dollar bills.

'You see, money means nothing to me,' said Crane, and then added hurriedly: 'Don't you touch those bills.'

O'Rourke collected them, however, and put them on the dresser. 'What are you going to do?' he asked.

'If I don't die I'm going swimming.'

'No, I mean about the girl.'

Crane swung his feet under the bed. 'I think we ought to talk to Tortoni and to the count. I'd like to find out if either one knows a gent with no lobe to his ear.'

'That was the guy who grabbed Camelia?'

'Yeah. I'll bet he's got something to do with Tortoni.'

'Tortoni *is* the guy behind all this,' O'Rourke said. 'I'd bet on that.'

'Not with me. Though I can't see him writing notes signed The Eye.'

'Maybe he's got a Poison Pen planted in the house.'

'Maybe. But let the cops work on that. Asking questions tires me.'

'Don't forget he's got seven hundred of yours.'

'He probably needs it to buy red ink.'

Crane went into the bathroom and put on his swimming trunks. He brushed his teeth with some difficulty, finding the blow had made it impossible for him to open his mouth more than a few inches, and drank a glass of water. He felt pretty good.

When he came out, O'Rourke was staring at the ceiling. 'What's the matter?' he asked him.

'Those placed in the ceiling . . . what are they for?'

Crane looked at the steel grilles in the four corners of the room. They were all about a foot square. 'Ventilation,' he said. 'I think I heard a fan going in the attic last night.'

'What good does a fan do up there?'

'It draws out the warm air in the house and lets cool air in the windows.' He scowled at O'Rourke. 'Got any more of that liquorice water?'

'You have breakfast first,' said O'Rourke.

'Maybe we get no breakfast. I remember the major being a little peeved with me last night.'

'How about the major?'

'That's right. Where was he when the trouble began?'

'The major told Tony Lamphier they slugged him, too.'

'I wonder.'

'Lamphier says the major told him he was out cold all the time we were in front of the joint.'

'I like Lamphier,' Crane said.

'Yeah, he's all right. He's certainly sunk about that girl.'

'I got an idea he sort of liked her.'

'Too bad a gal like that has to go for a phoney Spig.'

Crane put on his bath-robe and started for the door. He said: 'What she needs is a nice, steady fellow like me.' He went down to the beach.

The water was such a brilliant blue it hurt his eyes. It was warm and remarkably calm, and he waded out until he was no longer able to walk. With a long sigh he turned over on his back and allowed himself to float. The sky was also very blue.

He wondered what it was like to be a woman and held by kidnappers. He often wondered what it was like to be a woman, but never before in connection with kidnapping. He supposed it was pretty bad. In the first place, when you were kidnapped, man or woman, you were always in doubt wehther your captors would ultimately kill you or release you. But with a woman there was another consideration. With a pretty girl like Camelia Essex, especially, there was another consideration.

This flight into conjecture so agitated him that he failed to see an approaching whitecap. It tumbled over his face and, spluttering, he swam toward shore. Ordinarily he didn't worry much about a case he was on, but he was really disturbed about Camelia Essex. He hoped Count di Gregario had her.

On the shore, by his bath-robe, O'Rourke and Essex were talking. Essex spoke about the two notes. He looked very white and haggard. 'The fellow must have an accomplice in the house,' he said.

'There's no doubt of it,' said Crane. 'Your guess, though, is as good as mine.'

'The cops are going through our rooms,' said O'Rourke.

Crane was alarmed. 'They'll get the nine thou'.'

'I got it,' said O'Rourke.

'That's just as bad.' He put on his candy-striped robe. 'Is it all right if we have breakfast?' he asked Essex.

'Why not?'

'The major . . .'

'I've talked with him,' said Essex. His eyes were angry. 'You're working for the estate, not for him. He didn't hire you and he can't dismiss you.'

'That's fine. I *am* a trifle hungry.'

'I told him there's no reason why you should have

helped him against the count.   He admitted he started
the fight.'

'That's fine.'

'I'm not going to see you go just when we need you
most.'   He walked beside Crane toward the patio.
'Who do you think's got her?'

'The Eye,' Crane said.

'No, I mean . . .'

'I don't know as I even want to know,' said
Crane.

'What do you mean?' asked Essex.

'It may be dangerous to find out . . . for her.'   Crane
sat at the breakfast table, told the serving-man: 'Coffee,
toast and orange juice.'

Essex stood beside him.   'I don't understand.'

'Make that tomato juice,' Crane called after the
serving-man.   He faced Essex.   'You can bet The
Eye isn't holding her in person.   If he's caught, his
men may let her go, or . . .'

He drew his finger across his throat.

Essex sank into a chair, leaned his forehead against
his palms.   'This is terrible.'

Two men, walking heavily on the cement edge of
the swimming-pool, approached the table.   Both were
bulky, muscular, red-faced; both wore dark fedoras;
both looked as though they'd slept in their dark suits.
Crane knew they were policemen.   One of them had a
badly set broken nose.

'You're Crane, ain't you?' asked the man with
the crooked nose.   He was older than his companion.

Crane nodded.

'I'm Captain Enright, out of the bureau in Miami.
This is Slocum of the sheriff's office.'

'This is O'Rourke . . .' Crane began.

'We know O'Rourke,' said Slocum.   Black stubble
covered his bulldog jaw.   'We think you're a hell of
a fine pair of amateur detectives.'

'Now Slocum.' Captain Enright's deep voice was soothing. 'What's happened has . . .'

'Let 'em snatch a girl from under your eyes . . . it's a blot on the whole profession . . .'

'They did all they could, Mr. Slocum,' said Essex. 'If I hadn't keeled over we would have caught them easily. It's all my fault.'

The serving-man was pouring the coffee. 'Two lumps and no cream,' Crane told him.

Captain Enright said: 'We're not blaming you, Mr. Essex.'

Slocum had moved round so he could look at Crane's face. His black eyes were sharp. 'It's these imitation dicks . . .' he commenced.

'Have some coffee?' inquired Crane.

'Now look here. . . .' said Slocum.

'Listen, you big gorilla,' said Crane angrily, 'the taxpayers of Dade county are paying you, not us, to protect them. Why don't you get mad at yourself?'

O'Rourke got into a position to hit Slocum if necessary, but Captain Enright, authority in his voice, said: 'Don't make a fool of yourself, Slocum.'

As Slocum mastered his anger, O'Rourke said: 'I told you we'd talk with you, but if you're going to bawl us . . .'

Crane picked up a piece of toast, held it in front of his mouth and said: 'I won't talk to them.'

'Now, we're sorry, Mr. Crane,' said Captain Enright. His theory was that it didn't cost a policeman anything to be polite. Besides, you never knew who you were talking to. The mayor had a lot of funny friends. 'We're naturally upset about this thing.'

'All right,' said Crane, 'I'll talk to you. But not'—he pointed the piece of toast at Slocum—'with this orang-outang.'

O'Rourke got set again, but Slocum accepted the insult. The captain's failure to back him up frightened him. Maybe this mug with the smooth face was somebody. With the sheriff kind of mad at him over the load of smuggled Bacardi he'd picked up that he shouldn't have, he'd better watch his step. He scowled at Crane, but he didn't say anything.

Crane ate the piece of toast. 'What do you want to know?'

The captain, it seemed, wanted to know everything. He wanted to know exactly what happened at the Blue Castle before and during the kidnapping. He seemed to know everything already, but Crane patiently went over the story. He said nothing, however, of the man with no lobe on his ear. He was just describing the chase when Miss Day sat down at the table. She glanced at the serving-man.

'Coffee,' she said, 'and plenty of it.'

The yellow sunlight turned to henna in her hair, faintly outlined her body through the Chinese red pyjamas. Her face was tan; her lips scarlet; her eyes shaded with blue mascara. Her pointed breasts pressed against the tight red silk of her pyjama coat.

'Go ahead, boys,' she said, perfectly composed under their admiring scrutiny. 'Don't mind me. I'll just sit here with my headache.'

'Well,' said Crane, 'Mr. Essex fainted and we damned near turned over. When we got things straightened out the sedan was out of sight.'

'I dunno what we'd have done if we did catch 'em,' said O'Rourke. 'They probably had a Tommy-gun or two.'

'I don't want to seem critical,' said Captain Enright, 'but I think you should have called the police. We could've bottled them up when they came through town.'

'We didn't know which way they were going,' Crane smiled at Miss Day's sour expression. 'Besides, we knew Boucher would call you.'

Slocum said: 'In my opinion this Eye is a crank.'
He seemed to be speaking to Miss Day.

The serving-man was pouring Miss Day's coffee.
Crane leaned toward her. 'Jitters?' Miss Day replied:
'And how!'

'Crank or not,' said Captain Enright, 'you gotta
admit he's got Miss Essex.'

'Me, too,' said Crane to Miss Day. 'Do you know
what?'

O'Rourke asked the captain: 'How about Tortoni?'
Miss Day lifted the spoon with her little finger crooked.
'No, what?'

'We talked with him,' said Slocum. 'He's okay.
He wouldn't pull a thing like that in his own place.'

Crane said: 'They say brandy is awfully good in
coffee.'

Miss Day smiled. 'You got brains, big boy.' She
crooked a finger at the waiter. 'Pablo, a bottle of
your best brandy.'

'That's what I thought,' said O'Rourke, 'but you
never can tell.'

'Oh, we'll keep an eye on Tortoni,' Captain Enright
said.

'How about that count?' asked Miss Day. 'How
about him?'

'I believe you've put your finger on it, miss,' said
the captain gallantly. 'Yes, sir. I believe you have.'

'We're tryin' to find him,' said Slocum.

The serving-man came with the bottle of brandy.
Crane took it and poured a quantity in Miss Day's
coffee. Then he put some in his empty cup and
poured coffee over it. He put in a lump of sugar.
He stirred it with his spoon. He took a long drink.
It was fine. He grinned at Miss Day. She smiled at
him.

The others discussed the notes. They had them
all, including the two received by Crane, in front

of them on the breakfast table. Captain Enright maintained The Eye had planned to kidnap Miss Essex from the start. He said that was why the notes threatened Essex, to throw him off his guard. O'Rourke wanted to know why The Eye hadn't gone ahead, then, and kidnapped the girl without warning anybody.

'In my opinion,' said Slocum, 'this Eye is a crank.' Captain Enright said he didn't think so. He said, leaning over the table and speaking with an air of mystery, that he thought The Eye was right here in the house. Somebody you'd never suspect.

'You make me feel like there was a cold foot in the middle of my back,' Miss Day assured him, pretending to shudder.

Crane poured brandy in her coffee. He poured some in his cup, but did not add any coffee.

Slocum asserted that this was just the point about a crank. A crank was almost always somebody you'd never suspect. He'd had a lot of experience with cranks and he guessed he knew. Take the one he'd caught at the Biltmore. A religious crank. Guests had complained that somebody was writing on blotters and sticking notes under their doors. He looked around and one day he noticed people were coming from the bar with pieces of paper stuck on their backs. He went into the bar and grabbed an old gent that looked like a banker at the door. He was the guy, all right. He'd had his pockets stuffed full of stickers and on them was printed: HAVE YOU BEEN SAVED?

Crane was interested. 'From what?' he asked.

'Huh?'

'Saved from what?'

'Why,' said Slocum, 'that's all it said. "Have you been saved?"'

'You didn't ask the man from what?'

'Why, no.'

'So,' said Crane in a disapproving tone.

Captain Enright shifted impatiently. 'I don't see that we are gettin' anywhere,' he said. 'Our job is to catch the guy sendin' these notes, daffy or otherwise. We gotta protect the people in this house.' His bulging eyes sought Crane. 'They been frightened enough.'

'I'll say,' agreed Miss Day. 'When I saw that note on the pillow this morning I . . .'

Crane halted his cup half-way to his mouth, blinked at her.

Essex explained hurriedly: 'She looked in to see if I'd go swimming with her this morning.'

Miss Day giggled. 'It did sound a little bit . . .'

Crane said: 'You better have another drink.'

'What we gotta decide about is the ransom,' said Captain Enright. 'We gotta . . .'

Major Eastcomb pulled out a chair beside O'Rourke. 'Mind if I join the conference?' he asked. Two strips of adhesive tape criss-crossed the bridge of his nose, but otherwise his face, his head, showed no sign of injury.

'Glad to have you, Major,' said Captain Enright heartily. 'I don't believe you met Slocum of the sheriff's office. We were just speaking of the ransom.'

'Pleased t'meet you, Major,' said Slocum. He eyed the tape. 'Is that where they hit you?'

'Yes.'

'Quite a coincidence,' said Crane.

'What do you mean?' asked the major.

'To be hit on the same place on the same nose twice in the same evening.'

The major put the palms of both hands on the table. 'Are you intimating . . .?'

'I merely said it was a coincidence.'

'I don't like your tone.'

Miss Day said: 'Aw, come on, Majie. It's too early in the day to get mad.'

Major Eastcomb spoke to Captain Enright. 'I told you exactly what happened. I came out of the door and walked over to the Bugatti. A fellow came up and said, "Have you a light?" I reached in my pocket and the fellow hit me between the eyes. I came to in a clump of bushes by the drive.'

'Impudent beggar,' said Crane.

Miss Day said: 'Shush.'

Captain Enright looked at Crane with mild reproof. 'We wouldn't think of questioning *your* story, Major,' he said.

The major's face relaxed.

'When you came up,' Captain Enright continued, 'we were just speakin' of the ransom. I was about to say that Mr. Essex would be very foolish to pay it.'

'That's right.' As though he had palsy, Slocum's head jerked up and down. His neck was dirty. 'If this Eye's a crank he's gonna do what he's gonna do to Miss Essex, money or no money.'

Essex said: 'Oh, my God!' Miss Day patted his arm.

'Now, Mr. Essex, don't take it so hard,' said Captain Enright. 'We're handlin' this' . . . you can trust us. Like as not some of our men are on the trail at this very minute.'

Slocum added: 'They may even have got her.'

'Unharmed,' said Captain Enright, falling into the spirit of optimism.

'Except for the loss of a night's sleep,' continued Slocum.

Crane said: 'Now that you got her back, we don't have to talk about a ransom.'

Essex said: 'What do you think, Major?' His eyes were bloodshot. 'What are we to do when the directions for paying come?'

There was phlegm in the major's throat. 'You know I care for Camelia as much as anybody in the

world . . . as much as anybody.' He clenched his
fist. 'But what guarantee have we that she'll be
released after we pay the money?'

Essex's voice jangled in their ears. 'But we can't
just sit here . . .'

'But you won't be sittin' here,' Captain Enright
said. 'The whole world'll be lookin' for your sister.
Every newspaper in the country'll have her picture
in it. The police everywhere'll watch for her, Mr.
Essex. And they'll find her.'

O'Rourke took the bottle of brandy, filled a tumbler
half-way to the top. 'They never found a snatch-victim
yet,' he said.

Crane had forgotten about his brandy. 'Mr.
Essex,' he asked, 'is the fifty thousand available for a
ransom?'

Essex turned imploringly to the major.

'I talked with Mr. Hastings on the long-distance
phone this morning.' Major Eastcomb tilted his
head towards Captain Enright. 'He's president of the
Union Trust. He said the money will be deposited
immediately in the First National at Miami. There
now, I suppose.'

So tight were Essex's fingers on the table that the
skin turned white. 'But you're not going to refuse . . .?'
There was terror in his eyes.

'I think we ought to delay payment . . . at least for a
while.'

Captain Enright nodded approval. 'That's right.
Give us a chance maybe to save you fifty thousand
dollars, Mr. Essex.'

'Sure. Leave it to us,' said Slocum.

Crane pushed the coffee-cup out of his way. He
was genuinely angry. 'Do you want my opinion?'

Nobody did, apparently At least nobody spoke.

'I'll give it to you, anyway First you ought to
ask the Department of Justice for help.'

Major Eastcomb said dryly: 'We have.'

'Good. That's something sensible for a change. The second thing is to have the bank to get that fifty grand ready for you.' Crane was talking directly to Essex. 'Then put an ad in the papers. Say: "Money is ready. Please select contact man." And sign your own name to the ad.'

The major was aghast. 'But that'd throw us right in the swine's hands!'

'You're right in his hands now.' Crane spoke passionately. 'What do these cops care about Camelia Essex? What do they care what she's going through right now? How frightened she is? All they want is a chance to catch the kidnappers. Look at the publicity they'd get if they did.'

'How much cut you gettin' out of the ransom?' asked Slocum.

Crane ignored him. 'Then when the directions come, pay the money exactly as they direct.'

Slocum sneered: 'And what if they don't let her go?'

'You're no worse off than you were before.'

'You think throwin' fifty grand away puts you no worse off?'

'What's fifty thousand to the Essex estate?' Crane pushed the cup farther away. 'Possibly one-tenth of a year's income.'

'That's a lot of sugar,' said Captain Enright.

Now high in the sky, the sun toasted their backs. Wind rustled the palm leaves. Fresh water gurgled into the pool.

'It's her money, isn't it?' demanded Crane.

Major Eastcomb cleared his throat. 'I shouldn't care to pay out fifty thousand dollars needlessly,' he said stiffly. 'How can we know she will be returned?'

'Oh, God!' Crane's hands, palms upward, rose in

a huckster's gesture. 'Do you think you can sign a contract with them?'

'Penny, I think he's right,' said Miss Day. 'If they had me I'd want to be freed. I wouldn't want you to hold back the money.' When she leaned forward her breasts rested on the table.

Essex looked bewildered. 'I want to do what's right. . . .'

'Then you'll pay the money,' said Crane.

CHAPTER SEVEN

THE road to the Gulf of Mexico was rough and crowded with trucks carrying supplies for the Key West bridge. On the roadster's right was the old track of the Florida East Coast. In places there were stretches of warped rail, rusted a reddish-brown, but mostly there were only bare piles. Debris, blocks of stone, uprooted trees, boards, broken furniture, rags, littered the flat landscape.

'This where all them veterans were killed?' asked O'Rourke.

'It looks as though something had happened,' Crane said.

The sea, dotted with keys, was milky green.

'Williams is looking up Tortoni and the guy with no lobe to his ear,' Crane said. 'We'll see di Gregario.'

'I wonder how he picked out a phoney name like that,' O'Rourke said.

They passed some ruined stucco houses, swung the roadster round a forest of bent palm trees and came to the end of the road. There were two fishing-boats in a canal on their right.   Some people were looking at a black Lincoln sedan.

As they walked up to it, a man in boots, khaki trousers, and a brown flannel shirt turned toward them.   'Got a cigarette, buddy?'   He had a pistol in a holster over his right hip.

O'Rourke gave him one.

He lit it, blew out the match, said: 'Come to look at the car?'

'We were just driving down this way,' said Crane.

'You might as well give her a look,' said the man.

O'Rourke said: 'You mean that's the car they took Miss Essex in?'

'None other.'   The man pushed aside some of the spectators, opened the rear door of the sedan.   'Look at the blood.'

On the seat there were brownish stains.

'Somebody winged one of them,' the man repeated. 'Look.'

Under his finger, in the rear window, was a hole.

'Musta got his head,' the man said.

'I hope it killed him,' said a tanned man with bare feet, blue denim trousers and a torn white shirt.

The man with the bare feet was captain of the fishing-boat *Sally*.   The man with the gun was a deputy sheriff.   Both agreed there was little chance of discovering the kidnapper's boat.   The fisherman said it would be simple to hide by any one of a hundred keys between Port Everglades and Key West.

'Pile brush over the boat and nobody'd see it,' he said.

They went to the roadster and started back for the Essex house.

'I think that's the right dope,' said O'Rourke.

'They certainly could hide on a key.'

'No.   I mean about one of them torpedoes being wounded.'

'Why shouldn't he be wounded?' Crane stared at O'Rourke. 'You sound as though you were sorry about it.'

'Well, I hate to hit a guy on the head when I'm shooting at his tyres. That's pretty wild.'

'Wild, hell!' said Crane.

He knew O'Rourke was lying. This was one of the times he could put his finger on what O'Rourke was. What O'Rourke was he kept hidden most of the time. So did Doc Williams. And Eddie Burns. They were all alike. You learned about them only in an inverse manner. They boasted about how frightened they were at certain times, and you knew they had been brave. He remembered Doc Williams's account of his capture of Blackfoot Joe Staltz in a New York speakeasy before repeal. Joe had covered him with a pistol and Doc, in telling the story, said 'I am so damned scared that when I start to raise my hands the glass of beer slips out and hits Joe in the face. While he is wiping his eyes, I slug him with the bottle.'

If you were in on the secret you knew Doc had risked his life to capture Joe Staltz, and was proud of it. In the same way O'Rourke had made a very good shot and was proud of that. That was why he pretended he had been shooting at the sedan's tyres.

'This is funny country,' observed O'Rourke.

Even to Crane, who had been on the edge of the Everglades before, it appeared unusual. On either side of the road were canals, filled with brackish water and overgrown with coarse brown grass. In places there were large areas of the grass, but mostly on the opposite sides of the canals there was bush, very dense and as tall as a man's head. Near at hand it was brown and dull green: farther away it became grey. Once they saw a tarpon roll in the left canal.

'I'll bet there're plenty of snakes in there,' O'Rourke said.

'I hope I never find out,' said Crane.

It was five minutes before noon when they reached the Essex estate. The clean palms, with their bright green leaves; the fresh grass; the flowers were pleasing after the drab scenery. Far over to the right, surrounded by glowing hibiscus, was an *en tout cas* tennis-court, beside it were the two flamingos. The court and the flamingos and the hibiscus blossoms were almost the same shade of pink.

'We'll see what's happened,' said Crane, 'and then beat it for Miami.' He slammed the roadster's door. 'Better tell them we're going in to do some errands.'

They found the two policemen, aided by a Mr. Peters from the county attorney's office, questioning the servants. This promised to be a full day's job as there were eleven in all and Mr. Peters, a tall man with a thin nose and a large Adam's apple, was being very thorough. He talked with a lisp and he wrote everything down just as it was said.

Captain Enright asked Crane where they had been and Crane told him. He said he hadn't been able to learn anything from the sedan. The captain said it had been reported stolen three days ago. It had been owned by a doctor.

Mr. Peters was laboriously questioning a pretty French maid named Céleste and O'Rourke would have liked to stay, but Crane said: 'You can question her later, in private.'

They went out to the patio.

'You can ask better questions in private, anyway,' Crane said.

'You got me all wrong,' O'Rourke said.

'I suppose you didn't even see they were questioning a lady?'

'Was that a lady?'

Toward them across the patio came Imago Paraguay. She was wearing a dress of dark blue silk, high-waisted and printed with a flowered design in lighter blue. She moved in an effortless, gliding walk, turning her flat hips only slightly. Her lips were scarlet against the smooth cream of her skin.

'It is a nice morning, no?' she said.

Her face was really lovely. Through some trick of make-up she had removed its Asiatic aspect, made it more Latin than Chinese. It was patrician in an exotic way, with almond-shaped eyes, faintly arched eyebrows, slight hollows under the high cheek-bones. It reminded Crane of the painted death-mask of an Egyptian princess he had once seen in a Berlin museum. He had gone into the museum thinking it was his hotel.

'Swell,' said O'Rourke, 'and time you were up.'

'Oh, I ha-ave been up for some time.' Her voice was flat, without inflexion. 'I ha-ave been watching for you.'

O'Rourke said: 'If we'd known that we'd have hurried back.'

Her jet eyes fastened on Crane's. 'Sit down,' she said. 'I ha-ave a thing I wish to speak of.'

They sat down at the breakfast table.

'I am so surprised to hear you are detectives,' she said.

Crane said they were sorry to have deceived her.

'That is nothing,' she said.

When she looked at Crane the pit of his stomach tingled. She was seductive in a very strange way. She had not the animal appeal of Miss Day, but her slender body, her immobile face, her feline voice promised perverse delights, at once attractive and terrifying, of which she herself was contemptuous.

'I think perhaps I will help you,' she said. 'You wish to find Miss Essex?'

'Very much,' said Crane.

'Do you think Paul di Gregario may have her?'

'It is likely.'

'Do you know where he is?'

'Yes.'

'Good.   If you like I will go with you to see him.   I ha-ave an influence with him.'

'That would be nice, but I believe O'Rourke and I could obtain more from him.   Alone we can ask questions in a very direct manner.'

'You do not know Paul,' she said.   'He is afraid of no one . . . but me.'

Crane remembered the count's expression when he had encountered the dancer at the Essex table in the Blue Castle.   The man had been frightened.

'Maybe you *can* help us,' he said.

'I can, señor,' she said.   'When . . .?'

'Imago, dear!'

Sybil Langley, the actress, was approaching them from the other side of the patio.   Her long, horsey face was set, as though she were concentrating on the job of walking; her violet eyes were glazed.   She moved cautiously, making a great circle round a deck-chair and then barely avoiding a palm on her way back to the line of progress.

'Holy smoke!' whispered O'Rourke.

Completely black, Miss Langley's clothes hung from her as they would from a wire hanger, taking no shape except that caused by the action of gravity on them. Heavy powder whitened her face.   She halted abruptly by their table.   They stood up.

'Talking to the nice men?' she said.

'Yes,' said Imago.

'Such a terrible thing to happen.'   Miss Langley's mellow voice cracked a little.   'A terrible thing.' Abruptly she sat down, almost missing the chair Crane held for her.

'Mr. Cra-ane and Mr. O'Rourke have asked me to go to Miami with them,' said Imago.

'You are going to leave me?'   Miss Langley put her
hand on Imago's arm.   'Alone in this house?'   Her
face was alarmed.

Imago shrugged off the hand.   'Yes.   It is necessary.'

'The house is full of police, Miss Langley,' said Crane.
'You won't be alone.'

'Must you go, Imago?' pleaded Miss Langley.

The dancer ignored her, walked away.   They followed.
Miss Langley stared after them through her wide violet
eyes.

'She likes you a lot,' said Crane, coming up behind
the dancer.

'That is because I speak Spanish with her,' she said.
'She loves to speak Spanish.'

As they were getting into the roadster they met Miss
Day.   They told her they were going to Miami.   She
had on a tight black silk dress.

'Take me,' she said.

'Where's Essex?' Crane asked.

'He and Tony Lamphier and the major have gone
into Miami to see about an aeroplane.'

'To look for Camelia?'

'Yeah.   They think she's being held in a boat.
Tony's idea is they can spot it from the air.'

'How're they going to know it?' asked O'Rourke.

'Search me.'

'Why don't you come with us?' asked O'Rourke.

'I will if Miss Paraguay doesn't mind.'

'I do not mind.'

'Then let's be on our way,' said Crane.

It was a nice ride into Miami.   The sun was hot on
their heads, but the air stirred up by the movement of
the roadster was cool.   Along part of the road there
were lime trees and later they saw truck gardens.   There
were many red tomatoes on dark green vines.

In the front seat O'Rourke was telling Miss Day a
highly coloured version of the previous night's chase.

He pointed out the place where Essex had collapsed over the wheel. 'I was just about to jump from the running-board into the sedan,' he said, 'when Essex keeled over. It was an awful close thing.'

'Your friend is very heroic,' said Imago Paraguay softly. She was smiling a little.

'Don't think he's not,' said Crane. 'He's just fooling now.'

'Oh, yes. I know. I have se-en many brave men. I have seen many die.'

'Where? In China?'

'You think I am Chinese, señor?'

'Well . . .'

'Perhaps a thousand years ago there was a Chinese ancestor. But no later, of that I am sure.'

'You know your family a thousand years back?'

'Why not? The English do not alone keep records.'

'Yes, I know. The Spanish are very proud of their blood.'

Her eyes always gave him a nervous thrill. 'I am of two people older than the Spanish,' she said. Pride warmed her flat voice.

'Older?'

'My father was of Granada, a Moor. The people of my mo-ther lived many years ago—a thousand years—in Guatemala, in the city Piedras Negras. It lies now in ruins.'

'They were Indians?'

'If you wish.' Her flawless face was serene. 'My ancestor was the priest of Yum Kax, god of the harvest. When barbarians conquered the Old Maya Empire he fled with his family, carrying the sacred corn and many temple ornaments.'

'That was when the Spanish came under Cortez?'

'That was six hundred years before Columbus.'

Sliding from vitreous palm leaves, the sun's rays tinged white sidewalks with green. Heat-waves made

the pavement ahead a moving river of dark water.
There were elaborate signs on streets leading to vacant
lots. They were nearing Miami.

'I bore you?' Imago said.

'No. Please tell me the rest.'

She smiled and said in her flat voice: 'The grandson
of my ancestor led the family to Paraguay. There the
corn was pla-anted and to this day grows.'

'And the ornaments?'

'My mother's father has them. The temple robes,
of cloth much finer than silk, are gone, of course, and
the quetzal feathers in the head-gear, too. But there
is much gold and silver and jade.'

'Some museum would pay plenty for them.'

'Never! My grandfather would not sell.'

She was looking at the Miami river. Her face was
cold, composed, oblivious. The curve of her jaw under
her creamy skin, the perfect arch of her brows, the
clean line of her red lips, the soft hollows on her cheeks,
the strange black hair, so completely without life, gave
her an appearance at once alien and aristocratic. He
felt her strange allure. He wondered if she had been
telling him the truth.

Miss Day looked round at them. Her henna-blonde
hair was rumpled by the wind. 'Where are we going?'
she asked.

'Miami-Plaza,' said Crane.

'Oh, boy,' said Miss Day. 'Let's have lunch there.'

CHAPTER EIGHT

THEY left Miss Day, very demure, on a red leather
cushion in the bar, sipping pink planter's punch
through a straw. Crane asked her if she would be all
right while they were gone.

'Anybody bothering me better watch out,' she said.

He bet they had, too. Any one lured by her limpid
blue eyes, by her dimples, by her egg-yellow hair, cut
long so that the curls hung nearly to her shoulders,
was likely to find himself buying her champagne and
the two-dollar lunch in the main dining-room.

She smiled at him. 'Hurry back.'

O'Rourke was in front of the elevators. 'On the
eighth floor,' he said. 'I used the old telegram gag.'

In the elevator Imago Paraguay stood between them.
'You thi-ink it wise to bring her?' she asked. Her
body gave off an odour of sandalwood.

'She's very good company,' Crane said.

'Eight,' said the elevator man.

O'Rourke led the way. Their footfalls were muffled
by a thick rug on the corridor floor. They were walking
toward the ocean, and from a window at the end came
cool air. A stocky man in a brown suit, looking out
of the window, turned toward them.

Two paces behind Imago Paraguay, Crane shook his
head violently at the man. He was Eddie Burns, and
he had been watching the count.

Casually, the man put a cigarette in his mouth, lit a
match, held it in cupped hands to his face. His brown
eyes strayed over them, lingered for an instant on the
dancer, then passed on to the window. His cheek bore
a crescent-shaped scar.

O'Rourke turned left down another corridor and

halted at the third door on the right. He knocked with the knuckle of his forefinger. He knocked again, loudly.

'Who is it?'

'The telegram, sir.'

'Come in.'

Imago Paraguay paused in the corridor. O'Rourke opened the door and Crane went into the room. It was bright with sunlight, and the two large windows framed blue sea and sky. The bed had not been made. A pair of yellow silk pyjamas, trimmed with blue, lay across a chair.

Almost beside him, in the door to the bathroom, wearing trousers and an underwear top of ribbed silk, appeared di Gregario. Creamy lather covered the left side of his face; in his hand was a safety razor. His dark eyes were surprised.

'Who . . .?'

Before Crane could speak, di Gregario recognized him. His fist caught Crane's mouth, sent him sprawling against the ivory-white wall. Crane attempted to grapple with him as he came out of the bathroom door, but the Latin shook him off, ran for the bed. O'Rourke followed on his heels, hit the back of his head with a revolver, club-fashion, as his hands pawed the linen sheets. Like a celebrant about to pray, di Gregario's knees folded, slipped down on the floor. His outstretched arms, his head and chest, rested on the bed. O'Rourke felt the sheets with his left hand, found an automatic pistol, thrust it in his pocket.

'Tough guy,' he said.

Blood was trickling down a corner of Crane's mouth. He found a handkerchief and wiped it off. He tested his teeth with his fingers to see if they were loose. They weren't.

Turning his body so that he slipped off the bed to a sitting position on the floor, di Gregario scowled at them. His left eyebrow, his sideboard, were smeared with the shaving lather. Hate smouldered in his eyes, made the brown pupils grow like garnets.

'What do you want?' he demanded thickly.

'You oughtn't to leave your pistol lying about like that,' said O'Rourke. 'Very careless.'

Di Gregario's eyes were on Crane. 'Why do you follow me?'

'We'd like to talk with you.'

Suddenly di Gregario looked beyond Crane. Anger faded from his face; fear drained his colour, left him grey. He gasped: 'You!'

Crane turned and saw Imago Paraguay leaning against the hall door. She was smiling, but her jet eyes were cold. 'Si,' she said. 'Imago.'

Crane watched the count with surprise. He had thought him brave, very brave. He hadn't been afraid of the major, nor of him and O'Rourke. Why was he so afraid of the dancer?

'We're not going to hurt you,' he said to him. 'We'd like to ask some questions.'

Hooking one elbow on to the bed, the count got to his feet. His eyes reflected terror, but he was making an effort to control his fear. His skin was yellow.

'Señor . . .' he said, '. . . if I could write one last word to my family?'

Crane said: 'I don't understand.'

Imago Paraguay's laughter was brittle, like an old man's. 'He thi-inks we are of the Cuban secret police . . . that we will kill him.'

Crane daubed amazedly at his cut lip. 'What makes him think that?'

She had both hands on her hips now. 'For the government once I wa-as an agent.' Light gleamed from her glossy red finger-nails.

Di Gregario's voice exploded shrilly. 'Liar!' His fingers fluttered. 'You do not have to lie to me.

Every one in Havana knows the bed Imago Paraguay
sleeps in.' His face was wild. 'Where is he . . . your
Corporal Cabista? Or has he murdered so many school-
boys that he is a general now?'

Imago Paraguay hissed at him in Spanish.

'No, I am not afraid.' His body was shaking, but
his voice travelled down the scale. He pressed his
hands to his outer thighs. 'I die but once. How will
you kill me, Imago? As you did my cousin Roberto?
With that sharp little stinger you carry on your garter?'
He faced O'Rourke. 'Or is it to be this man's pistol?'

She said something to him in Spanish.

'Speak English,' Crane said.

She said: 'I tell him that he must learn to hold his
tongue or he will lo-ose it.' Her voice was barely above
a whisper.

'Listen,' Crane said. 'We are not going to kill you,
di Gregario. We won't hurt you if you answer our
questions.'

The Latin's face showed no relief.

'We want to know what's happened to Camelia
Essex,' said Crane.

As shiny white as bathtub porcelain, a steam yacht
nosed across the rectangle of blue water bound by the
left window. Up to them floated the cries of bathers
on the Miami-Plaza beach, in the Miami-Plaza pool.
The window curtains moved in the ocean breeze.

'Camelia Essex?' di Gregario whispered.

'Yeah, Camelia Essex.'

The count stepped backward, sank down on the bed.
There was sweat on his forehead. 'I did not know
anything had happened to her.'

'You didn't know she had been kidnapped?'

'No!' He stared up at Crane. 'And you think I
know something of it?'

'We're asking you.'

'I know nothing.'

'You don't even know she is gone?'

'I tell you I know nothing.' The passion faded from his eyes, was replaced by fear as he looked at Imago. 'This is a trick . . .'

'No,' said Crane.

Imago started to say something in Spanish.

'Speak English,' Crane said.

'I try to tell him re-ally Miss Essex is kidnap last night.'

O'Rourke said: 'Get a newspaper. That'll prove it for him.'

A small bag of navy-blue suede hung from Imago Paraguay's arm. 'There is no need,' she said. She took a piece of paper from the bag, tossed it at di Gregario. It fell on the floor, half under the bed, and he had to go down on one knee to reach it. His fingers had trouble unfolding it.

It was the front page of the morning's *Miami Herald*. While di Gregario read the Essex story under O'Rourke's watchful eye, Crane went into the bathroom and bathed his lip in cold water. Blood, now thicker, still oozed from the cut. He felt the hair rise on the back of his neck and turned to find Imago Paraguay's inscrutable eyes on him.

He tried to smile, but his lip throbbed. 'Big as a balloon tyre, isn't it?' he asked.

'It must be quite painful.'

'It isn't anything.'

'I should not like to ha-ave a man hit my mouth.'

'It isn't anything.'

'You are bra-ave.'

He let cold water run over the towel. 'Is what di Gregario said true?'

'What did he say?'

'That you are an agent for the Cuban government.'

'Once I was.' Her shoulders lifted in a shrug. 'But no longer am I interested.'

He turned off the water. 'And di Gregario's cousin?'

'Roberto Gomez?' Her teeth were small and very even. 'Yes, I killed him. Why not? He did not ca-are to give me some papers he had, so . . .' She made a small deadly movement with her wrist.

He felt again the peril that was so strange a part of her allure. That was her charm; to be as dangerous, as cold as a coral snake, and yet to be passionately seductive.

She was still smiling. 'Now you fear me?' she asked.

'I'll keep out of the way of your stinger,' he promised her. He tossed the bloody towel into the tub. 'What is di Gregario?'

'His family once owned much la-and in Cuba.' She spoke the country's name as if it were spelled Coo-ba. 'They lose all in the la-ast revolution. Now, I think, he heads a junta.'

'A junta?'

'Men who wish to overthrow the government.'

'Ah,' said Crane.

In the bedroom O'Rourke spoke. 'Now d'you believe us, Count?'

'Yes. But I know nothing of it.'

Crane came out of the bathroom. 'Mr. O'Rourke and I are in the employ of the Essex estate,' he said. 'We thought you might know something about Camelia. Miss Paraguay heard we were coming to see you and said she would come along. She said she knew you.'

The curtains fluttered in the breeze. The yacht had gone and there was only blue ocean in the window.

'What do you want me to tell you?' asked di Gregario.

'Where are the three men who were with you?'

Surprise widened the Latin's brown eyes. 'Gone . . . in a boat.'

'Where?'

For an instant di Gregario's eyes rested on Imago Paraguay. 'I do not know.'

Imago said: 'Liar!' Her voice was lazy. 'Tell them the truth. I am no longer interested in Cuba.'

'But the man with the lobeless ear didn't go with them, did he?' Crane demanded.

'The man with the lobeless ear?' Di Gregario held the palms of his hands open, as though about to catch a bundle. 'I do not know such a man.'

'All right,' Crane said. 'Where'd the boat go?'

Di Gregario shrugged his shoulders. 'A fishing trip, perhaps.'

'Look,' said O'Rourke. 'You come clean, dago, or I'll bat you right on the nozzle with this.' He brandished his revolver.

The drying lather made foamy splotches on di Gregario's face, showed the dark stubble on the unshaven left side. 'I give you my word, señores, the men in the boat have nothing to do with Camelia.' His voice was vehement. 'I know nothing about her.'

'Come on,' said O'Rourke, 'start clicking.'

'What does he mean, click?' di Gregario asked.

Crane ignored the question. 'You don't seem very worried about her . . . not for a guy who was so hot to elope a month or so ago,' he said.

'I am sorry, of course.' Di Gregario's brown eyes were frank. 'But it was over between us—she likes another.'

'Who?'

'I do not know. She told me last night that one was in her party.'

'Good lord! Not the major!' Crane exclaimed.

Imago laughed. 'Somebody younger, I thi-ink.'

'Why, she hardly knew me,' said Crane.

'Nuts,' O'Rourke said with disgust.

'Your friend lo-oves to joke,' Imago Paraguay told O'Rourke. 'He forgets Tony Lamphier.'

Di Gregario leaned against the foot of the bed. 'It is the truth when I say about Camelia I know nothing.'

'But the boat,' said Imago. 'Where is the boat?'

'I will not tell you.' His eyes were defiant. 'You are a spy for that devil Cabista.' His courage had returned and Crane thought he looked quite handsome with his regular features, his big dark eyes, his smooth skin and his glossy black hair.

'Want me to work on him?' asked O'Rourke.

Di Gregario stared defiantly at Crane. 'Kill me, but I will not tell you where the boat has gone.' Words popped from his mouth, brought flecks of spittle with them. 'I would not trust even an enemy to the mercy of this viper.' He pointed an elbow at Imago. 'My friends on the boat trust me.'

'That's just dandy,' said Crane.

'Want me to work on him?' asked O'Rourke.

'No.'

'You will not ma-ake him tell?' Imago asked.

'Not if he doesn't want to.'

'You believe I know nothing of Camelia?' asked di Gregario.

'I think I do.'

'But how do you know she is not on his boat?' demanded Imago Paraguay.

'Slut!' hissed di Gregario.

Imago spat Spanish at him.

O'Rourke reluctantly opened his linen coat, pushed his revolver in the under-arm holster. 'Then we're through with this guy?'

'Yes,' said Crane. 'Let's go.'

He held the door for Imago. As she passed him he could smell sandalwood sachet. She smiled a little at him. Di Gregario came as far as the bathroom door.

'I'm sorry I struck you,' he said to Crane.

'That's O.K.,' said O'Rourke. 'We're sorry we struck you.'

'I've been punched before,' Crane said.

'I am really sorry,' said di Gregario.

'That's all right,' said Crane.

'See you again,' said O'Rourke.

They left the roadster in a parking place and walked to the New York bar, where they were to meet Doc Williams. O'Rourke brooded about the count. 'He talks funny,' he said. 'What's a viper?'

'A windshield viper?' Crane asked.

Men loafing in front of shops, street-corner loiterers in shirt-sleeves, pedestrians, stared at them as they went by, ran wistful eyes over Miss Day's curves, ogled Imago Paraguay's exotic face. The sun blanketed the street, made the cement hot under their feet.

'Come on,' said O'Rourke.

'I guess it's a kind of snake.' Crane guided Miss Day across the street. 'He does talk like a guy in a melodrama.'

Doc Williams and a pop-eyed man with a round face were at a large table in the back of the grill. Williams waved at them. The man wore a mottled grey and white Palm Beach suit, a navy-blue shirt and a canary-yellow necktie. His face was red and his collar was too tight, causing a tyre-like bulge of flesh to circle his neck.

Crane presented Williams to the two women.

'And this is Mr. Joseph Nelson,'' said Williams.

'Pleased t'meet ya,' Mr. Nelson said, seizing a half-filled glass of gin and ginger ale and sliding along the leather cushion on his side of the booth. 'Sit down. I'm in the laundry business.'

He was, at the moment, very drunk.

'The Élite Laundry,' said Mr. Nelson. 'Finest in Miami. Yes, sir, or rather ma'am, as the case may be, the very finest. As I was just telling Mister . . . aah . . .'

'Williams,' said Doc Williams.

'Mr. Williams, here, there ain't a better man in the whole world to work for than old B.J.   Though I guess you ladies don't know what the B.J. stands for, now do you?'

They didn't.

'Benjamin Jenks,' said Mr. Nelson triumphantly. 'Benjamin Jenks. See? B.J.: Benjamin Jenks. President of the Élite Laundry.'

'What the hell is this?' demanded Crane of Williams.

'Yeah, Doc,' asked O'Rourke, 'what about Tortoni?'

'Tortoni?' said Mr. Nelson. 'Tortoni? Ha! I'll tell you what about him.'

'Tell 'em, Mr. Nelson,' said Doc Williams. 'Tell 'em what you told me.'   His button-black eyes gleamed with amusement.

'Well, I saw it this way . . .'   Mr. Nelson paused to take a drink.

'Saw what?' asked Crane.

'What?   I'm tryin' to tell you what,' said Mr. Nelson.

'Let him tell it,' said Doc Williams.

Mr. Nelson took a long breath.   'Whitey works in the diaper division,' he said.

Crane said: 'I must be crazy.'

'Let him tell it,' said Doc Williams.

'Whitey's my friend,' Mr. Nelson said.   'We been working for Élite for moren' ten years. Old B.J. said . . .'

'Tell 'em about Tortoni,' said Doc Williams.

'I am,' said Mr. Nelson indignantly.   'Whitey and me goes into this lunch-counter joint for a couple of sanniches and some java.   I woulda had beer only B.J. don't like for his people to drink. Not that B.J.'s a dry. No, sir. Well, this Tortoni's sitting on the next stool but one from us. I don't know him from Adam, but Whitey said: "You remember me, Mr. Tortoni?   A couple of years ago I sold you our towel service for the wash-room at the Blue Castle.   I bin promoted to the diaper division since then—tha's why I haven't been around t'see you."

'I don't know why, but he didn't warm up at all. He said: "I remember you all right." He didn't warm up at all.

'Whitey said: "Meet my pal, Joe Nelson."

'"It's a pleasure, Mr. Tortoni," I said, holding out my hand real friendly. "I heard a lot about you."

'Why, you'd think my arm was cut off at the elbow from the way he acted. He just sat there, not even lookin' at me. If he hadn't of been a friend of Whitey's I would have got mad.

'Well, after we got the sanniches, Whitey said: "And how's the towel service going? Everything satisfact'ry, Mr. Tortoni?"

'Now I ask you, ain't that a civil question? But wha'd he do? He just stared at Whitey like he never seen him before and started to get up from the counter.

'"What makes you so oblivious?" I asked him. "Is it your income tax, or are you composin' a poem, or is somebuddy after you?" I asked him.

'That's just what I asked him. I was sore, him being so upstage to Whitey. We're all citizens and can vote, and ain't we all equal under the skin, as the saying goes?

'But he didn't pay any attention. He had turned his back to me and was just startin' to walk away when it happened. The first thing I knew was when he stopped walking and stared at the door. I turned around to see what he was looking at, and there was a guy in a green suit with a gun in his hand. There was another guy behind this guy, but I didn't get a good look at him. Well, this guy shot Tortoni two times in the stomach and then when he falls on the floor he shoots him through the top of his head, holding his pistol right up close to . . .'

'He killed him?' O'Rourke's mouth hung open. 'Killed Tortoni?'

'That's what I bin trying to tell ya,' said Mr. Nelson. 'This guy in the green suit . . .'

'Imago!' cried Miss Day. 'What's the matter?'

The dancer's face looked as though it had been freshly dusted with rice powder. 'Nothing,' she said. 'It is nothing.'

'Here.' Crane handed her Doc Williams' glass of whisky. 'Drink this.'

'My God! Dead!' exclaimed O'Rourke.

Mr. Nelson said: 'That's what I bin trying to tell you. . . .'

'I am all right,' said Imago.

'That's terrible,' said O'Rourke.

'Terrible? I'll say that's terrible,' said Mr. Nelson. 'This guy in the green suit didn't pay any attention to Whitey or me. He bent over Tortoni and put a brand new buffalo nickel in his hand and whispered, but loud enough so Whitey and me could hear: "Use this on the slot-machines in hell, wise guy." That's what he said, me and Whitey could hear him. Then he and the other guy walked away. Yeah, I mean walked. They didn't run a step.'

Crane's eyes met Doc Williams' over the table. He was recalling that Williams had told him Tortoni was trying to muscle in on the Miami slot-machine racket.

'Whitey turned as green as that guy's suit,' said Mr. Nelson. 'I seen Tortoni was dead. The counter man was trying to get the police on the phone. "Why didn't they plug us?" I asked Whitey. "We're witnesses."

'Whitey said: "And just a minute ago we was talking to him."

'I said: "Let's get the hell out of here".'

'Did you?' asked Crane.

'I hope to tell you, mister,' said Mr. Nelson. 'I said goom-bye to Whitey and went to a place a couple of blocks down the street for a drink. I was kinda sick to my stommick. And as I was telling some of the

boys about what I seen, this genlman, Mister . . .
aah . . .'

'Williams,' said Doc Williams.

'Mister Williams here, said would I come down here
and tell the story to you folks, and I did.'

'His story ought to be worth another drink,' said
Williams.

'Hell, it's worth a whole bottle,' said Crane. 'Waiter!'

'Ah!' said Mr. Nelson.

'One thing,' said Crane. 'We don't have to see
Tortoni now. We can have lunch.' He looked at the
dancer. 'That is, if Imago feels like eating.'

'I am all right,' Imago Paraguay said.

CHAPTER NINE

THEY lay on their bellies in the warm sand, their
heads resting on crossed arms, the sun hot on their
bare backs and legs. In the east, whipped-cream
clouds floated on the blue Atlantic. The lazy breeze
was heavy with the perfume of tropical blooms; soft
with the rustle of palm fans; moist with traces of sea
spray. It was late afternoon.

'This is good,' said Crane.

'Picture of two great detectives at work,' said
O'Rourke. His voice, directed into the sand, was
muffled.

'I'm thinking,' said Crane.

'What about?'

'About a drink.'

'"Wine is a mocker, strong drink is raging,"' O'Rourke
said.

Crane groaned.

It wasn't my idea to learn all that stuff,' O'Rourke said.

'I made a mistake.'

O'Rourke pretended to be surprised.

'But now everybody knows we're detectives,' Crane went on, 'can't we forget it all?'

'I kinda like being able to say those things. It gives me class with the dames.'

'Not with Imago.'

'No, I guess not.'

Crane's arms were beginning to get tired from the weight of his head. He turned over on his back, rested his head on his peppermint-striped beach-robe.

O'Rourke said: 'That Imago's certainly got di Gregario's number.' He found a cigarette, lit it. 'What is she?'

'She says she's part Spanish and part Mayan.'

'What are Mayans?'

'High-grade Indians. They lived in Yucatan about a thousand years ago.'

'Maybe she thinks she's Mayan,' O'Rourke said, 'but I'll bet somebody from China stayed at her family's house once.'

'It's her make-up. She didn't look Chinese to-day.'

'You could tell she wasn't from Dublin.'

A big coast-guard amphibian, flying low and close to the shore, went over them on its way to Miami. It was going quite fast and it was very steady in the air. The two motors made a lot of noise.

'I suppose it's looking for Camelia,' said O'Rourke.

'I still don't see how anybody's going to know the boat she's in, even if they do see it.'

'Do you think di Gregario's got her, Bill?'

'Why would he want to kidnap her?'

'The fifty grand.'

'Yeah, that's so. But I think it would be too

dangerous for him.' He blew smoke at the sky. 'She'd be bound to recognize him and tell when he let her go.'

'Unless he killed her.'

Two gulls circled over their heads. The birds' feet were pink against their white underbodies.

'I hadn't thought of that,' Crane said.

O'Rourke pushed his cigarette into the sand. 'Have you got anybody in mind?'

'No.'

'What about Tortoni?'

'He wouldn't think of writing notes signed The Eye.'

'Not before he snatched her, anyway.' O'Rourke rested his chin on his right palm. 'A professional wouldn't work that way.'

For several minutes they lay in silence on the sand. Crane lay with his face towards the sky, his eyes closed. His half-smoked cigarette dangled from his mouth. O'Rourke poked holes in the sand with a disconsolate finger.

At last Crane said: 'O'Rourke.'

'What?'

'Did you ever drink usquebaugh?'

'No. Why?'

'I was just wondering how it tasted.'

The breeze seemed to be freshening. It shook the palm leaves, beat them against each other, making a noise like some one folding a newspaper. Far out at sea smoke from a freighter lay like a log on the horizon.

'Did you notice the way Imago took Tortoni's death?' asked O'Rourke.

'Yeah.'

'Could she have been a pal of that guy, too?'

Crane rolled over on his side. 'She knew him.' He told O'Rourke of his encounter with Imago in Tortoni's office.

'She must have been a pal . . . for him to cash a cheque for a grand,' said O'Rourke.

'If there was a cheque.'

The tide was coming in slowly.   A tiny roller nibbled tentatively at Crane's foot.   He crawled farther inshore.

'She certainly made good use of the grand,' said O'Rourke.

'She made a nice profit.'

'Say!' O'Rourke sat up.   'Where's your money? The Eye is probably . . .'

'Don't get excited.'   Crane fumbled with his beach-robe.   'I'm taking no chances.'   He held up the packet of nine one-thousand dollar bills.

'You better stick that in a bank.'

'Maybe I will.'

'How are you going to spend it?'

Crane thought for a moment.   'I think I'll go on a bender.'

'I'd like to know what you've been doing for the last six years.'

'Just warming up.'

O'Rourke pondered this bit of information, then said: 'I wish I could see you when you get going.'

'You're invited to come along.'

'No thanks.   I've been in jail.'

There were voices in the direction of the house. Coming towards them across the sand were Major Eastcomb, Essex and Tony Lamphier.   They all wore white suits.   Essex's face was haggard.

Lamphier asked: 'Have you heard about Tortoni?'

Worry had aged him, had somehow improved his appearance.   His face had lost its bland arrogance.

'Yes, a couple of hours ago,' Crane said.

'The afternoon papers say his death is connected with the kidnapping,' said Lamphier.

'What do you think?' asked Essex.

'I think they're wrong,' Crane said.

O'Rourke said: 'We think he got it for trying to muscle into the slot-machine racket.'

'That's so,' said Essex. 'One of his men was killed a week ago.'

Perspiration had wilted Major Eastcomb's collar. 'You think that he had nothing to do with the kidnappin'?' In contrast to the white bandage on his nose, his skin was brick-red.

'I don't know about that,' Crane said. 'I think he was killed because of slot-machines.'

'There's no news about the girl?' asked O'Rourke.

Essex said: 'We took a plane and flew down the keys. No luck. It was just an outside chance, anyway.'

'We thought we might see something suspicious,' Lamphier said.

'We were only one of about fifteen planes,' said the major. 'Whole country's in the hunt.'

Crane stood up and looped his beach-robe over his arm. 'I hope they find her.' He made sure his money was in the pocket.

'Beside lying on the sand, what have you been doing all day?' asked Major Eastcomb.

'I can't think why I'm telling you,' said Crane, 'but we saw di Gregario.'

'You did?' Essex's voice was eager. 'What did you get from him?'

'Nothing of any value.'

'You turned the beggar over to the police?' asked the major.

'No.'

'You didn't even tell them where he was?'

'They didn't ask me.'

'They requested me especially to order you to co-operate with them.'

'And did you?' Crane inquired.

The major eyed him angrily.

O'Rourke got up. 'How are your *two* punches on the nose, Major?' he asked.

'I'm tired,' said Essex. 'I think I'll go up to the house. Coming, Major? Coming, Tony?'

'I'll be along in a minute,' said Lamphier.

Essex and Major Eastcomb walked towards the house. Slowly, the others followed.

'You ought to be easier on the major,' said Lamphier. 'He really means well. It's just . . .'

'Yeah, I know. His manner is unfortunate.'

Lamphier tried to smile, but he wasn't very successful. He really was quite nice looking. He had a fine length of bone; the long legs of a hurdler; the sloping shoulders of a man good at fast games; sensitive hands. His crew-cut hair disclosed a well-shaped head.

'He does mean well,' he said. 'Despite his dislike of the idea, he arranged to have the fifty thousand ready for the ransom.'

'That's nice of him, especially as it isn't his money.'

'I know, but he could have held things up.'

O'Rourke asked: 'Has he got it with him?'

'No. It's at the bank.'

'Maybe I ought to lay off him,' said Crane.

'He does mean well.'

'I don't like him anyway.'

Lamphier's eyes wrinkled at the corners. 'Nor I.' They entered the patio. 'But I didn't mean to talk about him.'

'No?'

'I just wanted to say . . .' He hesitated, looking embarrassed. 'If anything comes up . . . if you ever need help . . . I wish you'd call on me.'

'Why, sure,' said Crane. 'We will.'

'I was pretty sour in the chase last night, but . . .'

'Who wouldn't be, with a sock like that on the head?' said O'Rourke.

'No, I was pretty sour.'

'We were all pretty sour,' said Crane.

'Well, if anything does come up . . .'

'We'll call on you.'

'You know, I feel terrible about this,' said Lamphier. 'I feel so damned impotent.'

'You just have to wait.'

'If there was only something we could do.'

'There isn't, though.'

'It's a terrible feeling.'

'Sure.'

'But you will call on me?'

'Absolutely.'

Tony Lamphier went into the house. The sun was still hot and the blue water in the pool looked cool and inviting. They put down their robes and dived in, and at once the lazy feeling caused by their sun bath disappeared. While Crane swam under water for rubber bricks at the deep end, O'Rourke tried jack-knives from the board. He got plenty of spring, and he was able to touch his toes, but his trajectory was wrong. Crane had heard that a good diver was supposed to go very high in the air and come down very close to the board. O'Rourke went out towards the centre of the pool, like a broad jumper.

Once, on his way back to the brass ladder, he paused beside Crane.

'I feel bad about that girl myself,' he said.

He resumed his diving and Crane admired his build. He thought O'Rourke would have made a wonderful boxer. He had long arms, powerful shoulders, a deep chest, narrow hips and a flat stomach. His legs were possibly too slender for maximum durability, but they would have a lot of speed. He had the blue-grey eyes of a marksman, too.

After a time they put on their beach-robes and went up to their room. Soon they would have to dress for dinner. They both felt fine. The liquor they had drunk before and at lunch had mostly been eliminated by the sun and water and the swimming, and all that

was left was a pleasant feeling and a mild desire for
more liquor.

Soft dusk had seeped into the room when Crane woke.
He would have liked to sleep longer, but he saw it was
time for dinner. The air was filled with the melancholy
sizzle of the surf. He swung his bare feet over the side
of the bed and sat there for some time. He thought
about Camelia Essex. It was a hell of a note, but what
could you do? If you were too smart the kidnapper
would become frightened and kill the girl. It didn't
make much difference as the penalty for kidnapping and
murder is the same. It was best to hold back until the
ransom had been paid. Not that he had anything to
hold back on.

There was still another difference between a murder
and a kidnapping case. At least for a detective. In
a murder case a detective could take an impersonal
attitude. Most of the time he hadn't known the corpse
and the chase after the murderer was like a nice game
of chess. The murderer had made the first move and
the purpose of the game was to forestall his future
moves, until, finally, he was check-mated. There was
rarely any personal feeling, but if there was, he thought,
it was more often favourable to the murderer. So
many corpses had it coming to them.

In kidnapping the victim was a living being, not a
corpse. The victim was suffering and would continue
to suffer until released, and stood a very good chance
of being murdered, besides. There was a great urgency
about kidnapping. Somebody was in trouble and the
detective had to get him out of it. Camelia Essex was
in trouble. He wished some one else had the respon-
sibility of getting her out.

At the same time he wished he could get his hands
on the kidnappers.

He combed his hair and bathed his lip in cold water,
and then dressed. The swelling on his lip had come

down a little.   He took a flash-light out of his suit-case
and went out into the hall.   Except for the murmur
of the sea there was no noise.   Quietly he walked along
the carpet past the stairs, hearing briefly the sound of
voices below, and entered the left wing of the house.
The door at the end of the hall he opened a crack,
saw it was dark inside, slid into the room.   Tall grey
rectangles on three sides of the room were French
windows.   He pulled the heavy curtains across these
windows and pressed the button on his flash-light.

It was a very large, very beautiful room.   The walls
were of rosewood, rubbed with oil until the surface
glowed like satin, and the floor, of polished yellow
pine, bore Cossack scatter rugs, barbaric with primary
colours.   The furniture was slip-covered in brick-red.

He swung his light around, feeling pretty sure he
was in the rooms occupied by Essex.   The French
windows to the right, he was certain, led to the balcony
from which the guard had watched him on the first
night.   Where was the bedroom?   He turned his back
on the fire-place and saw there was another door to
the room.   He started for it, but a glass-topped desk
with a telephone on it caught his eye.   He sat down
on a red leather chair and pulled a drawer in the rounded
red-lacquered pillar supporting one end of the glass
top.   He examined the letters inside, carelessly jumbled
advertisements, bills, invitations.   He had a feeling
Essex was holding some information from him, some
clue to the identity of The Eye.   If The Eye was really
a crank with a grudge wouldn't he have tried to reach
Essex in some way before writing those mysterious
notes?   He thought so.   He goggled at a bill for two
dozen voile shirts: $312.   There was another: thirty
cravats: $225.   A tailor, on bond paper, called Mr.
Essex's attention to two small items: three suitings
amounting to $600, one top coating at $275.

He was amazed at how much it cost to be rich.   He

closed the drawer and went through the other two. In one he found a left-hand golf glove and eight new balls; in the other a fountain-pen, envelopes, monogrammed paper and a bottle of ink. He held his flash-light to the ink. It was royal blue. He got up and opened the second door.

His light was dazzling on white structural-glass walls, on blue and white porcelain, on silver mirrors, on blue and scarlet tile. It was the bathroom. He went on through a small dressing-room with drawers built into the wall two-thirds of the way to the ceiling. The bedroom was quite large and there were French windows along one side. He saw a double bed of carved walnut, a white marble fire-place, some books on a table beside the bed. On it were also a green thermos decanter and two glasses. His feet sank into the thick green-grey rug as he crossed the room to the door on the other side. He opened it and flashed his light into the room thus exposed, and breathed through his half-opened lips: 'Ah!'

The room belonged to the early, fluffy Jean Harlow period. Everything was in white except the black composition floor. The walls were ivory, the ceiling chalk white, the furniture cream with white leather. On the bed, on a lazy comforter, was a white teddy bear. Long-haired white rugs scattered about the composition floor, looked like blobs of whipped cream on a blackberry tart.

This was really all he wanted to know: that Miss Day had access to Essex's bedroom. But he went on into the room. The cough-drop eyes of the teddy bear followed him as he went to a white writing-desk, examined the drawers. He found only one letter, addressed to Dawn Day and signed by a Rudolph Ginsberg. Would Miss Day be interested, Mr. Ginsberg inquired, in a nice spot at the Boulevard Yacht Club in Chicago? The salary would be $150 per on a ten-week contract. Apparently Miss Day would not since the letter was dated March 3rd. Nearly a month ago. Crane wondered if Miss Day had been with Essex then. Here was a possible explanation of the mystery of the notes.

He wondered what he would have done if he had caught Miss Day placing his note on his pillow last night. Shout for O'Rourke? Like hell!

Grinning in the dark, he remembered that he was supposed to be at dinner. He went back through Essex's room, carefully closing the connecting door, and entered the small dressing-room. His light, going up the high row of built-in drawers, disclosed a cream-coloured ceiling. Lines on one corner of the ceiling marked off a square with sides three feet long— a hatch leading to some sort of an attic. He didn't know houses had attics any more. He crossed the bathroom and was about to enter the big study when a noise made him halt. He drew back just as the lights were switched on.

A man came into the room and walked to the glass-topped table. He was a thick-set man in a dark suit, and he walked with a sailor-like roll. He bent in front of the table, pulled open the third drawer in the red-lacquered pillar, and thrust an object into it. When he came back to the door Crane saw that his nose had been broken and badly set. His face was sullen and there was a white scar over his left eye. He turned off the light and closed the door.

Crane waited for a full minute before going into the study. The man, he imagined was Brown, Essex's body-guard. He went to the desk, flashed his light into the drawer. Besides the fountain-pen, envelopes and monogrammed paper there were two bottles. He held one to the light. It was the bottle of royal blue ink. He held the other to the light. It was a bottle of red ink.

CHAPTER TEN

BY the time camembert and toasted crackers and brandy were served most of the early tension had gone. This was partly due to the cocktails and the Rhine wine with the dinner, and partly to Essex. While they were being served tomato juice in tall, ice-surrounded glasses, he urged them to discuss the kidnapping.

'Somebody might get an idea,' he said.

He looked quite ill, but he pretended to eat. His thin face was pale, and his eyes were red from lack of sleep. When any one spoke his eyes fixed on that person hopefully.

Crane and O'Rourke ate prodigiously. Crane discovered that crayfish, eaten with melted butter and lime juice, tasted like New England lobster. The shell was yellow instead of red, and perhaps the meat was tougher, but it tasted like New England lobster. He was disturbed about Camelia, too, but that didn't affect his appetite. That didn't affect his drinking, either.

'What are we going to do to-morrow?' asked Tony Lamphier.

All through the dinner he had persistently brought the conversation round to the kidnapping. He was slightly dramatic in his agitation, clenching and unclenching his hands, running a palm over his close-cut black hair, nervously drumming the table with long fingers, but Crane thought his emotion genuine. He liked the way the guy was standing up. It was a tough blow to any one who loved Camelia, but the boy was ready to fight. The only trouble was finding something to fight.

'What can we do?' Crane asked.

'You should say,' Major Eastcomb said. 'You're supposed to be a detective.'

'I am,' Crane said.   'I can prove it with a certificate.'

The major scowled at him.   He had been sullen all evening, had hardly spoken a word.   Instead of the hock, he had drunk three whiskies with water during the meal.

'It seems funny, us eating and drinking,' Miss Day said, 'and Camelia out somewhere. . . .'

'It does,' Crane agreed.   'But that's the way people act.'

Boucher finished his brandy, placed the inhaler on the table.   'What have the police been doing?' he asked.   His dark face, the hooked nose giving it a Levantine cast, was cunning.   Below the sleeves of his dinner-jacket his wrists showed, black with hair.

'They've been checking up on the servants,' said Major Eastcomb.   'Going over their references.'

'Why?' Mrs. Boucher asked.

For a long pull, Crane thought, she'd be the best of the women in the dining-room.   Her skin was good, her shoulders were athletic, yet feminine, her oval face was aristocratic, her brown eyes wise.   He said: 'Maybe the chief of police needs a butler.'   He wondered why she had married Boucher.   Money, maybe?

Major Eastcomb answered Mrs. Boucher.   'They think possibly some one inside the house is connected with the kidnap gang.   Particularly in view of the notes.'

'I think they're right,' said Lamphier.

'That's just what I said,' exclaimed Miss Day.   'Do you remember, Penn?'   At the very bottom of the V in front of her black satin evening gown her skin changed from golden brown to white.   'I told you that when you got the first note . . . at the Waldorf, in New York.'

Nervously Penn Essex daubed at his lips with his

napkin. 'That's right,' he said, and added: 'I told you the day after I received it, didn't I?'

'Why . . .' Miss Day's blue eyes widened for a second. '. . . Why, yes, I guess you did.'

O'Rourke glanced at Crane. Both were recalling Essex's denial that any one was with him in New York at the Waldorf. Of course, possibly Miss Day wasn't with him. But Essex had trussed, 'day after.' Naturally he'd want to protect Miss Day. But if she *had* been at the Waldorf it didn't look so good for her. That would make her the only person who had been constantly with Essex during the time he had been receiving the notes. The fighter, 'Buster' Brown, had been in New York at that time, but he was driving the Bugatti down to Miami when the second note came.

With what he had seen upstairs, Crane thought it very likely Miss Day had been at the Waldorf. O'Rourke, although he didn't know about the connecting rooms, came to the same conclusion. They both decided with satisfaction they'd better spend a little time on her.

Imago Paraguay had been listening to Miss Langley recount her English triumphs; relate what Tree said of her Juliet, of her Lady Macbeth; confide what Ellen Terry had told her of G.B.S.; describe the mannerisms of the divine Sarah. Now she turned to Crane and asked: 'Do you think I will be involved in the death of Roland Tortoni?'

'How do you mean?'

'The cheque. Do you remember the cheque I cashed?'

Crane remembered all right, but he didn't want to appear too bright. 'The cheque?'

'When you ca-ame to Mr. Tortoni's office.'

'Oh, sure. For a thousand dollars.' He finished his brandy. 'The police may ask you about it, but all you have to tell them is that he cashed it so you could gamble.'

'They will not arrest me?'

'Of course not. This isn't Cuba.'

Imago Paraguay smiled. 'I am glad.' Her teeth were very small, and very white and even. 'I was quite frightened when that funny ma-an was telling us of Tortoni's death.' Her sloe eyes lingered on his face. 'Did you not notice?'

She was contemptuously beautiful, like a temple-mask. The lids of her eyes were a faint violet-green and they had the lustre of worn silk, and her brows jet black, were arched like bamboo trees in a wind. Her lips matched the scarlet of her gown, drawn tight over her small, firm breasts and fastened over the left shoulder with an emerald-eyed serpent of twisted gold.

'Yes, I noticed,' he said.

The ladies left the room first, and he watched the dancer's back. He felt strongly attracted to her, but at the same time she frightened him. She was as slender as a boy and her hips moved very little when she walked, but there was a great deal of appeal. It was a perverse appeal, perhaps because she was so contemptuous of it. He wondered if there was passion under that contempt. He wondered about her needle-sharp dagger.

He and O'Rourke and the major had whisky. The others had more coffee. Tony Lamphier said: 'I'm never going to get drunk again.'

'Why not?' asked O'Rourke.

'If we'd all be sober last night they'd never have been able to take Camelia.'

'Sure they would,' said Crane. 'If we'd been sober we wouldn't have put up as much of a fight, as we did.

Boucher examined Crane. 'How much of a fight did you put up?' His eyes, small and black, were unfriendly.

'I didn't put this on with a paint-brush.' Crane showed him the bruise on his jaw.

'You're a damned poor excuse for a detective, anyway,' said Major Eastcomb. He looked at Essex. 'If I'd my way they'd have been fired long ago.'

'They're doing what they can,' said Essex. His tone was defensive.

Crane grinned at the major. 'You haven't got your way,' he said.

O'Rourke said: 'While we're talking, Major, suppose you explain now how you happened to get hit on the nose twice in the same place.'

'And maybe the brave Mr. Boucher will explain why he didn't take part in the struggle,' Crane said.

Boucher made a twitching movement with his shoulders, pulled his white shirt cuffs from under the sleeves of his dinner-jacket. 'I didn't get there in time.' He frowned at Crane. 'You know that.'

'I know you weren't there,' said Crane.

'Don't let's have a dog fight,' said Tony Lamphier.

Crane said: 'I'd like to know just what Boucher's position is here. Whose guest is he?'

'My wife is a close friend of Camelia' said Bouchier.

'And what are you?'

Eyes narrowed, jaw thrust out, Major Eastcomb was looking at Boucher. 'He'd like to be a close friend, too,' he said.

'This doesn't do any good,' said Tony Lamphier.

'Doesn't it?' The major leaned towards Boucher 'Why have you been payin' so much attention to Cam?'

Boucher looked worried. 'I've been polite to her, that's all.'

'You think it polite to dance with her all evening at Tortoni's?'

'She's a very good dancer.'

'How is she at kissing?'

Both Tony Lamphier and Boucher stood up. Boucher said: 'What do you mean?'

'I saw you on the balcony two nights ago.' The major was out of his chair, his palms on the table. 'She had to fight to get away from you.'

Boucher glanced apprehensively at Essex. 'I lost my head for a second.'

'You rat,' said Tony Lamphier.

O'Rourke grinned at Crane.

'You lost your head!' Major Eastcomb grunted. 'Not your head for figures. You know how much Camelia is worth to a penny. You'd like to marry her. You could divorce Eve and live comfortably then, couldn't you?'

'He's insane,' said Boucher.

'I was insane enough to have an investigation made of your financial rating.' The major turned triumphantly to the others. 'What do you think it was?'

'Zero,' said Crane.

'Worse. He has to have thirty-five thousand by the end of this month or the Baltimore banks will dispose of the Boucher estate in Virginia.'

Boucher looked as though he would like to hit the major, but didn't dare. He looked frightened. His mouth was compressed into thin lines below his hooked nose. He pulled at his cuffs.

The major slapped the table. 'The hunters put up at auction for the *nouveau riche* at Warrenton. The house where the Bouchers entertained Lafayette sold to some plumber from East Grange. No wonder he'd like to get Camelia . . . and her money.'

'Is this true, Greg?' asked Penn Essex.

'I am a little hard pressed.' He had to swallow before he could go on talking. 'But I swear I never had a thought of marrying Camelia. . . . You don't think I'd . . . I'd want to throw over Eve?' When he pulled down his cuffs the black hair on his wrists squirmed like eels.

'I don't know,' said Essex. 'I don't know what to think.'

'I know,' said Tony Lamphier.

'I swear I'm not trying to marry her,' Boucher said.

'You swear!' said Tony Lamphier.

'I did want some money,' Boucher said. 'I admit that.' He rotated his shoulders, making a wrinkle run across the back of his dinner-jacket. 'I was trying to get Camelia to make me a loan.'

'Why didn't you come to me?' Essex asked.

'You never have any money.'

'Has Camelia thirty-five thousand?' Crane asked.

'Close to that,' said Major Eastcomb. 'She's been saving part of her income.'

'Mother left her some money, too,' Essex said.

'I could give her good security,' said Boucher. 'I don't see anything unreasonable in that.'

'Why did you kiss her?' demanded Tony Lamphier.

'I told you. She's attractive. I lost my head.'

'Married men have tried to kiss girls before,' Crane told Lamphier.

The major said: 'But even a kiss didn't get him the money.'

'She said she'd consider it,' said Boucher.

'But you didn't wait,' said the major.

Crane blinked at Boucher, noted that he was pale.

The major went on: 'A fifty-thousand-dollar ransom would help, wouldn't it, Boucher?'

With a swift, underhand jerk, Boucher sent a water-glass into the major's face. The glass struck his jaw, fell to the table, smashed a coffee-cup, rolled from the table and shattered on the red tile floor. Coffee dregs made a mahogany stain on a white napkin.

The major came round the table. He held himself

like a football line-man, in a half crouch with his arms
dangling.

'Stop it! Stop it!' Penn Essex was hammering
the table.

O'Rourke moved in front of the major, blocked his
way. He hoped the major would get tough. For two
days he had been wanting to hit him.

'Let him come,' said Boucher.

'No,' said Essex.

'He can't accuse me of kidnapping Camelia,' said
Boucher.

'He didn't,' said Crane. 'He said fifty thousand
might be a help to you.'

'The implication was . . .'

'Hell,' said O'Rourke. 'Fifty thousand would be
a help to any one.' He had one elbow against Major
Eastcomb's chest.

'Let's drop it,' said Tony Lamphier.

The major looked around O'Rourke. 'I'll see you
later, Boucher.'

'Why not now?' Boucher asked.

'Come on; let's drop it,' said Lamphier.

Boucher no longer seemed afraid. He was angry.
He acted as though he could take care of himself.
Crane wondered if what he had been afraid of was the
revelation that he was in need of money.

'I'll see you later, Boucher,' the major repeated.
He stopped pressing against O'Rourke.

'I wish you would both forget it,' said Essex.

'You can't forget it when a man hits you,' said the
major. He fingered his jaw.

Craig, the butler, came into the dining-room. He
had a *Miami News* in his hand. 'The reporters outside would like to ask you about this,' he said. He
handed the *News* to Essex.

Essex examined the paper, said: 'Tell them I'll be
out in a minute, Craig.' He gave the *News* to Crane,

pointed a finger at a classified advertisement in the personal column.

It read:

> 'Money is ready.   Please contact.
> ESSEX.'

'So you did decide to pay the ransom,' Crane said, passing the paper to O'Rourke.

Essex said: 'We put ads in all the Miama papers.'

'It's going to be interesting when The Eye contacts you,' Crane said. 'I've never yet heard of a fool-proof way of receiving a ransom. Are you going to let the police in on it?'

'I don't know,' said Essex.

'Certainly we are.' Major Eastcomb was pouring himself a large drink of whisky. 'Do you think we'd take a chance of your bungling this, too?'

Crane ignored him. 'What are you going to tell the reporters?' he asked Essex.

'That I'm ready to pay the ransom.'

'I think it would be a good idea to say you intend to keep any messages received from the kidnappers secret until Camelia is returned.'

'Yes, I guess it would.'

O'Rourke said: 'I'd tell the police aren't going to be to be called in, even if it isn't true.'

'Sort of lull The Eye's suspicions,' said Lamphier.

'He's too smart for that,' said Crane. 'But it can't hurt to try.'

Essex said: 'Maybe we really should keep the police out.'

'I won't authorize the use of the money unless the police have full knowledge,' said Major Eastcomb.

'I guess the police are in, then,' said Crane.

O'Rourke said: 'I think they'll be reasonable. In New York when the Frachetti boy was snatched,

they didn't even try to trail the guy who took out the
ransom.'

'I'll speak to the district attorney,' said the major.
'He'll see the police don't jeopardize Camelia's safety.'

Essex said: 'We can probably arrange to have them
notified the instant the ransom is paid.'

'We better hold off until Camelia is safe,' said Tony
Lamphier.

'We better hold off until we get an idea how The
Eye wants the ransom paid,' said Crane.

'I'll see the reporters,' Essex said.

'Let's join the ladies,' suggested Boucher.

Chairs, feet, scraped the red tile floor. A serving-
man, Carlos, peeped in at them through the swinging
door to the butler's pantry. Their movement toward
the door made cigarette smoke swirl over their heads.
O'Rourke waited for Crane.

'I thought we were going to have a free-for-all,' he said.

'The major's certainly out for trouble.'

'He's eager t'put the snatching on some one.'

'Damn eager.'

'I'd like to slug him once.'

'You might as well,' Crane said. 'Pretty nearly
every one has.'

They walked toward the patio, and O'Rourke asked:
'What's on the programme?'

'We've got to find "Buster" Brown.' Crane told
O'Rourke about Essex's and Miss Day's bedrooms
and how he had seen Brown with a bottle of red ink.
'We have to find out what he was doing with it.'

'Questioning him ought to be fun,' O'Rourke said.
Over the patio, in a navy-blue sky, hung a three-quarter
moon. The milky light outlined shapes, made everything appear black and white, as in a photographic
negative. The wind was sweet and lazy; it sighed
through the palms and spread the odours of night-
blooming flowers and jasmine.

Crane pulled a metal chair over to Imago Paraguay.
'May I?'

'Of course.'

He sat down beside her. 'It is hard to believe in crime on a night like this.'

Her face was exquisite in the moonlight. 'Not for me.' Her skin was as pale, as perfectly textured as marble.

'Is something wrong?'

The moonlight was cream-coloured on the beach, chromium bright on the crests of breaking waves. The surf made a gentle whoosh at intervals, like a big animal exhaling. The murmur of other voices filled the patio.

'Yes.' Her voice sank to a whisper. 'Some one threatens me.'

'Who?'

'I think it best not to tell you.'

He gave her a cigarette. 'Is it di Gregario?'

'I will not tell you.' In taking the cigarette her fingers brushed his.

'What's he up to now?' He held a match in his cupped hands, leaned toward her. 'I thought he was afraid enough of you to try to do something to you.' The flame showed her scarlet lips, the blue shadows under her eyes, the hollows in her cheeks.

'I ha-ave told you nothing.' She steadied his hands with hers, lit the cigarette. 'I may later this evening, but now . . .'

'I don't understand.'

'I will do this with you.' When she stood up he was surprised, as usual, at her height. 'I will, if I do not say otherwise, give you some valuable information to-night.'

He stood up. 'When?'

'At two o'clock, say?'

'All right. But where?'

For an instant her hand touched his, pressed it slightly. 'You may come to my room.' She detached her hand, moved away, leaving a faint odour of sandalwood.

CHAPTER ELEVEN

O'ROURKE met Crane upstairs, in the hall outside Brown's room. It was quite warm and O'Rourke wiped the sweat off his forehead with a silk handkerchief.

'I could use some of that Dutch beer,' he said.

'We need something stronger than that,' said Crane. His knuckles hesitated three inches from the wood. 'Where do you want the body sent?'

'Nuts.' O'Rourke took his revolver from his under-arm holster, tucked it in his belt. 'I'll bump him if he gets tough.'

Crane knocked, his knuckles making a hollow sound on the door. 'Yeah?' said a hoarse voice.

Crane shoved open the door.

Chester Brown was reading on his bed. A lamp on a table beside his head outlined a zigzag scar on his right cheek, illuminated clasped hands tattooed on his hairy chest. He wore purple underwear shorts. His legs were hairy.

'Whacha want?' he asked Crane.

'We want to ask a couple of questions.'

He didn't seem particularly surprised to see them. His muscles bunched, unbunched, as he got to a sitting position. 'You're the dicks, ain't you?' His right ear looked as though it had been badly frozen.

'Yeah,' Crane said.

O'Rourke closed the door.

'Well, I got nothing to tell you.'

'Wait until we ask you somethin'.' O'Rourke said.

'I'll talk when I please.' He swung his feet to the floor. 'I got a belly full of cops.'

'Sit down,' said O'Rourke.

Brown sank back on the bed, his eyes on O'Rourke's gun.

'We aren't cops,' Crane said. 'We're working for Mr. Essex.' He sat in a straight chair. 'If you want to keep working for him you'll try to help us.'

'If you want to keep healthy you'll try,' said O'Rourke.

Sullenly, Brown said: 'What d'you want to know?'

Crane sat on the edge of the chair so that he could move quickly. 'What do you know about The Eye?'

Brown scowled at O'Rourke. 'Put that rod down and I'll show you what I know.

'Look,' said Crane. 'We want some help.'

'You pick a hell of a way to ask for it.'

'We were afraid you'll cool us.'

'I may.'

O'Rourke said: 'No, you won't.'

'Be reasonable,' Crane said. 'We're trying to get Miss Essex back. You're in favour of that, aren't you?'

'She's a nice dame.'

'It's swell of you to say so,' O'Rourke said.

Brown half rose from the bed.

'Sit down,' said Crane. 'I got a notion to throw you in the can.'

'Tell this Mick to lay off,' said Brown.

O'Rourke asked: 'What have you got on him, Bill?'

'The notes. He's the only person who could have stuck the note on Essex's bed in the Waldorf.'

'Oh yeah?' said Brown.

'Yeah.'

Brown leaned forward on the bed. 'How about that second note?' His hands were on his knees. 'I was in Richmond when that came.'

'You got a pal,' said O'Rourke.

'Probably that cute little French maid.' Crane nodded as though everything was becoming clear to him. 'That Céleste.'

'The hell!' Scar tissue on Brown's knuckles was the colour of pork rind. 'Just because I date a dame don't mean we're planning a kidnapping.'

'It doesn't look good.'

Brown's scowl was replaced by alarm. 'You guys don't really think I been writing those notes?'

'We don't know,' said O'Rourke.

'Your attitude,' said Crane. 'You don't seem to want to co-operate.'

'You got me all wrong. It's the way you come bustling in here . . . a guy'll stand just so much.'

'Stumble-bums!' said O'Rourke. 'Tough until you're in a corner.'

Brown's eyes glowed, but he took it. These guys wouldn't be so wise, he thought, unless they figured they had something on him. He'd better go easy: he might be in a jam.

'I'll help,' he said, 'but I won't take no gaff.'

'Well, what about those notes?' asked Crane.

'I don't know nothing.'

'Somebody in the house has been passing them out. You can't even guess who it is?'

Brown shook his head. He said he didn't know anybody in the house very well beside Céleste. He'd worked for Essex less than a year and he hadn't paid much attention to the regular servants. Besides, he and Craig didn't get along. He thought Craig was making plenty on the household accounts, taking a commission from the stores and stealing supplies, liquor and linen.

'Those two spicks, Carlos and Pedro, are on the take, too' he said.

'Do you think they'd have the connections to kidnap Miss Essex?' Crane asked.

'How do you know what connections a spick has?'

'Did you ever hear any of them mention Tortoni?'

'I thought of that myself,' said Brown. 'But these are Spanish spicks. Tortoni is ... was an Italian spick. The breeds don't mix.'

'How long has Craig carried a rod?'

'Just since the notes began to come.' Brown scratched his arm-pit. 'Essex had us all get guns.'

'Who's the guy who watched us arrive?'

'That was me.'

'And the other guy—the one on the balcony?'

'Me, too.'

'Hell, it looked like a different guy.'

'No, that was me.' Brown grinned. 'Essex wanted to be sure you weren't pretendin' to be detectives.'

'He isn't sure yet,' said O'Rourke.

'And you've got no idea how the notes have been arriving?' Crane asked Brown.

'I could make a guess.'

'Go ahead.'

'It's somebody who was around each time Essex got a note.'

'Who?'

'Well, it's a dame.'

'Miss Day?'

'Yeah, if that's her real name.'

'But Essex says nobody was with him at the Waldorf,' said O'Rourke.

'She had a room there.'

'So.' Crane nibbled at a finger-nail. 'Have you got anything on her?'

'No. Just that she's handy to deliver notes.'

'Deliver? You don't **think** she's writing them?'

Brown slapped a mosquito. 'She couldn't frame a kidnapping by herself.' The dead mosquito left a blob of bright blood on his arm.

'I guess you're right.' Crane settled back in his chair. 'If she's in it, she's working for someone.'

'What about the red ink?' O'Rourke asked.

'The hell!'' Brown got to his feet. 'That reminds me of something.'

He was a well-built, stocky man. His legs were short for great speed, but they were strong. He had been a hooker, able to hit from any angle, and his shoulders were wadded with muscles. From his breast-bone to the top button on his drawers ran a strip of black hair, as thick as a wolf's pelt. Layers of fat rounded his belly.

'This morning the major asked me for some red ink,' he said.

A current of air fluttered the curtain on the west window.

Crane asked: 'Did you get him some?'

'There was a bottle in Essex's study.'

O'Rourke asked: 'He tell you what he needed it for?'

Brown shook his head.

'Has he still got the bottle?'

'Naw. I put it back in Essex's desk just before dinner.'

'Looks like we got a date with the major,' O'Rourke said.

Crane nodded. 'Got any other ideas?' he asked Brown.

Brown had none.

'Well, thanks a lot,' said Crane, rising. 'This may come to something.'

'I hope it does. I'm sorry for that dame,' Brown said.

'I guess it isn't so swell to be kidnapped.'

'Not for a dame,' Brown said.

O'Rourke followed Crane out of the door. Brown scowled through the opening at him. 'I'd like to get you in an alley, Mick,' he said.

O'Rourke said: 'I never go in alleys.'

On their way downstairs they both had to dry their faces with handkerchiefs. The air was sultry; it felt as though it was going to storm.

'We're still alive,' said O'Rourke.

'But now I go to interview the major,' said Crane, 'And he doesn't like me.'

'He didn't like that telegram you sent him.'

'There's more than that. I think he's trying to marry Camelia for her dough.'

'Everybody is,' said O'Rourke.

'Except Tony Lamphier.'

O'Rourke transferred his revolver from his coat pocket to the holster. 'How'd you happen to know Brown was going with Céleste?'

'If you were working here,' Crane asked, 'who would you be going with?'

'You're pretty smart.'

'You don't have to be smart to figure that.'

'Remembering Céleste, I guess not.'

Mosquitoes had driven every one in from the patio. The Bouchers, Miss Langley and the major were playing bridge. Miss Day, who had been listening to Benny Goodman swing 'Sing, Baby, Sing' on the radio, hailed them with a cry of joy. 'Come on and dance,' she called. 'I've got the hottest band.'

Crane helped her kick away a rug in front of the radio. He took hold of her, swung her into a fox-trot. Her back was cool and firm under his palm.

'Nice music,' he said.

She snuggled closer. 'You said it.'

Her flesh was solid. She didn't have the slender, supple muscles of Imago Paraguay. She didn't have the dancer's perfect *tempo*, her intuitive anticipation of the steps, but she danced quite well. She was going to be heavy at thirty-five.

'What did you find out?' she asked.

'What do you mean?'

'From that fighter.'

In a corner of the room, on a divan, Imago Paraguay and Essex were talking. Essex was saying something; Imago's face was coldly composed.

'How'd you know we were going to talk to Brown?'

'Tom O'Rourke asked me where his room was.'

'We found out very little from him,' Crane said.

Benny was taking a lick on the clarinet. The music became hot. Only drum and clarinet were playing.

Crane cruised round the outside edge of the cleared space on the floor, whirling handsomely on the turns. 'Brown thinks you're dishing out the notes,' he informed her.

There was no break in her *tempo*. 'He would,' she said.

'After all, there's some reason. You've been with Essex all during the time he's been getting the notes.'

'Did Brown say that?'

'Yes.'

'Well, he's right. I have.' She was leading him now, her arm muscles tense. 'But that's not why he wants to get me into trouble.'

'No?'

'No. He's sore because I won't give him a tumble.'

'That would make a guy sore.'

'You don't have to be sarcastic.'

'I'm not.'

Imago Paraguay's eyes were on him. They had no expression in them at all. Her face reminded him again of a perfectly tinted ivory mask. Essex was still talking to her. She seemed bored.

Miss Day relaxed a trifle. 'What else that bum say?' She let him lead.

'He said you were at the Waldorf when the first note came.'

'What of it?'

'Essex told me you weren't'.

'He didn't want to mix me in this business.'

Benny Goodman's band had taken up the straight melody again. The music was fuller, smoother, less wild. He danced half-time.

'That was gentlemanly,' he said.

'But I don't care,' she said.

He accomplished a slow turn, using two two-steps.

'If I was putting those notes around I wouldn't put myself on the spot, would I?' she asked.

'I guess not.'

The music stopped and a fine mellow voice said there would be a brief interval for station announcements. O'Rourke came up to them. Another fine mellow voice said: 'You are listening to WQAM, Miami.'

Miss Day said: 'I'll tell you who you ought to watch.'

'Who?' Crane asked.

'That dame over there.' She jerked a thumb at Imago Paraguay. 'There's something funny about her.' Her thumb-nail was painted a blood-red.

'How do you mean?'

'Well, for one thing: what's she doing here?'

'What *is* she doing here?' demanded Crane.

'I'm asking you.' Miss Day adjusted a shoulder-strap, much to O'Rourke's disappointment. 'She's supposed to be Penn's guest, but he's scared of her.'

'Everybody is,' said Crane.

Carlos walked across the room to Essex. 'Telephone, sir,' he said. 'Will you take it in here?'

Essex looked frightened. 'I'll take it in the hall.' He stood up, stared round the room uncertainly, then followed Carlos towards the hall.

'Maybe it's the ransom directions,' whispered Miss Day.

O'Rourke switched off the radio. The people at the
bridge table stopped their game, craned their necks
toward the hall. The major started to get up, then
changed his mind. Miss Day and O'Rourke followed
Crane over to Imago Paraguay.

There was a decanter of whisky, a chromium siphon
and a silver bowl of cracked ice beside the divan. On
the same table were tall glasses. 'Will you have a
drink?' Crane asked Imago Paraguay.

'Tha-ank you.' Her smile showed her very small,
very even teeth. 'I will.'

'Make it four,' said O'Rourke.

Crane put three fingers of whisky in four of the
glasses. He smelt one of them. The liquor was
Scotch.

Imago said to Miss Day: 'It is exciting, is it not?'

Miss Day said: 'I'll take the races any day.'

Crane put in the ice, added charged water. He
handed a glass to Imago, another to Miss Day, gave
O'Rourke his choice of the remaining two.

'Here's how,' he said.

They were drinking when Essex came back into the
room. 'Just the police,' he told the bridge players.
'Wanted to know if I'd heard anything.'

He walked over to the divan and Miss Day gave
him her glass. 'You need it, baby,' she said.

'Where's Lamphier?' Crane asked.

'He went upstairs to lie down,' Essex said. He
was unnaturally pale; almost a greenish white. 'He's
done up.' He took a long drink of the whisky.

'He should be?' O'Rourke said. 'No sleep since
night before last.'

'And very little then,' said Crane, remembering the
pursuit of the flamingo.

'I think I'll lie down on the couch in the library,'
Essex said. 'Then I'll be handy if any one wants
me.'

'You ought to take a nap,' said Miss Day.

'I can't sleep.'

'I have some sleeping-powders,' said Imago Paraguay. 'They are excellent. I take two capsules every night before I turn off my light.'

Boucher, at the bridge table, laid down four cards, said: 'That's game and rubber.' He and the major appeared to have been reconciled.

'Sleeping-powders give me a headache,' said Essex. 'Besides, I don't want to sleep.'

Miss Day asked Imago: 'Aren't you afraid you'll get a habit from taking them?'

'I ha-ave already.'

They were adding up the score at the bridge table. Crane kept an eye on the major. He didn't want him to get away.

Essex asked: 'But don't they give you a headache?'

'Never,' said Imago Paraguay.

Crane started to move toward the bridge table. Imago asked him: 'You ha-ave not forgotten our date?'

'Of course not,' said Crane.

He caught the major in the hall. 'I'd like to speak with you,' he said.

'What about?'

'It's a private matter.'

The major scowled at him. 'Come to my room, then.' Without waiting for Crane, he turned and went up the stairs.

CHAPTER TWELVE

AT quarter to two O'Rourke came into their suite.
He was surprised to see Crane. 'Thought you'd
gone to bed,' he said. There was lipstick on the bosom
of his shirt.

Crane was lying on his bed. He had taken off his
coat and shoes. 'I wish I had,' he said. There was
a half-filled bottle of whisky and a glass on a table
beside the bed. He had been reading a copy of *Exciting
Detective Tales*.

O'Rourke removed his coat, jerked off his black tie.
'I'm going swimming . . . with Miss Day.'

'In this thunder-storm?'

'Hell, the thunder's thirty miles off. The moon's
out.'

Crane got off the bed, looked out of the french
windows. The moon was to the right, low on the
horizon. It was just above a bank of milky clouds.

'I'd go too,' he said, 'only I've got a date.'

O'Rourke brought his trunks out of the bathroom.
'Who with?'

'Imago.'

'You better be careful she don't stick you with
that little dagger.'

'It isn't that kind of date.' Crane stared at the
path the moon made across the black water. 'At least
I don't think so.'

'These feel clammy,' O'Rourke said, pulling up his
trunks. 'What did you find out from the major?'

'Nothing. Exactly nothing.'

'What was he usin' the red ink for?'

'To balance the estate's books. He showed them
to me.'

'Was he tough?'

'No more than usual.'

'Is he clear?'

'I'm afraid so.'

'Maybe we'll get something on him later,' said O'Rourke hopefully.

There was a distant growl of thunder. The wind seemed to be fresher; it rustled the palms and started the french window swinging shut. Crane stopped it before it slammed, said: 'You better get going or there will be a storm.'

O'Rourke had on his beach-robe and an orange and white towel was draped over his arm. 'Will you be needing all that whisky?' he asked.

'I guess not.' Crane filled the tumbler, gave the bottle to O'Rourke. 'Don't let Essex catch you.'

O'Rourke grinned. 'He's dead to the world. He's sleeping under a green blanket on the couch in the library.'

Alone again, Crane glanced at his watch. It was nearly two. He sat on the bed and pulled on his shoes. He tied his black bow-tie and put on his coat. He drank about a quarter of the glass of whisky, then had a water chaser out of the thermos by his bed. He felt pretty good.

He left the rest of the liquor for a night-cap, and went out into the hall, and found Imago's door and knocked softly. He knocked again. Then again. There was no answer. He waited fully two minutes, then, for the fourth time, knocked. No reply. He went back to his room and sat on the bed. She had definitely said she would see him at two o'clock and he felt slightly angry. He drank about half the remaining whisky in the glass and debated whether or not he should go to bed.

Off in the distance the storm snarled and growled and broad flashes of lightning fitfully illuminated the pale cloud-banks. The sea looked ink-black beside the clouds. The atmosphere was humid.

He went to his suit-case and took out an oustiti, an instrument shaped like an incredibly thin pair of pliers and designed to open locks. He dropped this in his pocket and went back to Imago's room. He felt he would like to see the interior of her room and he had a good excuse for breaking in. If she was there he could explain that he had become alarmed when she failed to keep her appointment with him, had entered to make certain nothing had happened to her. Reaching the door, he knocked again. There was only silence. He dropped on one knee, deftly inserted the oustiti, unlocked the door.

Once inside, he bolted the door. Where was the light switch? He thought of using his flash-light, but decided that his appearance in the room would seem more innocent if he turned on the lights. His handkerchief-covered hand rubbed the wall, encountered the switch; he pushed the button.

On the double bed, a sheet pulled up to one creamy shoulder, lay Imago Paraguay. Her black hair clung to the pillow beside her, like a smudge of soot on snow. He looked at the electric clock on the table beside her, and saw that it was twenty minutes to three. He moved closer to the bed and glanced down at her face. She was lying on her back and her ebony-black eyes were wide open. Her skin, usually pale ivory, was the colour of claret wine. Startled, he touched her bare shoulder, then shook it violently. It didn't do any good. She was dead!

His first thought was of flight. He'd be in a jam if any one found him in the room. It would make a really fine scandal. He started for the door, then halted. The unnatural flush of Imago's skin stirred his memory. He went back to the bed, knelt on the floor and put his nose to her cerise lips. There was

a faint bitter odour. It reminded him of almonds.
Cyanide of potassium!

His surprise made him forget his own danger. Beside her, on a small table, was a thermos bottle, a
glass half-filled with water and a small box of white
cardboard. He smelt the thermos, then the glass.
Both were odourless. He opened the box and took
out three of the dozen or so capsules inside. He opened
these and smelt the grey powder with which they
were filled. It was odourless. The label on the box
read VERONAL. He frowned and looked at the dead
woman.

Suicide? Would she kill herself? He didn't think
so. The door had been locked from the inside, and
the key had been in the lock. He looked out the
french windows. From the balcony to the patio was
an impossible jump. From the roof to the balcony
was another long jump. No one could have come
and gone that way. Back beside Imago's bed he
stared down at the body. He had an impulse to close
the purple lids over the indian-ink eyes, but he decided
he'd better not touch her. It was a hell of a time to
commit suicide, he thought, but how could any one
have got into the room to poison her?

With his handkerchief over his hand he lifted the
box marked VERONAL. She said she always took
sleeping-powders, and the half-filled glass was evidence
she had this night. There were two small scars on the
veronal box, almost as if some one had started to cut
it with a pair of scissors. He wondered if a cyanide
capsule had been slipped in with the veronal. That
would be a way of murdering her, but not a very good
one if the murderer was in a hurry. She might not
come to the cyanide until the last two or three capsules;
not for a week or so. No, suicide seemed the . . .

There was a gentle knocking at the door.

He stood absolutely motionless, holding his breath.

His heart beat in his ears; his body was suddenly covered with goose-flesh. He waited. At last he had to swallow to clear his throat so he could breathe.

The knocking was repeated. A low voice said:

'Imago.'

He recognized the voice as that of Miss Langley. He kept as quiet as he was able, breathing through his open mouth. He was frightened.

'Imago,' said Miss Langley, knocking again.

There was a long pause.

'All right,' said Miss Langley.

He could hear the departing swish of her night-gown.

He found he was still grasping the box of veronal with his handkerchief. He put it back on the table. He pulled the sheet over Imago's body. He knew he'd better get out of there. He didn't want to try to explain just what he was doing in the room.

He took one last tour of the room. The door had been locked from the inside. With Essex's guards outside, he was confident no one could have reached the balcony from the roof or the patio. There was no other balcony near it. The bathroom window was locked from the inside. There was no window in the dressing-room. He looked at the ceiling in the bed-room. It was calcimined white and there were only the four foot-square ventilators in the corners, just as in his room. There were absolutely no marks on the clean surface of the ceiling. He stared up at the ventilator over the bed. It would be impossible for anything larger than a monkey to come through that. Certainly nobody had come into the room through the ceiling.

The clock read 3.05. He'd better be going. On his way to the door he paused beside the dancer's body. Her face was strange under the soft light. It was like the face of an Asiatic doll: fragile, serene and

impassive; cold and inhuman. Over her brow the skin
was blue-white; on her cheeks and neck it was pink;
a result of the poison. Her mouth was a crushed-
raspberry red; lilac mascara shadowed her eyes; the
brows were charcoal curves. The soft rise of her
breasts was just revealed by the sheet. He resisted
an impulse to close her eyes.

He let himself out of the door, then locked it with
his oustiti, and hurried down the corridor to his room.
He took off his clothes and got into bed without bothering to put on pyjamas. He set the alarm of the travelling
clock in the pigskin case for quarter to nine, drank
the whisky in the glass and turned off the light. He
exhaled deeply, wearily.

CHAPTER THIRTEEN

O'ROURKE shook him, said: 'Wake up, Bill.' Ex-
citement made his voice high. 'Wake up. Things
have happened.'

No matter where he moved the sun was in Crane's
eyes, like the beam of a search-light. It made his
eyeballs hurt. His mouth tasted as though he had
held threepenny nails in it all night. His head ached.
He did not feel at all well.

'Come on.' O'Rourke pulled him to a sitting position.
'I'm going to have to throw water on you.'

'I am not well,' Crane said.

'Are you awake?' O'Rourke asked.

'Yes, but I am not well.'

'Imago Paraguay is dead,' O'Rourke said.

Crane sank back on the pillow.

'You hear me?' O'Rourke asked. 'Imago Paraquay is ...'

'I hear you.' Crane closed his eyes, buried his face in the pillow.

There was a pause. Then O'Rourke said: 'You knew it already.'

Crane asked: 'What time is it?'

O'Rourke glanced at his wrist-watch. 'Eight-twenty.' He sat on the edge of the bed. 'How'd you find out she was dead?'

'She was dead last night.'

'You didn't talk with her?'

'No.'

'You didn't knock her off?'

Crane opened one eye. 'Do they say she was knocked off?' The light was paler now; a cloud had passed in front of the sun.

'No. The cops think she took poison.'

Last night's storm had roused the surf. It wasn't heavy, but it was coming in fast, making a hissing noise. In the sun, just outside the French window, a butterfly examined the yellow interior of a trumpet-vine blossom.

'Were you there right after she killed herself?' O'Rourke asked.

'I don't know.'

While Crane took a bath and shaved, O'Rourke described the discovery of the body. Miss Langley couldn't get an answer to her knocking, had one of the servants break open the door, he said, and found the body. Her screams woke the household. So far the theory was suicide, although a careful search had been made of the room. No note had been found.

There was another piece of news, O'Rourke continued: from di Gregario. Eddie Burns had called to say the count had again given them the slip during the night, but they had learned he was in Key West.

Williams was now flying there on the Pan-American plane to pick him up.

'Those guys are swell shadows,' said Crane.

'It's tough to hang on to somebody day and night,' O'Rourke said.

'I suppose so.' Crane let hot water run over a washcloth. 'Anyway, I'll go to Key West, too.'

'To see di Gregario?'

Crane pressed the dripping cloth against his face. 'Yeah.'

'You think he and Imago are connected in some way?'

'It's possible. Maybe they put on all that cat-and-dog stuff for our benefit.'

'I get the idea.' O'Rourke was leaning against the bathroom door. 'She put the finger on Camelia Essex for di Gregario, then killed herself in remorse.'

'She was killed.'

The bathroom door swung back and O'Rourke nearly lost his balance. 'How do you figure that?'

Crane pretended to be mysterious. He put his finger to his lips. 'It came as a revelation.' As he put on the coat to his double-breasted linen suit, O'Rourke asked: 'When do we start?'

'You aren't going.' Crane adjusted his brown tie. 'I wouldn't think of tearing you away from Miss Day.'

'Miss Day won't give a damn to-day,' said O'Rourke.

'Why not?'

'She's going to be a cripple, unless she's tougher than I think.' O'Rourke smiled reminiscently. 'After we had a swim and polished off the whisky I took her up to her room. She was locked out, so we went in by way of Essex's rooms. In that sort of dressing-room, just past the bathroom, she fell over a chair and damn near broke her neck.'

'Where was Essex when this was happening?'

'Down in the library, asleep.'

'Well, you can't go, anyway.' Crane got his panama from the cupboard shelf. 'I got a job for you in Miami.'

He told O'Rourke that he wanted to know if Imago's cheque for one thousand dollars had been found either in Tortoni's bank or among his effects. 'See if you can find out how well they knew each other,' he added.

'O.K.,' said O'Rourke. 'Now how about a spot of breakfast?'

'Oh, my God!' said Crane. 'I'm never going to eat again.'

After an hour's ride over turquoise water dotted with uninhabited grey-green keys, Key West appeared very large. The hired amphibian passed a beach with thatch-roofed *cabañas* on it, an hotel with gardens and tennis-courts, a crumbling red fort, and circled for a landing in calm water outside the entrance to the submarine-basin. Deftly the pilot met the water in an easy glide, then guided the amphibian to the landing-dock, passing within a few yards of the regular Miami-Key West seaplane. Two men in blue overalls caught ropes, eased the ship to the dock.

The pilot grinned at Crane. 'Not a bad trip,' he said. He had blue eyes.

'It was fine,' Crane said.

Tony Lamphier stood up. 'You're sure you don't mind my coming along?' he asked.

'No. I'm glad to have you.'

'Really?'

'Yes. Really.'

The pilot asked: 'When will you be going back?'

'Not until after lunch.'

'O.K.'

They jumped to the wooden dock and climbed a flight of stairs to the pier. To their right, past a grey Coast-guard cutter and two neat white and mahogany cruisers, people were swimming. On the left, pulled up to a series of piers, were other boats, some of them quite large, and in the distance were the yellow walls of an hotel, half hidden by palm trees. The name of the hotel appeared to be La Concha. There was an odour of fish about the pier.

Crane caught sight of Williams half-way down the dock. 'This way,' he said to Tony Lamphier. He walked up to Williams. 'Hi, Doc.'

Williams was carrying his green gabardine coat over his arm. His tan silk shirt, opened at the collar, was damp with sweat. 'Hi,' he said. He wiped his neck with a handkerchief. 'This place is hot.' He told them the count was on a boat.

'Which boat?' Crane asked.

'That tub with the green paint on it.'

The boat was fat and grimy and there were uncoiled ropes on the deck. *Sylvia* was printed in black letters on the bow. Forward, two dark men in olive-brown trousers lounged with cigarettes. From the copper-red funnel floated thin smoke which disappeared almost at once in the bright sunlight.

Followed by the others, Crane jumped to the deck. Their feet were noisy on the wood. One of the men came towards them.'

'Who do you want?'

'Di Gregario,' said Crane.

The man was a Cuban and his bare feet were dirty. 'There is no one of that name here.' He had a hammer-toe on his left foot.

'I saw him come aboard,' said Williams.

'No, señor. There is no one of that name.'

'We'll look around,' said Crane.

'What's the matter, Frank?' The other Cuban was coming towards them. 'What's the matter?' He was stocky and there was a long white scar along his belly. It looked as though he had been gored by a bull.

The first Cuban said something in Spanish.

'No. No one here by that name,' said the stocky Cuban. 'Now please go.'

'Where's the captain?' asked Crane.

'You will please go,' said the stocky Cuban.

The other Cuban started to move away. Williams stepped in front of him. Under his coat he held a revolver. 'Stay here, spig,' he said.

Both the Cubans were frightened at the sight of the revolver. They rolled their eyes and the stocky one asked: 'What does this mean?'

'Keep 'em here, Doc,' said Crane. 'We'll go below.'

The main cabin stank of wine and garlic and sweat. At a round mahogany table in the centre sat di Gregario and an elderly man with white hair and a grey beard. They were looking at a map. In front of them was a wicker jug of Bacardi and two glasses. The portholes were draped with frayed red velvet.

Startled, di Gregario pushed back his chair. 'You!'

In the copper light from dim overhead bulbs the elderly man looked distinguished. His linen suit was well tailored; his beard had been trimmed and brushed; his eyes and arched nose were haughty. 'What is this?' he asked.

'I came to ask di Gregario where he spent last night,' said Crane.

'Who are you?'

'He is an American detective,' said di Gregario. He made no attempt to move from his chair. 'He believes I have kidnapped Camelia Essex.'

'So.' The elderly man frowned. 'That is not good.'

'He is also a friend of Imago Paraguay,' said di Gregario.

Water, lapping against the bottom, sounded like some one pouring a drink. There was a noise of pounding in the engine-room. Tony Lamphier, beside Crane, moved nervously.

At last the elderly man asked: 'Why do you wish to know where di Gregario was last night?'

'I'll tell you after he answers,' said Crane.

Di Gregario leaned over the table. 'Camelia has come back?'

'Listen,' said Crane. 'If you don't want to answer my questions, just say so. Then I can take you over to the sheriff's office.' He scowled at di Gregario.

'You better talk here,' said Tony Lamphier.

The elderly man said: 'Di Gregario was in Key West last night. He had a room adjoining mine at the Colonial Hotel.'

'Is that so?' Crane asked di Gregario.

'Yes.'

'And you didn't murder Imago Paraguay?'

Tony Lamphier gave a startled gasp.

'Imago Paraguay murdered?' Di Gregario straightened up in his chair, then relaxed. 'You are joking me.'

'No.'

Di Gregario's white teeth gleamed. 'Then I am glad.'

The elderly man said: 'She was an enemy to the Cuban people.'

'What rooms did you have at the hotel?' Crane asked.

'We have them yet.' Di Gregario tossed a key on the table. Crane picked it up. It was for room 410. 'That is mine,' said di Gregario.

'You were there all night?'

'We went to bed soon after one o'clock,' said the elderly man.

'I guess that lets you out.' Crane took his clenched hand from his coat pocket. 'At least as far as Miss Paraguay's concerned.'

'You still believe I kidnap Camelia?' di Gregario asked.

'This boat would be a good place to hide her.'

The elderly man and di Gregario looked at each other.

'In fact,' said Crane, 'I'd like to look it over.'

Di Gregario and the elderly man exchanged glances again.

'I give you my word she is not aboard,' said the elderly man. 'Is that not sufficient?'

'No,' said Crane.

Di Gregario spoke in Spanish. The elderly man replied. Then di Gregario said: 'We are going to trust you.'

'Good.'

'In this boat we have weapons.'

'Ah,' said Crane.

'We are planning to deliver them to a certain country. If the officials of the country learn of this it will become very difficult to do so.'

'We don't care about gun-running,' Crane said. 'All we're interested in is Camelia, aren't we, Tony?'

'That's all.'

Di Gregario said: 'If we allow you to search the boat you will say nothing?'

'Not unless we find Camelia.'

'You will not find her.'

'Than we can look?'

The elderly man said: 'Yes.'

'Good.' Crane spoke to di Gregario. 'Two of your men would like to make trouble on deck. Will you tell them it is all right?'

They blinked in the sunlight. There was a mixed smell of salt and fish and tar in the air. Doc Williams and the two Cubans were in the bow. The stocky Cuban's forehead was bruised, blood had stained his cheek. Doc Williams grinned at them.

'One of the spicks got kinda fresh,' he said.

Di Gregario spoke to the Cubans in Spanish. Sullenly they watched the three Americans go below

again. '*Cabrones   Americanos!*' said   the   stocky
Cuban.

After talking to the clerk at the Colonial Hotel,
which turned out to be the one with the yellow walls,
they walked down Duval Street towards a place called
Sloppy Joe's. On their way they discussed di Gregario's alibi.

'He's out,' Crane said.

'I'm afraid so,' Tony Lamphier agreèd. 'Both the girl
clerk and the night bell-boy were positive he was there.'

Williams said: 'It's funny they'd have a girl for an
hotel clerk.'

Crane was admiring a cottage completely covered
with bougainvillaea blossoms the colour of Burgundy
wine. 'I don't think he'd mix gun-running and kidnapping,' he said. 'And murder, too.' Only the peak
of the cottage's roof was visible.

'Not a bad looking girl, either,' Williams said. 'What
was her name?'

By another, larger house, thousands of hibiscus flowers
stuck out scarlet tongues at them.

'What makes you think Imago was murdered?'
asked Lamphier.

'I got a hunch,'said Crane.

The street was massed with tropical blooms; the air
was thick with tropical odours. Flowers in beds beside
the wooden houses were insignificant beside the explosive
colours of vines and trees. Magentas, ochres, creams,
ultramarines, lemons, ecrus, coquelicots, hennas made
a sub-tropical tartan of the city. The tints were dew-
fresh, bright.

Williams asked: 'What was the name of the clerk in
the hotel?'

'Miss Sharpley,' Crane said.

'Oh, yeah.' Williams grinned. 'I was thinking it
ought to be Miss Shapely.'

They turned the corner towards the telegraph office and found Sloppy Joe's. 'Three Bacardis,' said Crane to a gaunt, red-faced man behind the bar. The man said over his shoulder to a coloured man in a white coat: 'Three Bacardis.' The coloured man said: 'Three Bacardis.'

Three natives were talking over beer at one end of the bar. One of them was saying the tarpon had gone out to spawn. 'That's why there ain't none in the channel,' he said.

The coloured man poured the Bacardis. Crane gave him a five-dollar bill and said: 'Three more.'

'What's on the programme?' asked Williams.

'You'll have to stay down.' Crane tasted his drink. 'Make sure the count does sail to-morrow.' The drink tasted fine; it was smooth and tart.

'That's O.K. by me,' Williams said.

'Is he really a count?' asked Lamphier.

'No.' Crane finished his drink. 'I think he used his real name at the hotel: Paul Lopez.'

'What'll I do if he does leave?' asked Williams.

'Give me a ring,' Crane said. He watched the coloured man fill the glasses again. 'Just keep them filled,' he told him.

The coloured man looked surprised. 'You mean, just keep on making them? Like I'm doing?'

'Exactly.'

The gaunt man said: 'Make 'em up a batch, Skinner.'

'No,' said Crane. 'Three at a time. They're better fresh.'

Skinner began to squeeze limes.

The man who had said the tarpon had gone out to spawn said: 'I know I'm right. Captain Luther was out with a party the day afore yestiddy. He seen hundreds of 'em rollin' . . . right in the stream.'

'It's too early for spawnin',' said the second man. The third man had a round face and spectacles.

His face was red up to the point where his hat circled his forehead. 'Captain Luther could a seen anythin',' he said. 'He was carryin' a load.'

'No, he was sober,' said the first man.

Skinner filled Crane's glass. 'Let me know when the five is used up,' Crane said. He was listening to the three men.

'Yes, sir,' said Skinner.

'I know he was loaded,' the man with the spectacles said. 'He tried to tell me he seen a man killin' fish from a boat with a machine-gun.'

'He told me that, too,' the first man was forced to admit.

Outside it began to rain furiously. Water screened the open side of the bar, changed from grey to white as it struck the sidewalk. The air became cool.

'Maybe he seen Ernest,' said the second man.

'He said the man would hook a sailfish,' the man with the spectacles said. 'Then, when the sail'd jump, he'd shoot at it.'

'Captain Luther said that?' said the second man.

Williams went over to a slot-machine and put a dime in it. A lemon showed. He put another dime in it. Another lemon showed. 'Hell!' he said.

'It must have been Ernest,' said the second man.

The man behind the bar said: 'No, it wasn't.' His eyes were pale blue. 'Ernest'ud never shoot at a sail.'

Tony Lamphier said: 'I wonder if they've heard anything at the house.'

Crane was listening to the three men.

'Ernest only uses the Tommy-gun on sharks,' said the man behind the bar. 'And besides, Captain Luther knows Ernest's boat.'

'I reckon you're right, Captain Joe,' said the second man.

'I know Goddam well I'm right,' said Captain Joe. 'Besides, Ernest don't keep his gun in this country.'

Skinner, the coloured man, poured another round of drinks. 'Your five dollars is up, mister,' he said. His brow was damp with sweat.

Crane handed him another five dollars.

'All I know,' said the second man, 'is that it's too early for spawning.'

'Then what're they doin' out in the stream?' the first man wanted to know.

'I wish we could get hold of something,' said Tony Lamphier.

Crane said: 'Huh?' He had been listening to the three men.

The rain stopped and the sun came out. It was hot again. Skinner poured another round of drinks. Water running down drains made a gurgling noise.

'Captain Luther was loaded,' said the man with spectacles.

'I feel terrible about Camelia,' said Tony Lamphier.

'So do I,' said Crane.

'It's too early for spawnin',' said the second man.

'Why don't they bite then?' asked the first man.

'Let's start back,' said Tony Lamphier.

'In a minute.' Crane held his glass out to Skinner.

'What about lunch?' Williams asked.

Crane raised the full glass to his mouth. 'To hell with lunch.'

CHAPTER FOURTEEN

MISS DAY came to the door as Crane steered the roadster through the clutter of police cars in the driveway. She was wearing French blue slacks, rope sandals and a grey sweater, and her hair was the colour

of butter. Her lips and finger-nails were the colour
of blood oranges.

'Howdy,' she said.

Crane halted the car in front of the marquee, shut
off the engine and said: 'Howdy.'

'You will please help us into the house,' said Crane.

'Not me,' Miss Day said. 'This baby is a cripple.'

'So I heard.'

'Imagine a dope leaving a chair right in the middle
of a passageway!' Miss Day pulled up her slacks to her
thighs. 'Look.' There were black and blue marks
on both her shins, on her tanned left knee. 'It's a
wonder I didn't break something.'

'I think you're beautiful,' said Crane.

Tony Lamphier got out of the car. 'I'm going
upstairs. His face was pale; there were liver-coloured
smudges under his eyes; new wrinkles had aged him.
'I'm tired.'

Miss Day came and sat beside Crane. 'He's taking
it hard,' she said. An aroma of My Sin surrounded her.

'I don't blame him.'

'I didn't know he was that goofy about Camelia.'

'I feel bad about her myself,' Crane said.

'Oh, you!'

'Well, I do.'

'You feel worse about Imago.'

'I feel bad about her, too.'

'You went for her, didn't you?'

'I found her . . . interesting.'

'Why do you think she killed herself?'

'I don't know.'

'They say inside'—Miss Day jerked her bright
head toward the house—'she was mixed up with The
Eye.'

'Maybe she was.' Crane gave Miss Day a cigarette, pushed the electric lighter on the roadster's dashboard. 'I'd like to know what she was doing in this

house . . . why Essex invited her.'   He lit her cigarette, then his own.   'Where is Essex?'

'He and the cops are working up a plan.'

'A plan?'

'To catch The Eye when he collects the ransom.'

Crane let smoke run through his nostrils. 'Why don't they wait until they know how The Eye's going to try to collect it?'

'But they do know.'   She stared at him in surprise. 'Haven't you heard?'

'Heard what?'

'Penn got a ransom note.'

'The hell he did!'

'Sure.   That's what the confab's about.'

'So.'   Crane shoved the wheel with his hands, pushed himself against the leather cushion. 'What did the note say?'

'I'll show you.'   She twisted her body into an S, drew a piece of paper from her hip pocket. 'Here's a copy of it.'

He took the paper from her. 'How come you got the copy?'

'Penn had me make it.   He thought maybe the cops would take the real note away.'

Crane unfolded the paper. Sunshine, reflecting from the white surface, made his eyes blink. Miss Day had evidently tried to make an exact copy of the note.   On the paper was printed:

'Essex

'Directions. . . .   Wrap the fifty thousand in oil-skin. . . .   Put in a box. . . .   Take box at 10 a.m. to-morrow to cement bridge 12.3 miles south of Homestead on Key Largo road. . . .   Leave box on canal bank under exact centre of bridge. . . .   Drive away.

Camelia will die if you fail. . . .   No one must ride

with you. . . .   No one must follow you. . . .   No one
must be near bridge.

Camelia is well but unhappy. . . .   She says please
save her. . . .   She says remember Froggy.

'THE EYE.'

.

Crane gave the paper to Miss Day. 'Who the hell's
Froggy?'

'You got me.'

'How'd the note come?'

'Penn found it in with some mail on the breakfast
table.'

It hadn't been mailed, just put there, Miss Day
told him. The servants had been questioned, she
said, but they denied all knowledge of it. Craig had
put the mail on the table himself, and he was sure it
hadn't been there then. For about half an hour
before Essex had sat down, there had been no one
near the table and the police thought, she said, that
The Eye, or an aid, had put it there then.

'What are they going to do about it?' Crane asked
her.

'They're figuring out a way they can hide a party
of men around the bridge, but Penn's been fighting
them. He thinks it would risk Camelia's life.' She
turned and looked at him curiously through her big
blue eyes. 'What are *you* going to do?'

Crane opened the door. 'Get us a drink,' he said.

Crane told O'Rourke all about di Gregario and
the ransom note, the interview with Miss Day. They
were having sandwiches and Holland beer at the table
by the swimming-pool. A yellow and blue umbrella
gave them shade. 'What luck did you have?' he
asked.

'Plenty.' O'Rourke poured beer into his glass. 'In
the first place there is no cheque.'

'No?'

'And there never was.'

Crane was interested. 'How do you figure that?'

'Imago was Tortoni's girl friend.'

Crane put his beer glass down. 'I never thought of that.'

O'Rourke was pleased with himself. 'I got the dope from a guy I used to know at Saratoga, a guy named Dan Grady. He works for Bradley's, up at Palm Beach.'

'A croupier?'

'Yeah. I thought he might know some gossip so I drove up there. He'd heard from a guy working in Tortoni's joint that Imago was his doll. They been going together for a year.'

Crane frowned. 'That doesn't seem to make things easier.'

'It looks as though Imago and Tortoni had something to do with the snatching after all.'

'It doesn't have to.' Crane put mustard on his sandwich. 'Maybe the same guys that killed Tortoni killed her.'

'If she was killed,' O'Rourke said. 'But why?'

'Maybe she knew too much. Maybe she knew who killed Tortoni.'

'That could be. But what was she doing staying here?'

'That's what gets me. I'll have to ask Essex.'

'Maybe she was watching Essex for Tortoni . . . to see what he was doing about the gambling debt.'

'She could have been.'

'And on the other hand she could have been watching Camelia, ready to put the finger on her.'

'You're certainly a big help.'

'Well, you have to look at the angles.'

Crane took a long drink of the cold beer. 'I'd rather look at the curves.'

'Meaning Miss Day?'

'She'll do.'

'How's her ankle?'

'It's all right. A fall over a chair doesn't stop her.'

O'Rourke seemed pleased at this information. 'What's next on the programme?'

'I don't know. The cops won't let me in on their conference.'

'Big secret stuff?'

'Yeah. They even got a G-man in there.'

'What are they doing?'

'Miss Day tells me they're figuring out how to nab the Eye after he gets the ransom money.'

O'Rourke said: 'Let's take a look at the bridge where Essex has to leave the dough. It's not far.'

'O.K.' Crane tilted all four of the beer-bottles over his glass, but they were empty. 'Let's go.'

They drove all the way into Homestead and at the intersection of the town's two streets they set the roadster's speedometer at zero. Then they turned back to Key Largo. It was late afternoon, and part of the way they drove with the sun directly in front of them. The yellow light made their eyes smart. There was almost no wind and it was still very hot.

O'Rourke watched the speedometer. 'Ten miles.'

The country was absolutely flat. On the left, a mile distant, was the sea. Marshes led to the blue water. On the right grey tundra stretched until it merged with the horizon, broken only by clumps of palmettos and scrub pine. In places brown grass grew almost waist high. Along the asphalt road the ground was pin-pointed by small yellow flowers.

'That's it ahead,' O'Rourke said.

A sickle-shaped bay, filled with pale green water and coarse marsh grass, pressed its back against the left side of the road. From a point near the middle of the bay a thirty-foot canal drained water, and over

the canal was a cement bridge. Crane brought the
roadster to a stop just short of the bridge and glanced
at the speedometer. It read 12.2.

They got out of the convertible and walked up to
the peak of the bridge's arch. Tar oozed from cracks
in the cement. The tide was ebbing and the dark
blue water in the canal was running out to sea, carrying
brown grass, foam and twigs, moving very rapidly.

O'Rourke leaned on the rail and said:

> 'Oh, yellow's forsaken, and green is forsworn,
> But blue is the sweetest colour that's worn.'

'Oh, God!' Crane said. 'I thought you threw
that book of quotations away.'

'Threw it away?' O'Rourke pretended to be
horrified. 'A man of my culture wouldn't do a thing
like that.'

'Look,' Crane said. 'I'll give you two-fifty for the
book. That's what it cost.'

'I wouldn't part with it for ten dollars.'

'I'll give you three bucks for it.'

'Ten.'

'All right. Ten. But you've got to promise me
you won't spout another one of those things.'

'Sold for ten dollars.'

'O.K.' Crane drew some bills out of his watch
pocket, handed O'Rourke one. 'Now shut up.'

O'Rourke put the bill in his wallet. 'Where've you
got that nine grand?' He put the wallet in his hip
pocket. 'You didn't leave it in your room?'

'Right here.' Crane patted his inside coat pocket.
'I got it pinned in.'

'Anyway,' O'Rourke said, 'that quotation fitted.
The water is as blue as hell.'

'That's because the canal is deep. I guess it'd be
over a guy's head.'

On the side where they had left the car, the water

ran against the cement base of the bridge. On the opposite side there was an earth bank which sloped from the bridge's base to the water. They crossed the bridge and walked down this slope and went under the bridge. The earth was soft under their feet.

'This must be the spot,' Crane said.

By bending a little, a man could walk under the bridge on the canal bank. Moisture had turned the cement of the arch yellow, and mould grew where the base touched the earth. Damp, dank air clogged their noses.

'How the hell's The Eye going to pick the money up here?' O'Rourke demanded.

'It does seem odd.'

'In broad daylight, too.'

Behind them was the canal. It disappeared two hundred yards away in a jungle of palmettos, sugar-cane and tall brush. They were unable to see how much farther it went. Ahead was the bay, pale green, and farther the Atlantic. It was very bright outside the shadow of the bridge.

'He must be going to use a boat,' Crane said.

'Which way would he go?'

'Out to sea, I'd say.' Crane was feeling the cement under-surface of the bridge with his palms. 'They could trap him if he went up the canal.' The cement was cool, damp.

'He'd have to have a fast boat to get away by sea.'

'Maybe he has a plane.'

'You mean, land in the bay with it? Here?'

'Sure.' Crane moved along the bank, still palming the cement. 'He could land here, jump ashore, grab the money and scram, all in a minute.'

'Where would he go?'

'There must be lots of places. In the Everglades. Or on a deserted key. Or over on one of the British islands.'

'What the hell are you doing?'

'What do you mean?'

'Feeling around.'

'Oh.' Crane reached the sea end of the bridge, wiped his hands on a handkerchief. 'I wanted to see if the cement was solid.'

'Why?'

'I thought maybe The Eye had a hiding-place in the bridge.'

A gull started to come through the bridge, wheeled at sight of them, uttered a shrill cry and flew away.

'That's not a bad idea,' O'Rourke said.

'Not good, either. Of course, he could sneak out and get the dough, but how would he ever get out of his hiding-place within the bridge?'

'Wait until night, maybe.'

'There'd be cops around.'

'He could wait a couple of days.'

Crane sighed. 'He'd starve to death. He might have another way out, though.'

'It sounds phoney,' said O'Rourke.

Crane led the way out from under the bridge. 'It is phoney.' He slid on the bank, smeared mud over the knees of his linen trousers. 'It's either a boat or a plane.'

'Or a submarine,' said O'Rourke.

CHAPTER FIFTEEN

SWIMMING in the pool at dusk, with the air quiet and tangerine clouds rising over the sea, Crane found himself watching for Imago Paraguay. Momentarily he expected to see her come gliding across the patio, to hear her mocking drawl. It was almost impossible to believe she was dead. There had been something hard, impervious, assured about her; something that seemed beyond the reach of such a commonplace as death. He wondered if she really had been of priestly Mayan stock. What an end, if she had, for so ancient a blood-line! He was sorry . . .

O'Rourke interrupted his thoughts. 'They really hand you a sunset down here, don't they?' he said.

The clouds were splendid. They towered high above the horizon, giving the effect of a city on fire. Heliotrope smudged their bases, but the tower-like peaks were bright with scarlets, roses, salmons and oranges. Above, the sky was sapphire.

'Pretty gaudy,'' Crane said. 'It looks as though Sam Goldwyn had a hand in it.'

Slowly, using a quiet side-stroke, they swam the length of the pool. The water felt cool against their skin, made them feel fresh and clean. Out of the corner of their eyes they watched a serving-man put Bacardi, lime juice, powdered sugar and ice on the table by the pool.

'We got a friend in the house,' O'Rourke observed.

'I told Craig to send the makings out,' Crane said, 'when I got through my little chat with him.'

'Did he admit getting a cut on the groceries?'

'Yeah. He even offered me a slice.'

'He was scared, then?'

They began to paddle towards the side of the pool nearest the drinks.

'Plenty. But he said all good butlers got commissions on stuff they bought. He said it made no difference in the price the estate paid.'

'Did you tell him what Brown said?'

'I didn't have to.' Crane clung to the side of the pool. 'He told me Brown tried to muscle in on the buying racket.'

O'Rourke put his hands on the edge of the pool, pulled himself out of the water, put his feet on the edge, stood up. 'What about Craig and the snatching?' He leaned over, pulled Crane out of the water.

'I think he's clear.' Crane seized the bottle of Bacardi, filled a glass with the brown liquid. 'He's been working as a servant nearly all his life.' He filled another glass one-sixth of the way up with lime juice, added a tablespoonful of sugar. "He's got a house all paid for outside of Jersey City and he showed me his savings deposit book.' He began pouring the lime juice and the Bacardi from one glass to the other.

'How much was in it?' O'Rourke asked.

'Eighteen grand.' Crane filled two glasses with cracked ice. 'He's been putting away nearly a grand a year for the last twenty years.' He poured the mixture of lime juice and rum over the cracked ice.

O'Rourke accepted the filled glass. 'I'm going to be a butler.'

'Me, too,' said Crane.

They were drinking their second when Essex and three men came out of the house. 'Here they are,' Essex said.

Crane recognized one of the men as Captain Enright of the Miami police. He remembered the captain's broken nose, his dirty shirt. The other men were County Attorney Osborn and Mr. Wilson, representing the Department of Justice.

'You're the private detectives?' asked Wilson. He was neatly dressed in an Oxford-grey suit and his black hair was slick. He looked like a recent graduate of a law school.

"Yes," Crane said.

'You haven't done so well.'

'No.'

'Why haven't you offered to help to check the servants?'

'We're working on our own lines.'

'You're drinking on them, anyway.'

District Attorney Osborn looked as though he would have liked to look like Abraham Lincoln. He was tall; he had a big head, a large nose; his black hair was uncombed. He asked: 'How do you think the ransom will be collected?' One of his teeth was discoloured.

'O'Rourke and I decided the man would have to use a boat, or a plane.'

Osborn nodded. 'Those seem the only possibilities.' He pulled a chair to the table, sat down. 'It's curious he would want the money delivered in broad daylight . . . at ten o'clock in the morning.''

Essex was looking under the table. Finally, he found the electric buzzer, pushed it with his toe.

'It fits with an aeroplane,' Crane said. 'It would be much easier to land by day.'

Osborn said: 'The pilot could make sure there were no policemen hiding by the bridge, too.'

Pablo, wearing a white coat, approached the table. Essex told him to bring glasses and Scotch.

Twitching slightly, Wilson asked: 'What course of action would you recommend, Mr. Crane?' His face was small and pointed.

Crane shrugged his shoulders. 'I don't know. It would be pretty dangerous to càtch the person picking up the ransom . . . at least for Miss Essex.'

Osborn's deep voice echoed in the patio. 'We don't plan to apprehend this man, to act, until Miss Essex is released.' He sounded as though he were beginning a political speech.

'The idea is to follow him.' said Wilson.

Crane said: 'That will be hard.'

'He's bound to know,' said O'Rourke.

'Not if we are careful,' Wilson said.

He told them of the police plan, and Crane, listening, admitted it was a clever one. It was based on the use of an aeroplane and two-way radio communication between it and the ground. A very fast plane would be hovering high over Miami around ten o'clock, Wilson said, and its radio would be in contact with a portable police set on the Homestead water-tower.

Crane eyed O'Rourke. Both remembered the tower they had seen from the bridge.

Watchers on the tower, Wilson went on, would inform the plane the moment the ransom was picked up. It could then, still flying at a very great height, race toward the bridge and pick up the kidnapper's plane or boat. 'It will take only six minutes for it to get here,' he explained.

Osborn said: 'The kidnapper would hardly have time to get the money and lift his plane off the water.'

'What if he uses a car?' O'Rourke asked.

'There'll be radio-equipped cars all along the road,' Osborn said.

Pablo appeared with a tray. He poured four Scotches from a pinch bottle, added soda, ice. He started to fix small Bacardis for Crane and O'Rourke, but Crane said: 'Never mind.' He went away.

'What if the man has a small boat, goes up the canal and loses himself in the underbrush?' Crane asked.

'We've allowed for that,' Osborn said. 'We'll have men hidden up the canal.'

Crane divided the remainder of the rum equally between O'Rourke and himself. 'If The Eye comes from that way, won't the men alarm him?' he asked.

'They'll be quite a way from the bridge,' said Wilson. 'And they'll be well hidden.'

'How will they follow him?'

'He can't make any more speed over the Everglades than they can.'

'What if he circles round to the road and uses a car?'

'They can notify one of our control cars and we'll pick him up.'

Crane was drinking the Bacardi straight. 'It sounds all right.' The liquor was smooth. 'The only thing is to keep him from spotting you.'

'We can do it,' Osborn said.

'What'll you do when the guy goes to cover?' O'Rourke asked.

Captain Enright said: 'Pinch him as soon as Miss Essex is safe.'

Wilson was looking at Crane. 'Have you any suggestions?'

'I think it's risky for Camelia,' Crane said.

'Mr. Essex is willing to trust us,'' Wilson said.

'Are you?' Crane asked.

'Yes, I think so.' Essex's eyes went from Crane to Wilson. 'Mr. Wilson has had more experience and . . .'

'It's this way,' Wilson said. 'If they were going to harm Miss Essex they would have done it long ago. The only safe victim of a kidnapping is a dead one.'

Essex paled. 'You must face the facts, Mr. Essex,' Osborn said.

'If she is dead,' Wilson went on, 'we want to bring them to justice. The best chance is to follow the man who collects the ransom.'

He and Osborn had evidently used this argument before. Osborn supplemented: 'If they haven't killed her, they aren't intending to do so.'

'So we aren't really risking her life,' Wilson said.

Crane shrugged his shoulders. If Essex believed this, there was nothing he could do. 'Who's Froggy?' he asked.

Essex said: 'A Teddy bear Camelia had. I spilled green paint on it and we named it Froggy. It was a secret name.'

'Then she probably is alive,' said O'Rourke.

'Sure,' said Wilson.

Crane asked: 'Anybody else know about Froggy?'

'Aunt Sybil . . . Miss Langley.'

Crane said: 'Ha!'

'Why do the directions say to wrap the money in oilskin?' O'Rourke asked.

'I imagine he's afraid the money will get wet under the bridge,' Wilson said.

'Have you got a cardboard box?' Crane asked Essex.

'I've just the thing. One that had been filled with prunes.'

'Fifty thousand is a lot of money,' O'Rourke said.

'A king's ransom,' Wilson said.

'A queen's ransom,' Crane said.

Each time he lifted his glass, Captain Enright cocked his little finger. 'It will fit in the box all right.'

Crane looked at Wilson. 'You've taken the numbers of the bills?'

'Of course.'

Osborn finished his drink, stood up. 'It's time we were going.'

Crane asked: 'Would you mind if O'Rourke and I watched with you from the water-tower?'

'You can if there's room.'

Wilson was still seated. 'One more thing. Crane, what do you know about Miss Paraguay?' His voice was sharp.

Crane was frightened, so he took his time answering. Did some one know he had been in Imago's room? Did the police know? 'Very little,' he said.

'Did you know she was the . . . aah . . . friend of Tortoni?'

'Not until this afternoon.'

'And you've no idea why she killed herself?'

'None.'

O'Rourke's eyes were amused; Wilson's angry.

Osborn said: 'Do you think she knew the kidnapper?'

'She did if Tortoni had a hand in it.'

'That's obvious,' said Wilson.

'Sure.'

Captain Enright moved uneasily. 'We better get going if we want to get things arranged for to-morrow.'

Wilson got to his feet. 'All right.' His eyes were on Crane's face. 'See you to-morrow.'

'Fine,' said Crane.

A nurse with a soap-and-water-bright face met him at the door to the room and said: 'You must be careful. She's had a terrible shock.'

'I know,' he said.

Rustling, the nurse stepped aside. 'Only for a minute,' she said. She smelt of laundry soap.

Drawn curtains made the room dim. Like a cord, face to the ceiling, great violet eyes open, Miss Langley lay in the double bed. 'Who is it?' she whispered. Tiny wrinkles circled her neck.

'William Crane.'

'Oh, yes.'

'Could you help me?'

Her skin was so tight over her nose the yellow bone showed through. 'How?' she asked. White powder was thick on her face, on her neck. 'How?' she asked. 'How?'

'I believe Imago was murdered.'

One of the drawn curtains, sucked inward by a current of air, made a rasping noise.

'You are right.'

'How do you know?'

Her thin lips trembled. 'I know.' The violet eyes, followed by no motion of the head, turned upon his face.

'But how?'

The eyelids fluttered, closed, and when they opened again the violet eyes were staring at the ceiling. 'How does one know anything?' On either side of her mouth the skin hung in pouches.

'Oh,' he said.

'I see death everywhere,' she whispered. 'Death . . . everywhere.'

'But who killed Imago?'

She stared at him, her eyes like a sleep-walker's. 'I am afraid . . . afraid.' Her voice grated on his ears. 'I see death . . . Imago . . . Camelia . . .'

'Yes, Miss Langley, but do you remember Foggy?'

'Froggy? . . . Froggy? . . . No.' Her body shook. 'I see death. Who will be next?' Her voice was louder, tremulous. 'Who?'

The nurse touched his arm. 'You are exciting her.'

'This awful house.' Miss Langley tried to sit up. 'This awful house.'

'Please go,' said the nurse.

'It is not finished.' Miss Langley's arm was dry, frail withered. 'There will be more.'

Crane went out of the room, carefully closing the door behind him. He took out a handkerchief and wiped his forehead.

Essex came out of the swimming-pool and collapsed in a chair. 'If only Camelia . . .' His voice was weary.

'It should be over to-morrow,' Crane said.

'How do you mean?' Essex looked up. 'Have you . . .?'

'No. I mean that you'll pay the money and Camelia will be freed.'

'Oh.'

Pablo came up to the table. 'A telephone call for Mr. Crane or Mr. O'Rourke.'

Crane said: 'You get it, Tom.'

For a moment after O'Rourke left they sat in silence. The air was soft and humid and perfumed; it was languorous. It made their eye-lids heavy, their movements sluggish, their voices drowsy. It was all Crane could do to reach for his drink.

Finally, finding himself half asleep, he asked: 'How
did Imago Paraguay happen to be in this house, Mr.
Essex?'

'A friend of mine, Charley Beauchamp, knew her in
Paris.' Essex poured himself a whisky. 'He gave her
a letter to me. That was in New York. When I found
she was going to be in Miami in March I invited her to
stay out here.'

'Did you know she was a close friend of Tortoni?'

'I didn't even know they knew each other.'

Crane yawned. 'Do you think Tortoni had her come
here to watch you'?

'No. Why should he?'

'The debt.'

'He'd given up all idea of trying to collect that.'

'You're sure?'

'I'm positive. Look.' Essex removed his wallet
from his hip pocket, drew out three pieces of paper.
'Tortoni gave me my I O Us over two weeks ago.'

Crane examined the papers. One of the I O Us was
for six thousand dollars. The others were for nine
thousand each. They were all signed Penn Essex.

'Then you weren't lying when you told me you didn't
have any large debts?'

'Of course not. Why would I lie to you? You're
on my side.'

'I did think it was queer.' Crane gave him back
the notes. 'Why didn't you tell Major Eastcomb you
had them?'

'I didn't think it was any of his business.'

'I guess it wasn't."

Lights had been turned on around the swimming-pool
and Crane saw coming toward them a man in blue
overalls. The man was old; his face was brown and
wrinkled; he had a drooping straw moustache; he walked
with a shuffling gait. He was carrying a woman's bag,
made of dark blue beads.

He halted three yards from them and said tentatively:
'Mister Essex.'

'What is it, Fritz?'

The man held out the bag. 'This I find in the rose
bushes.' The movement made the beads glitter.

Essex got up and took the bag. 'It looks like one of
Imago's.' He emptied the contents on the table. There
was a red lacquer cigarette-case, a metal lipstick,
possibly platinum, and a red compact. On a fine lace
handkerchief was a smear of lipstick. 'Nothing to tell
who's it is, though.'

'Give it to me,' Crane said. 'I'll tell.'

A heavy odour of sandalwood clung to the bag.

'It *is* Imago's,' Crane said.

Essex turned toward the man. 'Where did you find
it, Fritz?'

'Here by the patio, Mister Essex.'

Crane said: 'Could you show us where?'

'Yah. I show you.'

They were just starting to leave the table when
O'Rourke came out of the house. 'Where're you
going?' he asked.

'Just over here.' Crane waited for him. 'Who
was it?'

'Doc Williams. He said the police have picked up
di Gregario.'

'Ha!' Crane moved his head vertically. 'That's
why the G-man wasn't interested in what I knew about
him.'

'Doc says he'll wait and see what they do with
him.'

'Good.'

They went across the patio. The man pointed out
a clump of rose bushes. 'Here.'

Crane looked up at the white wall of the house.
'That's my room up there, isn't it, O'Rourke?'

'Yeah.'

Essex asked: 'Do you think some one threw it down?'

Crane was examining the bushes. 'It's a hell of a funny place to drop a purse,' he said.

The man said to Essex: 'It is good I find it. That Garcia, he give it to a girl.'

'Thank you for bringing it in, Fritz,' Essex said.

'That Garcia,' said the man, leaving them.

Essex asked: 'But why would any one want Imago's bag?'

Crane started towards the house. 'She must have had the nine thousand she won at Tortoni's in it.'

'That's right.' Essex's voice had new vitality. 'The police didn't find the money.'

'They're not mentioning it if they did,' Crane said.

'Do you think some one found her dead in her room, took the money and tossed the purse away?'

'It's possible.'

They walked through the French windows into the living room. 'Who's Garcia?' O'Rourke asked.

'The assistant gardener,' Essex said. 'Fritz doesn't like him.'

Crane glanced at his watch. 'I think I'll take a nap before dinner.'

Essex said: 'I wish I could sleep.'

'Didn't you sleep last night?'

'I took some dope, but I felt worse when I woke up than I did before.'

'It's a terrible strain.'

'It wouldn't be so bad if we could do something.'

'You'll be able to do something to-morrow,' Crane said.

'Yes. To-morrow,' said Essex.

Crane led the way up to his room. It was cooler than the patio and a current of air was coming in through the window. A pumpkin-coloured moon, almost full, was rising above the cloud banks on the horizon. From it to the house, over water the colour and texture of navy-blue silk, extended a tongue of pale gold, contrasting with the silver shimmer of breakers and the salt-white beach. It was bright enough outside to see the palms.

O'Rourke went into the bathroom and washed. Crane took off his shoes and coat, unfastened his collar and lay down on his bed. O'Rourke came out of the bathroom. 'Where're you going?' Crane asked.

'I thought I'd look up Miss Day.'

Crane yawned, sighed comfortably, let his head sink into the pillow, closed his eyes. He wondered if Imago's purse had been planted under his window. It looked as though it was an effort to implicate him in her death. A sudden thought occurred to him. He slid off the bed, seized his coat, then sighed with relief. His nine thousand, at least, was safe. He took the money out of the coat and put it in his trousers. What he didn't understand was how anybody could have got into Imago's room to steal the money. But then he didn't understand how The Eye had left the two notes he and O'Rourke had received. Or how he had taken his wallet with the hundred-dollar bills in it. He got back on the bed and closed his eyes. It was a hell of a case.

CHAPTER SIXTEEN

9.40 A.M.

THE Bugatti's engine, throttled down, went chug-chug . . . chug-chug-chug. Blue vapour, a fine drizzle of gasolene, came out of the exhaust. The carburettor had a rich adjustment.

Major Eastcomb opened the black valise. 'Here.'

Green bills, tied with rubber bands, were slick in the sunlight. He helped Essex to wrap the money in yellow oilskin, put the package in the brown cardboard box. 'Fifty thousand dollars.' There was a clean piece of adhesive tape on his nose.

Wilson, the government agent, pulled his coat sleeve from his wrist. 'You've got twenty minutes.' His sharp face was excited.

Essex put the box beside him on the front seat. 'I'll drive slowly.'

Even before ten the sun was hot. In the glare, pebbles on the drive looked as though they had been chalked. From the fountain the two flamingos watched them.

Miss Day, in flowered beach pyjamas, was standing between Crane and O'Rourke. Her hair was the deep colour of honey which had been a long time in the comb. She said: 'Take care of yourself, Penny.'

Essex's nervous foot pressed the Bugatti's throttle, made the engine purr. 'I'll be all right.' His face was pale; his lips mauve. He looked frightened.

Major Eastcomb took the valise into the house. An elbow on the tonneau, Wilson asked: 'You'll come to the water-tower as soon as you've left the money?'

Essex nodded.

Crane touched O'Rourke's arm. 'Take the roadster and pick him after he leaves the money.'

Miss Day asked in alarm: 'You don't think they'd try to kidnap him, do you?'

'You never can tell,' O'Rourke said.

'The Eye won't try anything before he leaves the money,' Crane said. 'The police would be alarmed if he didn't show up at the bridge.' He smiled at Miss Day. 'If anything does happen, it will happen after he leaves the bridge.'

'*You* certainly seem worried,' Miss Day said angrily.

'It's all in the day's work.'

The major came out of the house and went up to the car. He patted Essex's shoulder. 'Cheerio,' he said.

Essex put the Bugatti in gear. Wilson took his elbow off the tonneau. He said: 'Good luck.' The Bugatti sneaked away, sunlight making a nimbus on the black engine hood.

'You'd think he was going on a trans-Atlantic flight,' said O'Rourke.

9.56 A.M.

From the observation balcony of the water-tower, Florida looked like one of those infra-red photographs taken from a balloon. The tower was much higher than Crane had realized and he was still out of breath from climbing many steel ladders. He hung on to the rail and tried to see the west coast. A faint blue haze prevented this, but he was able to see far into the Everglades, to distinguish oases of palms and pine trees and pools of brown water. In one place a brush fire was going, smudging a section of the horizon with smoke.

Wilson pulled back his sleeve, looked at his watch. 'Three more minutes,' he said.

Toward the Atlantic, Crane could actually see the curve of the earth's surface. He could see freighters plodding along the edge of the Gulf Stream, the closer ones completely visible and those farther away less and less visible, until of one he could see only smoke and the tips of masts. Behind him was the smoke of Miami.

'Two more minutes,' said Wilson.

With Wilson on the balcony were Osborn, the County Attorney, a dark, fat man from the sheriff's office and the radio operator. All were near the portable set the man was using, all watched the bridge through binoculars Crane moved up to the set.

'Getting close to the deadline, Mark,' the radio operator was saying into the mouthpiece.

Crane tried to see the aeroplane hovering over Miami,

but he couldn't find it. There was a small bank of clouds toward Miami and he thought the plane was probably above them.

'One more minute,' said Wilson.

'I see him,' said Osborn.

Crane lifted his binoculars to his eyes. They were a fancy pair and it was necessary to adjust each eye separately. He got the right eye immediately, but the left gave him a lot of trouble. When he finally did get it fixed, Essex had reached the bridge. Parked in the centre of the road, the Bugatti looked like a beetle on a gauze bandage.

'Stand by, Mark,' the radio operator said.

Essex climbed out of the car and walked to the canal-bank. Crane could see the brown cardboard box under his right arm. He went down the bank sideways, using the edges of his shoes to check his descent, and disappeared under the bridge. He looked about the size of a toy soldier.

'Right on the dot,' said Wilson.

Essex reappeared and scrambled up the bank on hands and knees. He walked briskly to the Bugatti, got in, started toward the water-tower. Crane figured he would make the eight miles in about ten minutes.

'Are you standing by, Mark?' asked the radio operator.

'O.K.,' he said.

Wilson said: 'Everybody keep their eyes peeled.'

All of them leaned over the rail, binoculars to eyes.

10.13 A.M.

O'Rourke at his heels, Essex stepped off the steel ladder to the balcony. 'Anything happen?' he asked. He pulled a white handkerchief from his coat pocket, wiped his face.

'No sign as yet,' said Wilson.

Crane lowered his binoculars. 'Want to take a look?' he said to Essex. The binoculars hurt his eyes, anyway.

'Thanks.'

Crane asked O'Rourke: 'Anything funny on the way over here from the bridge?'

'Not a thing.'

'You didn't see any mysterious cars or people?'

'Not a thing.'

The radio operator asked: 'Still standing by, Mark?' Apparently Mark was, because the radio man didn't say anything further.

'It's hot as hell up here,' said Crane.

10.30 A.M.

'Stand by, Mark,' said the radio operator.

A vegetable truck was going down the road.   It crept over the bridge and continued on south.

'Another truck, Mark,' said the radio operator.

'He's certainly taking his time collecting the money,' said O'Rourke.

County Attorney Osborn said: 'He's probably waiting to make sure no police cars are hiding by the bridge.'

'We can wait as long as he can,' said Wilson.

11.30 A.M.

'I wish they had a bar up here,' said Crane.

11.56 A.M.

Sweat made the sheriff's man's shirt cling to his chest. He lowered his binoculars.   'D'you suppose he could have swum up the canal?'   He rubbed his eyes with the back of his right hand.   'I'm damn near blind.' Thick black hair showed through the damp shirt.

'We can see both sides of the canal,' said Wilson.

The strong midday heat made them all perspire. Direct rays from the sun and reflected rays from the big silver water-tank toasted their skin like flames in an open fire, dazzled their eyes, made the steel rail round the balcony too hot to touch.   Inside, shoes treading the steel floor burned their feet.

'*I'd* like to swim up that canal,' said O'Rourke.

Crane wistfully regarded the big tank.   He supposed it was utterly full of water.

The radio operator said: 'Standing by, Mark? . . . O.K..'

Now there were only clouds on the horizon and a haze over Miami.   Overhead the sky was turquoise.

The sheriff's man raised his binoculars. 'Give us some action.'

Wilson said: 'We just have to wait.'

12.20 P.M.

'My God!' Essex said.   'Why doesn't he come?'

'Take it easy, pal,' said O'Rourke.

'I wonder if he's wise to our plan?' asked the sheriff's man.   His face was beet-purple.

Wilson said: 'We have to stick it out.'

12.31 P.M.

The radio operator took off his earphones. 'Mr. Osborn.'

'Yes?'

'Mark says he'll have to come down for gas.'

Osborn lowered his glasses.   A lock of black hair hung over his high forehead. 'What's the matter? Can't a plane stay up more than three hours?'

'Yes, Mr. Osborn.   But Mark says he won't have enough gas to follow another plane unless he re-fuels?'

'Well, Wilson . . .?'

'I suppose he'll have to land.'

Crane said: 'While he's down, suppose we go by the bridge and see if everything's all right.'

'And alarm the kidnapper?'

'Hell!   He's either alarmed right now, or he's waiting until dark.'

Osborn said: 'We can't stand here all day.'

'All right.'   The heat had paled Wilson's face.

'Block, you stay here with the radio man.' He started for the ladder.

The radio man said: 'It's O.K. to go down, Mark.'

Block was evidently the sheriff's man. He didn't like being left behind. He scowled at Wilson's back, but he didn't say anything. The others followed Wilson down the ladder.

They took the roadster rather than the police car. Essex sat in the back, between Osborn and Wilson. O'Rourke drove and Crane sat beside him. 'This is the hottest place in the world next to Death Valley,' said Crane.

Osborn said: 'Miami has a very even summer temperature.'

'Even unto Death Valley,' said Crane.

'You're quite a wit, aren't you, Crane?' said Wilson. His voice was sharp.

'I think so,' said Crane.

'My God! I wish this were over with,' said Essex.

They swung out on to the road leading to the bridge. Crane thought Essex looked ill. Certainly the last two days had taken most of the vitality out of him. His eyes were dull; his skin unhealthy; his manner listless. He almost seemed, Crane thought, to have abandoned hope of having Camelia returned.

The bridge was ahead of them. 'Which side?' asked O'Rourke.

'Cross it,' said Wilson.

O'Rourke pulled the roadster to a smooth stop just past the bridge. Wilson opened his door and stepped out on to the pavement. 'You can come with me, Crane.'

The tide was barely coming in, but the water in the canal was blue and clear. A few pieces of seaweed, brown and covered with red berries the size of peas, floated near the edge of the bank. They went down the slope together, being careful to keep their weight on their heels.   Near the bottom Wilson started to slip, but Crane steadied him.

'Thanks,' Wilson said.

They inclined their bodies and peered under the bridge.   It took them a moment to adjust their eyes to the gloom.   The air was damp, cool.   The tide made a gurgling noise.

'It's gone!' Wilson exclaimed.   'Gone!'

'Box and all,' said Crane.

CHAPTER SEVENTEEN

EVERYBODY agreed it certainly was a mystery. It was a very great mystery. Captain Enright, who had been hiding five miles up the road with a squad of his Miami detectives, came the closest to summing it up when he said: 'It don't hardly seem possible.'

It didn't, but the money was gone.

Nearly fifty detectives, deputies and other law enforcement officers stood around on the bridge while Osborn and Wilson questioned Essex.   It was now one o'clock.

'But you saw everything I did,' Essex said.   'I simply put the box on that flat place under the bridge and came out.'

'And you're sure it couldn't have slipped off on to the water?' asked Osborn.

'I'm certain.   The only thing that could have moved it was wind and there wasn't any.'

'And there was nobody waiting under there?'

'I should say not.'

Two of the detectives came up from under the bridge and reported to Captain Enright that there was no hiding-place within the cement structure. 'It's solid as rock,' one said.

Crane and O'Rourke were examining the canal bank for the seventh time. The tide was almost completely full now, and the seaweed hardly moved at all. Two gars, small, thin, green fish with bill-like mouths, were harassing a school of minnows.

'It looks as though he did use a submarine,' O'Rourke said.

'Maybe he's got a cloak that makes him invisible,' Crane moved along the bank, farther from the bridge. 'If there were any footprints these cops have tramped over them all.'

'Elephants and cops are a lot alike.' O'Rourke bent over a small recess in the bank. 'Hello! What's this?'

There was almost a bay where the bank had crumbled away. The tide, coming into this bay, sent the water into a slow spiral. On the back edge of the bay was a soggy piece of brown paper. O'Rourke picked it up.

'It looks like a piece of paper,' said Crane.

'It's cardboard.'

'So.' Crane took it from O'Rourke. 'There's printing on it.'

On the damp piece of cardboard, about the size of a business envelope, was printed: LIFO

'What the hell does that mean?' asked O'Rourke.

Crane lifted his shoulders.

'Is it a clue?' asked O'Rourke.

'How do I know?' Crane pressed the water out of the cardboard, put it in his pocket. 'I'm a stranger here.'

They moved back toward the bridge. Osborn was staring at Essex, was saying:

'You're sure you didn't throw the box into the canal instead of putting it on the bank?'

Essex, very pale, said: 'You don't suspect that I'd jeopardize my sister's life by not following instructions, do you?'

Captain Enright said: 'You could've had some other instructions from the kidnapper. Secret ones. He could've told you to throw it in the water.'

Crane said to O'Rourke: 'Not so dumb.'

'Don't you see?' Captain Enright turned to Wilson. 'The tide's been going in. The box could've floated to somebody hiding in those bushes inland.'

Every one looked at the green clump of palms, palmetto, sugar cane and scrub pine a quarter of a mile inland. The canal disappeared in the centre of this oasis on the grey-green tundra of the Everglades, its water cloaked by marsh grass and hanging trees.

'Let's take a look,' said Wilson.

'But it's no use,' said Essex. 'I didn't throw the box in the water.'

'Let's look, anyway,' said Wilson.

Crane touched O'Rourke's arm. 'I got an idea. While I go with those guys you find out a couple of things for me. Find out if cyanide of potassium is used for anything in the Essex house. Find out what the gardener, Fritz, uses to trim the trees with.'

'I know one answer now.' O'Rourke's eyes followed the police moving along the bank toward the oasis. 'They use cyanide to clean the silver.' He glanced at Crane. 'What's your idea?'

'I'm getting tired of this case.' Crane mopped his face with a handkerchief. 'I think I'll wrap it up. It's too hot here.'

'You've really got something?'

'I've got an idea. Where'd you hear about the cyanide?'

'I heard the cops asking Craig.'

'Then anybody could have got hold of some?'

'Yeah.' O'Rourke's face was alert. 'You think Essex did float the box along the canal?'

'No.'

'Then what do you think?'

'I've just got an idea.'

'All right, wise guy. Keep it a secret.'

Osborn, Wilson, Essex and Captain Enright were a hundred yards inland. They were walking slowly along the canal-bank, keeping their eyes on the water and on the edge of the bank. Even at that distance Essex's face was grey.

'I'd better go with them,' said Crane. 'You find the gardener.'

'I'll miss our pal, Wilson.'

'You go with them then. I'll talk to the gardener.'

'No, thanks. It looks like snake country up there.'

'My God! It does. And I haven't any whisky.'

'Hell.' O'Rourke grinned at Crane. 'Whisky doesn't help you with snakes.'

'It does before they bite you,' said Crane.

He hurried and caught up with the group round Essex. On both sides of the canal policemen had strung out, were examining the brush. They were nearing the clump of trees. Beside the pine, the thick growth of sugar-cane was luxuriant. The leaves were a lovely combination of pale green and silver. A crane, flying heavily, came out of the marsh grass, flapped inland. Its cries echoed in their ears.

Essex pointed at the marsh. 'A floating box wouldn't get past here,' he said.

Captain Enright's voice was unfriendly. 'How do we know?'

Wilson was a little ahead of them. 'Some one must have lived here once,' he said. 'I see banana trees.'

'I see a shack,' said Osborn.

The banana trees were an emerald green and they

leaned against the side of a frame shanty, their trunks arched.   The heavy leaves looked like folded elephant ears.   There was a cut through trees and palmetto bushes to the shack.   Sunlight through the branches made a zebra effect on the ground.   The shanty's door stood open; the windows had been blown out; one side of the roof had collapsed.

'Deserted,' said Wilson.

They went round the shack toward the canal.   They could hear the policemen talking on the other side, the rustle of leaves.   'Look,' said Osborn.

He was pointing at a place twenty yards up the canal.   There, on a rectangular sandy beach, just in the water, was a diver's suit.   In the filtered light the suit's wet rubber was slick, the glass panel in the helmet diamond bright.   A hose led from the helmet to a self-contained air outfit, the straps of which, meant to be fastened over the diver's shoulders, trailed in the water.

'So that's how he got under the bridge,' said Osborn.

Wilson's thin lips were compressed, his sharp face angry.   'Clever,' he said.

'Damn clever,' said Crane.

Captain Enright turned to Essex.   'I want to apologize for doubting your word, Mr. Essex.'   He rubbed the back of his neck with a dirty palm.   'It was just that I couldn't figure out any way to get rid of that box besides having you throw it in the water.'   He laughed. 'I guess I'm plain dumb.'

'You aren't the only one,' said Crane.

Wilson gave him a sharp, oblique glance.

Captain Enright said: 'No hard feelings, Mr. Essex?'

'That's all right.'   Essex was bending over the diving-suit.   'I don't care what happens as long as Camelia comes back.'   His voice sounded as though he were going to cry.

CHAPTER EIGHTEEN

CRANE and Wilson rode home with Essex in the Bugatti. Osborn followed in his car, but Captain Enright stayed to supervise a widespread search of the area round the shack where they had found the diver's suit.

Wilson was angry. 'Whoever heard of a melodramatic stunt like that?' he demanded. 'Using a diver's suit?'

'It's right out of a story-book,' Crane said. 'It's like the whole damn business. It's too phoney to be true.'

Essex swung the Bugatti round an erosion in the asphalt. 'But will he return Camelia?'

'We'll have to wait,' said Wilson.

'I'm not going to wait,' said Crane.

'What do you mean?' Wilson's eyes were sharp. 'I thought you were the one who advised Major Eastcomb to wait.'

'I'm tired of waiting.'

'What are you going to do?'

'I'm going to grab The Eye.'

'Don't be funny,' said Wilson.

Essex said: 'Do you really know who The Eye is?'

'I've got a good idea.'

Essex turned the Bugatti into the gravel driveway. 'I'd give anything to get hold of him.' His lips, compressed, were like white cord.

Wilson asked: 'Who do you think he is?'

'Don't be funny,' said Crane.

Miss Day, O'Rourke and Major Eastcomb met them at the front door. O'Rourke was carrying a ten-foot pole on his shoulder. Crane asked him: 'What are you; a spear-bearer in *Julius Cæsar*?'

The pole had a steel scissors on its end and from one blade dangled a small rope. When the rope was jerked the scissors closed, something like the operation of a lobster's claw. 'You told me to get this from the gardener,' O'Rourke said.

'Oh, yeah. The pruning pole.'

Wilson asked: 'What are you going to do, Crane?'

Essex explained to Miss Day: 'Crane thinks he has a line on The Eye.'

'Ooo! Isn't he smart?' said Miss Day.

Crane said: 'I'll try to put a finger on the guy. Suppose we have everybody come into the living-room.'

'It's nicer on the patio,' Miss Day said.

'O.K. The patio.'

'More melodrama,' said Wilson. His voice was sarcastic.

O'Rourke asked: 'What do you want me to do with this pole?'

'Bring it along.'

Miss Day said: 'Isn't this exciting? I'll get everybody.'

Essex started to follow her, but Crane stopped him. 'I think you better stick with us. We've had too many people bumped off already.'

Osborn, the County Attorney, and a detective joined them on the patio. Major Eastcomb asked Crane: 'Is this some more of your bloody foolishness?'

Miss Langley, her bulging eyes looking like balls of vanilla ice-cream on which caramel sauce had been poured, arrived with her nurse. Tony Lamphier, wearing white slacks and a horizontally striped green and white jersey, appeared with the Bouchers.

'What's up?' he asked.

'You'll see,' said Crane.

'Do you want the servants?' asked Miss Day, thrusting her head out of a door.

'You might have one of them bring us a drink,'

Crane said. 'I seem to be thirsty.' He added: 'Might as well have Craig and Brown join us.'

Crane helped Pablo place a tray with cracked ice, glasses, limes, Bacardi and charged water on the table by the swimming-pool. 'Anybody have one?'

While he was mixing drinks for every one except the nurse with Miss Langley and the detective, Miss Day appeared with Craig and Brown. Both the men appeared apprehensive. Craig looked at Essex. 'You wanted me, sir?'

'I did,' said Crane. Ice tinkled in the glasses as he passed them.

'Well, get on with whatever you are going to do,' said Wilson.

Crane took a long drink of his Bacardi rickey. 'Good,' he said.

Miss Langley gulped hers. 'Some more, please,' she said. 'I feel a little faint.'

'No,' said the nurse.

'I got everybody here,' Crane said, 'because I want a lot of witnesses to what I'm going to do.'

They stared at him. 'What are you going to do?' asked Wilson.

'I'm going to accuse some one of kidnapping Camelia Essex.' Crane finished his glass. 'Fix me another, will you, O'Rourke?' He gave O'Rourke the glass. 'In fact, I am going to accuse Essex of kidnapping his sister.'

'You can't mean that,' said Tony Lamphier.

'Good!' said Major Eastcomb.

Essex looked at Crane in bewilderment. 'What . . . what?'

'Penn!' said Miss Day.

Mrs. Boucher's brown eyes were wide. 'This is a joke.'

'Oh, that isn't all,' Crane said cheerfully. 'I further accuse him of being The Eye.'

'This is monstrous!' His face cherry-red, Major Eastcomb moved toward Crane, an arm raised as though he were going to strike him. He looked at Wilson. 'Isn't it enough that Penn's gone through what he has without being harassed by a lunatic?'

O'Rourke stopped making Crane's drink, watched the major. He was thinking: Now's my chance to slug him.

'Let him go on,' said Wilson. 'We'll soon see if he's a lunatic.'

'What proof have you of this?' demanded Osborn.

O'Rourke poured Bacardi in with the ice and lime. Crane said: 'I have quite a bit of proof.' O'Rourke handed him the glass, saying: 'Here.' Crane took it in his hand. 'But first I want to give you my reasons for picking on Essex.' The glass was cold, moist.

'Gad!' said Major Eastcomb. 'Do we have to listen to this?' He looked at Osborn.

'What are you so scared about, Major?' asked O'Rourke.

'Go ahead,' said Wilson to Crane.

Crane was watching the major. 'Well, in the first place there are the notes. They were always being found on Essex's pillow or in his pocket or some place like that. Who could put them there easier than himself?'

'All right,' said Osborn. 'Go ahead.'

'He needed money,' said Crane. 'Tortoni was after him for nearly twenty-five thousand dollars. He couldn't get it from the trust company.'

Essex spoke for the first time. 'That's foolish, Crane.' His voice did not sound angry. 'I had the I O U's. I didn't need the money to pay Tortoni.'

'You have them now, but you didn't have them a couple of weeks ago. You told me yourself.'

'Yes, but . . .'

'Never mind.' Crane took a sip of the Bacardi.

'You and Tortoni figured you could kidnap Camelia and make fifty grand. I suppose you were going to split it between you. Then Tortoni would call the debt square.'

'This is very pretty,' said Wilson. 'But have you any facts?'

'Wait.' Crane was still talking to Essex. 'You thought you could write notes to yourself, signed The Eye, and establish the fact that some one, probably a maniac, was threatening the Essex family. Thus the kidnapping would be blamed on The Eye.

'Then Tortoni's men kidnapped Camelia. You put up a phoney fight and one of the men socked you.'

'But he did his best to catch them in the Bugatti,' Tony Lamphier said. 'Don't you remember?'

'I remember, all right. I remember that he collapsed just as we were about to overhaul Tortoni's men. It was funny he should pick that particular time to fold, wasn't it?'

'I don't know,' said Tony Lamphier.

'When Tortoni was killed it left Essex alone in the plot, but he decided to carry it through. The fifty grand would come in handy. So he wrote the note giving the directions for the delivery of the money.'

Every one was listening quietly now.

'Then he went out under our eyes,' Crane continued, 'and made the gesture of paying over the money to The Eye. He returned to wait with us for the release of Camelia, but I don't think that will ever happen.'

'Why not?' asked Tony Lamphier.

'I think she's dead.'

Voices rose in incredulous conversation. Essex said: 'No! No! She can't be dead.' His face was wild. Major Eastcomb said of Crane: 'The man's mad.' Miss Langley said in a graveyard whisper: 'I knew she was dead, I knew. . . .'

Wilson demanded: 'Why do you think she's dead?'

'When a kidnapper sends a ransom note he usually has the victim write on it to prove he or she is alive.'

Major Eastcomb said: 'But The Eye mentioned Froggy, a toy only Camelia would know about.'

'Essex, writing the note, would know about Froggy.'

Osborn pushed black hair off his forehead. 'But who is the accomplice? Who collected the money?'

'Nobody.'

'But the diver's suit . . .?'

'It was a plant. Essex put it there last . . .'

Miss Day screamed. Her voice echoed shrilly in the patio. With an overhand sweep, like a soldier throwing a hand grenade, O'Rourke flung a Bacardi bottle, hit Essex a glancing blow on the top of his head. He fell, spinning, to the tile floor, lay there under every one's astonished eyes. An automatic pistol slipped from his outstretched right hand, skidded across the patio, came to rest at the base of a boxed palm. The Bacardi bottle shattered against the side of the swimming-pool.

'Thanks, tutz,' O'Rourke said to Miss Day.

Crane walked over to Essex, jerked off his linen coat. He ripped off Essex's shirt, not bothering to unbutton it, and then pulled his underwear top over his head. Essex's skin was pale. He undid Essex's belt, tore open his trousers. The nurse with Miss Langley uttered a cry, averted her eyes. He unfastened a brown canvas inner-belt around Essex's hips, emptied the contents of the rectangular pockets on the red tiles in front of Wilson.

'Money,' said Wilson.

The bills were so clean they looked counterfeit. Essex groaned. The bills were cabbage green.

'There's your proof,' said Crane.

Osborn and Major Eastcomb knelt on the floor, began to count the money. Wilson asked: 'How does he have it?'

Crane said: 'He hid the money on the way to the bridge. Under the bridge he tore up the cardboard box, tossed the pieces in the canal.'

'How'd you figure it?'

'Easy.' Crane fumbled in his pocket, found the water-soaked piece of cardboard. He gave it to Wilson. 'This spilled the beans.'

Wilson read the printing on the cardboard. '"lifo." What does that mean?'

'He had a prune box. Where do prunes come from?'

'California.'

'Sure. "lifo" is part of California. Californian prunes. I found this piece, or rather O'Rourke did, right near the bridge.'

Miss Day was kneeling beside Essex, was offering him a drink of rum. 'This'll make you feel better.' O'Rourke had retrieved the pistol, was standing with it behind Essex.

Wilson's face was puzzled. 'I still don't see what finding a piece of the box by the bridge proves.'

'The tide.' Crane got his drink from the table. 'It runs six hours one way, then six the other. It was running inland when we reached the bridge around one o'clock, but it had almost stopped. That meant it was running pretty fast inland when Essex was under the bridge at ten o'clock. If there had been a diver he would have grabbed the box and hurried back to the bushes with it. He wouldn't have waited under the bridge to open the box.'

'No, I guess not,' Wilson said.

'Well, if there had been a diver it would have been impossible for O'Rourke to find a piece of the box near the bridge. The tide was going inland, so any pieces he threw in the water by the bushes would have gone toward the Everglades.'

'I get it.' Wilson nodded his head. 'The piece by

the bridge indicated the box had been torn up by the bridge.'

'That's what gave me the idea about Essex,' Crane said. 'And then, when we found the diver's suit, it was too much like a plant. I also wondered if a diver could walk under water against the tide. It goes pretty fast in that canal.'

Hands full of bills, Osborn came up off his knees. 'This can't be the ransom money,' he said. 'There's only nineteen thousand dollars here.'

Crane said: 'Have some one look in the Bugatti.'

Osborn and the detective went into the house. Essex sat up, pressed his head with both hands. There was a smear of blood on his blond hair where the bottle had struck. His eyes went from one to another of them in dazed appeal. 'Brown . . .' he began.

'Not me.' Brown was standing beside Craig. 'You're all alone in this jam, buddy.'

The sun was bright in Miss Day's yellow hair. 'Take some more,' she said, holding the glass of rum in front of Essex. He pushed it away.

Wilson said: 'Then you think the men who actually kidnapped Miss Essex were hired by Essex?'

'By Tortoni,' Crane said.

'That's the same thing.'

'Not exactly.'

Miss Langley suddenly began to babble. 'This is impossible . . . The Essex . . . such a disgrace . . .' disconnected sentences, phrases came from her lips. 'I knew it . . . my poor sister . . .' Her violet eyes seemed as large as the tops of two mason jars.

'Take her away,' Crane told the nurse. 'Put her to bed.'

Miss Langley allowed the nurse to lead her to the house. Her voice faded into silence.

'A rummy,' Crane explained to Wilson.

Osborn and the detective came running on to the

patio. 'Here's the rest of the money,' Osborn said. His voice was excited.

'Forty thousand dollars,' said the detective. Bills in rubber-banded bundles were heaped like kindling wood in his arms. 'And the oilskin wrapper, too.'

'That's nine thousand extra,' said Wilson.

Crane said: 'This is the first time in history a cop ever got back more money than was lost.'

'I guess we can arrest him,' said Osborn.

Crane took a long drink of Bacardi. 'Why not?'

Wilson asked: 'Why'd he put part of the money on him?'

'Safety, I guess. If something happened to the Bugatti he'd still be well heeled.'

Satisfaction made Osborn's voice oily. 'We'll charge him with kidnapping.' His voice sounded as though he were already talking to the grand jury.

'How do you know?' asked Crane.

Essex struggled to his feet. 'No! No!' O'Rourke got ready to club him with his pistol. 'She's not dead. She can't be dead.'

'How do you know?' asked Crane.

'Tortoni told his men to take care of her. They weren't to harm her.' Essex's face was the colour of mashed potatoes; his lips trembled; his hands were clenched. 'I wouldn't kill my sister.'

'Not much,' said Crane.

Osborn said: 'A man who would be coadjuvant to the kidnapping of his only sister would be capable of any crime.'

'She's safe,' said Essex. 'I'm sure of that.'

'Where is she then?' asked Wilson.

Essex walked stiff-legged to a chair, sat down. 'I don't know. Tortoni had charge of the hiding-place.'

Osborn said: 'Then you do admit conniving with Tortoni in the kidnapping of your sister?'

'Yes.' Essex pressed his head with his palms. 'Tortoni forced me to help him.'

'Like hell,' Crane said and asked: 'What makes you so sure Camelia's safe?'

'Tortoni promised nothing would happen to her.'

'And you believed him?'

'Of course.'

Crane disgustedly drained his glass. 'I wish I was as dumb.' He turned to Wilson. 'Tortoni probably had Miss Essex murdered.'

Essex came to his feet. 'He wouldn't dare. He knew I'd have him hung.'

'Would you put your own head in a noose to get him for your sister's murder?'

Essex was silent.

Wilson asked: 'If your sister is alive, how will we get her back?'

'We'll just have to wait.'

'Will they return her without word from Tortoni?'

Essex's voice cracked with anguish. 'That's what I don't know. I thought if they heard the ransom was paid they'd let her go. That's why I collected the ransom.'

'Sure,' said Crane. 'You were just trying to help your sister. You didn't want the money for yourself.'

'I was trying to help her.'

'Sure,' said Crane.

Tony Lamphier spoke for the first time. He had been watching Essex, contempt in his eyes. He said: 'This is terrible. Now we haven't anybody to pay a ransom to.'

Osborn was wrapping the money in the oilskin. 'We'll take him down to the detective bureau. Maybe somebody can make him talk there.'

'No!' Essex cried. 'Not there. I've told you all I know.'

Major Eastcomb walked round Miss Day to Essex.

'Don't worry, Penn. I'll get a lawyer. We'll have you out on bail.'

Crane stared at him in amazement. 'Don't you think he's guilty?'

'Yes,' the major said. 'But I'm still his trustee.'

'We'll make the bail high,' said Osborn. 'Kidnapping comes high.'

'Make the charge murder,' said Crane. 'You can't bail out a murderer.'

Osborn shook his head. 'I'm afraid we can't. At least not until we have reason to suppose Miss Essex is dead.'

'Well, hell!' said Crane. 'Charge him with the murder of Imago Paraguay.'

CHAPTER NINETEEN

SUNLIGHT, coming through the open French window in Imago Paraguay's room, cast a white rectangle on the floor. In the palms there was a sough of wind, husky and soothing. It was hot.

Crane sat on the green chaise-longue, propped one of the satin pillows behind his head, covered a yawn with the back of his hand. 'The big show'll continue in a minute, gentlemen,' he said.

Wilson and Osborn stood in the middle of the room, their eyes admiring the grey silk curtains round the French windows, the huge rose, blue and grey Chinese rug, the hand-carved double bed with the emerald silk spread. Behind them, by the door, were Tony Lamphier Miss Day, Major Eastcomb and the Bouchers. Essex, handcuffed to the Miami detective, had been left downstairs.

Crane admired Miss Day and her flowered-silk pyjamas. Her hair was the colour of a new penny. She was looking at the ceiling.

Presently O'Rourke's voice came through the nearest of the steel ventilators to the bed. 'This the one?'

'Yeah,' said Crane.

O'Rourke's fingers hooked themselves round a portion of the steel grille, lifted it out of its place.

The foot-square hole in the ceiling looked black.

Wilson said: 'You can't tell me anybody got through that.'

'They didn't.' Crane sat up on the chaise-longue. 'I'll show you.' He looked from Miss Day to the major. 'Where's Céleste?'

'Here, monsieur.' Céleste had evidently been standing in the hall. She was trim in her black and white maid's uniform.

'Did you not put Miss Paraguay's sleeping-tablets on the table by the bed each night, Céleste?'

'Yes, monsieur.' Her face was pert. 'It was at her orders.'

'Thank you.' Crane's eyes went to Wilson and Osborn. 'Essex came in here after dinner and replaced her sleeping-capsules with similar capsules filled with cyanide. Then at bedtime Imago took her usual capsules with water just before she turned off the light. The gelatinous material of which the outside of the capsules is made took some time to dissolve in her stomach—perhaps ten minutes—but when it did, bang!' Crane snapped his fingers. 'The cyanide would take less than two minutes to do the job.'

'Why didn't she scream out?' asked Tony Lamphier.

'My guess is that she was already asleep . . . that she died in her sleep.'

'Very fine,' said Osborn. 'But how do you account for the fact that the box found on the table was filled with harmless sleeping-capsules?' His beard, growing in patches, was coal black and it had come out since morning. It made his long face look dirty.

'That's what I'm going to show you.' Crane got off the chaise-longue, put an unopened package of cigarettes on the table beside the bed. 'This is the box filled with cyanide capsules.' He bent his neck, eyed the ceiling 'Do your stuff, O'Rourke.'

The pruning pole which O'Rourke had obtained from the gardener appeared through the hole in the ceiling, stretched to the table. Slowly, the claw-like blades closed over the packet of cigarettes, gently lifted it off the table, pulled it through the hole in the ceiling.

'There!' said Crane.

Osborn gaped at the hole. 'Clever. Then all Essex had to do was to put the regular sleeping-capsules in the box and lower it to the table.'

'Exactly,' said Crane.

'But what made you sure it was murder?' Osborn asked. 'Why couldn't it have been suicide?'

'There were two small scars on the veronal box, as though somebody had tried to cut it with a pair of scissors. That's how I got the pruning pole idea.'

Mrs. Boucher's aristocratic face was pale. 'I suppose that's how Penn got the notes on your bed, Mr. Crane?' She was a handsome woman.

Crane nodded.

'I get the idea.' Wilson's shoulders twitched. 'But why does it have to be Essex up there? Why couldn't it be anybody in the house?'

Crane began: 'I'll tell . . .'

O'Rourke's voice came through the hole. 'Do you want anything more? It's hot as hell up here.'

'Give me those cigarettes,' said Crane.

'The Eye returns nothing,' said O'Rourke's voice in a graveyard basso. 'Good-bye.'

Crane went back to the chaise-longue. 'One reason I suspected Essex was something that happened to Miss

Day.' Her blue eyes rounded in astonishment. 'On the night Imago was killed she barked her shins on a chair in Essex's dressing-room.'

'I'll say I did,' Miss Day said.

'Her door was locked, she had forgotten the key, so she went in through Essex's rooms.'

Wilson began: 'But . . .'

'The chair she fell over was under a trap-door to the attic.'

'Aah!' said Wilson.

Crane continued: 'I think Essex was up in the attic at that time.'

Major Eastcomb said: 'He was asleep in the library. He'd taken a sleeping-powder.'

'So he said. But did anybody see him there?'

'I saw his shoes,' said the major. 'He was sleeping under a green blanket.'

'That's what I heard from Miss Day and O'Rourke.' Crane scratched the back of his head. 'And that's what made me certain he wasn't there. Can you imagine sleeping under a blanket in this weather?'

'By Gad!' exclaimed the major. 'Just his shoes—eh?

'Still another thing gave him away,' Crane continued. 'He told me, when I first came, that Tortoni had his I O Us, but wasn't trying to collect them. Then Essex showed me the I O Us, said Tortoni had given them to him two weeks ago. That meant he had lied, one way or the other.'

'Those the I O Us we found on him?' asked Osborn.

'Yeah. Twenty-four thousand worth. He got 'em from Imago.'

'How do you figure that?'

Crane leaned against the back of the chaise-longue. 'They weren't found among Tortoni's effects. Imago was Tortoni's mistress, and she had been put in the house to see Essex didn't try any funny business. She'd be likely to have them.'

Tony Lamphier looked very tall, very handsome, beside Miss Day. His black hair, his black arched eyebrows, contrasted with the pallor of his skin. 'You think Penn got the I O Us when he exchanged the tablets?' There was good strength in his jaw.

'I think after she had taken the poison. She probably had her purse on the table beside her bed. All Essex had to do, after he had put back the harmless tablets, was to grab the purse with that pole of his.'

Wilson said: 'It works out very well, but it's all supposition.'

'Not all.' Crane adjusted the pillow under his neck. 'The purse was found in the patio, under my window. I think maybe Essex planned to incriminate me in some way. In this purse, along with the I O Us, had been the nine thousand dollars Imago had won at the Blue Castle. She and I were both paid in thousand-dollar bills.'

'Ah!' Wilson's thin face was pleased. 'The extra nine thousand dollars we found on Essex. If we could only prove it was her money.'

'Get out the thousand-dollar bills you found on Essex,' Crane said.

Osborn undid the oilskin packet, sorted out the thousand-dollar bills. 'There's nine of them, all right.'

'Smell them,' Crane said.

Osborn held the bills to his nose. 'Sandalwood!'

'Imago's sandalwood!' Miss Day exclaimed.

'Sure.' Crane took out his money. 'They picked up the smell of sandalwood in her purse.' He held the money towards Osborn. 'Mine doesn't smell, and I won it at the same time.'

Osborn sniffed the money, said: 'No, it doesn't.'

Crane put his bills back in his inside coat pocket, fastened them with a safety pin. 'Is that convincing enough?' He caught Miss Day's eyes on him, grinned, patted the pocket.

'Yes.' Osborn put the bills back with the ransom

money. 'But I don't see Essex's motive for murdering Miss Paraguay.'

'There was plenty of motive. She was undoubtedly trying to force Essex, after Tortoni was killed, to cut her in on at least half the ransom money. She was holding the I O Us over his head. And she was in a position to blackmail him the rest of his life.'

Wilson agreed: 'She had him, all right.'

Crane was thinking Imago had made the date with him, primarily, to frighten Essex. She had probably threatened to reveal the plot. Essex, then, had pretended to grant whatever she wanted.

Osborn asked: 'Do you think Essex had a hand in the actual kidnapping?'

'No. Tortoni hired the men. They probably don't know Essex is involved in any way.'

"It's funny, now Tortoni's dead, that the men don't let Miss Essex go.'

'I wonder if they know he's dead.'

'They must have heard of it.'

'If they're in a boat, or on some island, they may not have heard anything.'

Wilson said: 'We better take Essex to the county jail.'

Osborn persisted: 'But what will the men do if they don't get word from Tortoni?'

'God knows,' Crane said.

Tony Lamphier said: 'We've got to find her.'

Osborn asked: 'Do you think Essex knows where they are?'

'I'm sure he doesn't.'

'But how will we find her?'

'I wish I knew.'

Wilson said: 'Let's be going.' He held out a hand to Crane. 'You're clever. We'll let you know if anything develops.'

'Thanks.'

'If you ever come to Washington, look me up.'

'I never come to Washington,' said Crane.

Every one except Tony Lamphier left the room. Crane rested on the chaise-longue, wished he had a drink. These one-man shows always tired him.

Lamphier's long face was worried. 'What about Camelia?'

'I'm a lousy detective,' Crane said.

'You're swell. But I wish you could get her back.'

'I wish I knew how.'

O'Rourke came into the room. 'They've lugged Essex off to the bastille,' he reported.

'That's good,' said Crane.

O'Rourke's voice was brisk. 'Now that the case's washed up, when do we start spending that nine grand?'

Crane closed his eyes. He felt drowsy. 'Pretty quick.' He wished Miss Day would rub his head.

In dismay, Lamphier asked: 'You're not going to give up on Camelia? Not until you're sure she's . . . dead?'

'No,' said Crane. He cocked one eye at O'Rourke. 'What have you been doing, my man?'

'Talking to Essex.' O'Rourke walked over to the French window, leaned his weight against it. 'I was asking him about his sister. I don't feel so good about her?'

'What did he tell you?'

'He thinks she's in a boat.'

'Well, for God's sake,' Crane said. 'We know that.'

'I'm just telling you what he said, wise guy.' O'Rourke's manner was aggrieved. 'He said he gave Tortoni two rods and reels for the guys that took her to use.'

'Rods and reels?'

'Yeah. You know. Rods and reels.'

Crane sat up abruptly. 'Moses!' he exclaimed. 'I know where she is.'

CHAPTER TWENTY

THEY cruised across a *crème de menthe* ocean under a sky so brilliantly blue it hurt their eyes. Far astern, like spears on the horizon, were the palms of Key West, and ahead, was a flat sea. Afternoon sunlight fell in a golden flood on the trembling deck of the fishing-boat, and danced in silver flashes on foam flung from the boat's bow. In their ears was the beat of the engine, the irregular cough of the exhaust.

'It's calm, isn't it?' said Tony Lamphier.

Crane was leaning over the stern. They were in shoal water and he could see alternate patches of weed and sand on the bottom, six fathoms below. 'It's a good thing,' he said. Two small jacks, moving like rays of light, fled from the thrashing propeller.

'Are you a bad sailor?'

'I'm not any kind of a sailor.'

His face so rough, so crimson it looked like raw hamburger, Captain Luther Binton stood by the wheel, kept his boat pointed towards Dry Tortugas. He was an old man, but his back was stiff, his blue eyes keen. He had on brown shoes, blue serge trousers and a white shirt, and on his right arm was tattooed a blue anchor.

Crane asked him: 'Do you think you can find it?'

Captain Luther wasted few words. 'I kin if anybody kin.' His hair was perfectly white.

'You'll certainly know the boat, won't you?'

'I said I seen 'em. I seen 'em shootin' sailfish with a Tommy-gun.'

No breeze marred the smooth green surface of the ocean, nor brought them relief from heat hanging over the deck. Beside them the water mirrored the white side of the boat, the orange cabin. It was so utterly calm it seemed almost as if the boat and its shadow were standing still and the water was being rushed under them. There was no sensation of motion.

Engine vibration made the metal water-cooler by the cabin door rattle. Crane filled a glass, offered it to Lamphier.

'Thanks.' Lamphier drained the glass. 'It is hot, isn't it?'

'Hot as hell. Have some, Captain?'

'No.'

Crane had some.

Lamphier asked: 'What are we going to do if we spot them?' New lines at the corners of his eyes gave his long face maturity. He had a good jaw-line, wide-apart eyes under arched brows, pleasant lips. Crane wondered why he had disliked him at first.

He replied: 'Just spot them. O'Rourke and the other boys are getting a boat with a machine-gun.'

'Won't seeing us alarm them?'

'They'll think we're a fishing-party on our way to Tortugas. After dark we can turn round and sneak back to Key West.'

'And pick up O'Rourke?'

'Yeah.'

They were in deeper water now and the colour of the sea had changed from cucumber-green to a rich blue. It was no longer possible to see Key West. A school of flying fish skidded across the bows of the boat, made white dots of spray when it returned to the sea. It was hard to breathe in the heat.

'I thought the ocean was supposed to be cool,' Crane said.

'My God, I hope we find her,' said Lamphier.

Navy-blue water glided by the boat.

In the west, almost ahead of them, the sun looked like a red-hot coal. The water was blue-black. It was still hot. Captain Luther grunted, turned the boat slightly to the starboard.

'See something?' asked Crane.

'A vessel.'

Crane squinted at the setting sun, but he could make out nothing on the viscous surface of the ocean. The water appeared oily. Beside him, Tony Lamphier asked in a tense voice: 'Where?'

'You'll see,' said Captain Luther.

Presently, so close it surprised them, they saw a black and mahogany cruiser. It was a larger boat than theirs and it looked as though it were part of the ocean. It was motionless in the water, and two men, seated in wooden chairs, were fishing from the stern. KATE— MIAMI was painted on the stern.

'That's her,' said Captain Luther.

They passed within forty feet of her. Crane could hear Tony Lamphier's breath wheeze through his nostrils. One of the men was fat and he had on a white shirt with the collar tucked in, so that he appeared to be clad in his underwear. The other man was a blond with a face like granite. Both men looked hostile. Crane waved a hand, but neither replied.

The pair watched them as the gap between the boats widened. Suddenly the fat man stood up, ducked into the cabin, reappeared an instant later with another man. This man cast a quick glance at Crane and Lamphier, spoke angrily to the two men, darted back into the cabin.

'Can you get a little more speed out of her?' Crane asked the captain. 'I'm afraid we've been recognized.'

'She'll burn out a valve if I give her any more.'

'You better burn out a valve.'

The *Kate* was getting under way. She had powerful engines and the spray mounted her bow. She swung in a quick circle, started after them. There were four men on her deck now.

'They better not hurt my boat,' said Captain Luther.
Ahead of them the entire sky was yellow. The
engine, racing, shook the boat, made the metal water
container clang. Beside the bright sky the sea was
swarthy. Salt spray flecked their faces, rose in a henna
mist over the bow. The *Kate* came up fast.

Captain Luther shut off the engine, let the boat coast.
'They got the legs,' he said. He reached up on a shelf
behind the wheel and took down a three foot piece of
pipe.

The roar of the *Kate's* engines ceased; the *Kate* slid
up beside them. The plump man with the turned-in
shirt pointed at Crane. 'That's him, ain't it, Frankie?'
he said. He had a tiny red mouth, like a blood-sucker.

Frankie had no lobe on his left ear. His bare chest
was tanned nigger black under coarse hair. 'Bring 'em
on board,' he snarled. His face was pock-holed. He
was a stocky man. There was a plaster bandage on
his left shoulder.

The boats rubbed sides, clung together. The plump
man started to leave the *Kate*. Frankie had a sub-
machine-gun in his hands. Captain Luther moved toward the plump man, lifted the piece of pipe, and said:
'No, you don't.' The boats, deck touching deck, made
a creaking noise like a rusty door.

The plump man suddenly had a pistol in his hand;
he fired it once. An angry welt appeared on the side
of Captain Luther's forehead; the pipe, released, clanged
on the deck. Captain Luther fell forward, hit the deck
on his left side, and rolled over on his back.

The plump man stood over him. 'The old fool,' he
said.

Blood came from the welt on the side of Captain
Luther's forehead.

'Come on.' The plump man jerked the pistol at
Crane and Lamphier. 'Get in the other boat.'

They got in the other boat. There was anger in

Frankie's voice. 'Wise guys, hey? Catchin' up with us, hey?' Three bullet wounds had left white scars on the right side of his chest. 'Watch 'em, Dopey.' He looked over at the plump man. 'Anybody else on board?'

'Naw,' said the plump man. He was standing over Captain Luther. 'Nobuddy except this old fool.' He put the pistol in his hip-pocket. His skin had the pallor of a consumptive.

Dopey was a very thin man with an Adam's apple, a smudgy face and irregular teeth. The hand holding the pistol he had pointed at Crane shook. He had a neck-tie bound round his head.

At the *Kate's* wheel was the blond man with the granite face. 'For Christ's sake, Toad,' he said, 'why'd you shoot the old dope?'

'You seen him try t'hit me, din'ya?'

'Yeah, but now what'll we do with him?'

'Is he dead?' Frankie asked.

'Naw.'

Frankie said: 'Bring him on board, then. We may wanta talk with him. An' sink the boat.'

As though he had an ague, Dopey's gun hand trembled.

Crane said: 'For God's sake, point that somewhere else. It'll go off.'

Frankie said: 'Shaaat aap, wise guy.'

The plump man's eyes peered out from folds of unhealthy flesh. 'How'll we sink the tub?' He had a soprano voice. 'Bust out the bottom,' said the blond man at the wheel. He got an axe from the wall of the black cabin, jumped into the boat beside the plump man. He kicked Captain Luther's body. 'Tie the old pooper in a bung, Toad. I'll sink the boat.'

'I can't lift him,' said Toad.

'Aaw, nuts . . .'

Crane stepped towards Dopey, wrestled the pistol

from his hand. He turned to cover the man with the missing ear-lobe, saw something descending on his head, tried to duck . . .

Being tossed down the steps to the cabin floor brought him to. His hands and feet were bound with cord. He could feel the heat of the two engines, could smell gasolene and oil. A voice said: 'You two move and we'll plug ya,' and Tony Lamphier dropped heavily beside him, half across his feet, half on the cabin floor.

He could feel warm blood trickling over his forehead, down his cheek. His ears roared; his head was filled with exquisite pain; he would have liked to hold his head with his hands, but they were tied. It was dark in the cabin.

A woman's voice, frightened, whispered: 'Who is it?'

Tony Lamphier got to a sitting position. 'Camelia!'

'Who is it?'

'Tony.'

'Oh!' Her voice was glad. 'Oh, Tony!'

'Darling.'

'I knew you'd come.'

'Darling.'

I knew you'd come, Tony.'

'Are you all right, darling. Where are you?'

'I was so frightened.'

'Where are you?'

'On the bed.' There was a pause and then she said: 'Come up, Tony.'

'I can't. I'm tied.'

There was another pause.

'They've tied me, too,' she said.

'Poor darling.'

Crane moved his position so that his head was near the cabin entrance. He could hear voices outside. It was almost dark now. A voice which he recognized as that of the granite-faced blond was shouting:

'Come on, Toad! Scram! She's sinkin'!'

'I'm all right,' said Toad.

Frankie, authority in his voice, said: 'Come on, Toad.'

Tony Lamphier had moved to the other end of the cabin, just below Camelia's bunk.

'Who's with you?' she asked.

'Crane.'

'Did they shoot him?'

'No. They wounded our captain.'

'Badly?'

'I don't know.'

'How did you find us?'

'Crane heard about men shooting sailfish with machine-guns.'

'Yes. They do it every day.' Her voice was soft. 'Oh, Tony, I'm so glad you've come.'

'I'm afraid we're not much help.'

'Oh, you are. I've been so frightened.'

'Darling.'

Some one came down the cabin stairs, stepped on Crane, almost fell. He kicked Crane heavily in the stomach, then shoved him farther into the cabin, 'Keep outa tha way,' he growled. By hand he started first one engine, then the other. He turned a flashlight on Captain Luther.

'Gran'pappy's still out cold,' he called up the stairs.

He turned the flashlight on Camelia Essex. 'Holdin' up, kid?' he asked.

She didn't reply.

He said: 'Still givin' us tha Ritz,' and went up the stairs.

About ten o'clock the *Kate* put in at Little Hog Key. At least, that was what Crane heard the man with the granite face call it. The man with the granite face was named George, and he had apparently been a rum-runner in the old days. He piloted the boat, and held himself

aloof from the whispered conversation of the others.
They were trying to determine what should be done with
Crane and Lamphier. All were drinking rum out of
a jug.

They were quite close to shore. Crane could hear the
mewling of disturbed sea birds, the rustle of branches
being pushed aside, the lapping of water on land. His
ears still roared from the noise of the engines and his
skin burned from their heat. The engines ran hot
and once George had come down and tinkered with
them. After a time he had wiped his hands on a piece
of oil waste, thrown it in a corner of the cabin and
gone up the stairs.

'It's either timin' or the water-pump,' he reported to
Frankie.

Camelia Essex had gone to sleep.

'Poor kid,' said Tony Lamphier to Crane. 'She's
been scared to death.'

'I don't blame her,' said Crane.

For ten minutes the *Kate* lay at rest. Cool air came
in the port holes, fanned away some of the engine heat,
gradually took the cherry-red glow from the muffler and
the exhaust pipe. Waves murmured faintly under the
boat, against the shore.

Two men appeared at the head of the cabin stairs.
The voice of Frankie said: 'Bring wise guy out here.'

The men grasped Crane under his arm-pits, dragged
him up the stairs. They flung him on a leather-covered
seat by the port rail. 'Here's wise guy,' one of them
said.

Moonlight bathed the deck, the dark quay, the ocean,
with silver. The sky was lavender and the great moon
was the colour of a honey-dew melon. It was the colour
of a very pale lemon. Behind cordage on the deck,
behind chairs, behind the four men, were inky shadows.

'Search him,' said Frankie to the plump man named
Toad.

The man's hands were soft and clammy. He ran them over Crane's body, found the wallet pinned in his inside coat pocket. He opened the wallet. 'Jeeze!' His voice was reedy.

'What's the matter?'

'Nine grand,' said Toad.

'Wise guy had nine grand?' Frankie's voice went up the scale. 'Nine grand? Give it here.'

The tropic sea, in the path of light from the moon, looked as though it had been frozen.

'Where'd you get the nine grand?' asked Frankie. He was wearing a black suit coat over his bare chest and he put the bills in an inside pocket.

'Expense money,' said Crane.

'Jeeze,' said George. 'Maybe we should 'a' been dicks.'

'How'd you find us, wise guy?' asked Frankie.

'Some fishermen reported you as looking funny,' Crane lied, his eyes on Frankie's coat.

'I tole ya,' said Toad. 'I tole ya it wasn't safe to stick here.' His voice was alarmed.

'Shaaat aap,' said Frankie.

Around Little Hog Key were mangroves. Other foliage choked the shore. The mangrove roots, like the gnarled fingers of old men, were thrust into the salt water. It was impossible to see land on the quay.

Frankie asked: 'Why dinja have more people with ya?'

'They're coming in the morning,' Crane said. 'They've got all kinds of boats.'

'I tole ya,' said Toad. 'I tole ya.' His skin was greenish in the moonlight. His blood-sucker mouth was puckered.

'I think we oughta scram our of here,' said George. 'It'll be tough.'

'Yeah,' said Toad. 'Yeah.'

'We gotta lie right here,' said Frankie.

Dopey had taken the neck-tie from round his head. His hands no longer trembled. He must have had a shot. He said: 'If we ain't here the Boss can't give us the office.' His Adam's apple bobbed when he talked.

'Tortoni's never going to reach you,' said Crane.

'No?' said Frankie.

'He's dead.' Crane wondered how it was they did not know this.' 'He was shot for trying to muscle into the slot-machine racket.'

At first they did not believe him. The reason they had heard nothing was that their radio was broken. George had been unable to fix it. They hardly believed him, even when he went into details.

Frankie walked over to him when he had finished telling them. 'You lie.' His gold teeth flashed in the moonlight.

'No.'

Frankie hit him on the cheek-bone and then had to pick him off the deck. 'You lie,' he repeated.

'All right. I lie.'

'Yah!' Frankie scowled at him. 'You're yellow.'

'Sure, I'm yellow,' he said.

Frankie hit him again, knocked him against the side of the boat. 'Wise guy's yellow,' he said.

Crane's head spun, but he did not faint. The gnarled roots of the mangroves seemed to writhe in front of his eyes. The place on his stomach where George had kicked him suddenly began to hurt.

'I think he's giving it to us straight,' said George.

'A dick wouldn't give his mother tha right time, said Toad.

'I don't know,' said Dopey. He sounded frightened.

Frankie asked: 'How'd you find out about Tortoni if they knocked him off?'

Crane told them about Essex's part in the plot.

'That's the angle Tortoni was talkin' about,' said

George. ''Member he said there'd be no rap in tha case?'

'Yeah, I remember,' said Frankie.

'What'll we do?' asked Dopey.

'Les talk,' said Frankie.

He took Crane by the waist and lifted him off the seat. The hair on his chest tickled Crane's face; a smell of stale liquor, of sweat, was in Crane's nose. He threw Crane down the cabin stairs.

Landing on his right shoulder, Crane rolled past the engines. The ropes cut his ankles, his wrists. He lay absolutely quiet in the dark. The fall had started the blood flowing again from the cut on his head. His stomach pained him terribly.

Tony Lamphier whispered: 'Are you all right?'

'I'm fine,' Crane said.

CHAPTER TWENTY-ONE

A FAINT breeze, hardly more than a slow current of air, moved through the hot cabin, and Crane fell into a fitful sleep. He had bad dreams. He kept pulling bodies out of a burning house; hundreds of black bodies which crumbled when he tried to lift them in his arms. When he awoke there were moonbeams in the port holes on his right. The odours of oil, sea water and scorched paint filled the cabin.

What wakened him also wakened Camelia. She whispered: 'Tony.'

'Yes, dear?'

'I'm so glad you're here.'

'I'm not much help.'

'You are, though.   Now you're here I don't mind.'

'Really?'

'Darling, I don't care what happens as long as you're here.'

'You're brave.'

'No, I'm not.   I'm scared.'   Her voice suddenly went off key.   'Oh, Tony, get us out of here.'

Water murmured under the boat for almost a minute.

'I'm sorry, Tony,' she said.   'I won't do that again.'

'That's all right, darling.'

'Tony, do you love me?'

'Oh, yes, Cam.'

'I love you, too, Tony.'

Not far away Crane heard the sound of a boat being rowed.   The oarlocks grated and the oars made a sucking noise in the water.   He could hear men's voices. He decided the kidnappers must have landed on the quay and were now returning to the boat.

He heard a noise in the lower bunk to the left, saw Captain Luther Binton's head roll over to one side. The captain's eyes, open in the moonlight, were the colour of watered milk.   He was conscious.   Crane moved along the floor in his direction.

Camelia Essex said: 'Don't mind our talking, Bill Crane.'

'I don't.'

'Tony and I have such a short life ahead of us.   We have to be soupy, don't we, Tony?'

'Darling, we'll have a long life together.'

'A long, soupy life?'

'A very long, very soupy life.'

Camelia said: 'Don't mind our talking, Bill Crane.'

'I don't.'

'You're witnessing our love life.'

'That's all right,' said Crane.

'The short, happy love life of Camelia Essex and Tony Lamphier.'

'Darling,' Tony Lamphier said. 'Don't.'

The rowing-boat was alongside. George called: 'Everything all right, Dopey?' His voice was loud.

'Sure,' said Dopey. He sounded as though he had been asleep.

There was a noise of oars being shipped. Frankie said: 'Good ole Dopey.' He was very drunk. 'Trust him.'

The deck creaked under feet. Dopey asked: 'Wha'd you decide?'

'We're goin' t' croak 'em,' said Toad.

'That's good,' said Dopey.

'We figured it out.' Frankie's voice was thick. 'We croak 'em and scram for Miami.'

'The girl, too?' asked Dopey.

'Why not?' said Toad.

'Sure, we gotta croak her,' said George. 'She knows too much.'

Crane reached the captain's bunk, whispered in his ear: 'Are you all right, Captain Luther?'

The captain's voice was barely audible. 'No. What happened to my boat?'

'They sank it.'

The captain's hands were free. He said: 'Damn 'em.' Rope still bound one wrist. Crane, for the first time, felt hopeful.

Outside, Frankie's voice said: 'We take the nine grand and divide it up. That's only a grand less'n Tortoni was t'give us.'

'And we're in the clear,' said George.

'Clear as hell,' said Frankie. 'Clear as hell.'

'When do we kill 'em?' asked Dopey.

'Right away,' said Frankie. 'Before the sun comes up.'

'We gotta go out in the stream,' said George. 'The bodies'll never come up out there.'

'Sharks,' Toad explained.

'Le's get goin',' said Frankie. 'Wha's keepin' us?'

George came down in the cabin to start the engines. His breath smelled of Jamaica rum. He kicked Crane in the small of the back and turned his flashlight on Camelia. 'How ya doin', kid?' He turned to the engines.

One of the engines wouldn't start.. Presently Frankie came down. 'Wha's tha matta?'

'I'm damned if I know.' George spun the cast iron wheel viciously. 'But I'll make her go. See if I don't.'

Between drinks they finally got it going. The cabin reeked of rum and spilled gasolene. It was almost daybreak and Crane could see the men's dirty faces. They were both sweating. George threw a piece of oil rag in the corner of the cabin and said: 'Let's scram.' Crane could see a pile of oil rags in the corner. The men went up the cabin ladder. There was a long scar on Frankie's nigger-tanned back.

'They're going to kill us?' asked Camelia.

For the first time Crane was able to see her. Her blonde hair was tangled; her lips were pale; the tan had faded from her skin. Her hands were tied with linen strips in front of her and she was touching Tony Lamphier's head with them. Her white chiffon evening gown was soiled and one side had been ripped open, exposing half a peach-coloured brassière and part of her stomach. Fear had made her blue eyes luminous.

'Don't give up hope,' said Crane.

'What can we do?' asked Tony Lamphier.

'Can you untie your feet, Captain Luther?' Crane asked.

The captain tried to sit up, to reach his feet, but he was unable. He had lost a great deal of blood.

'How long has he been conscious?' asked Tony Lamphier.

'Shush,' Crane said.

The *Kate* was heading out to sea and the engines, racing, were getting hot. The cabin floor vibrated. On deck Frankie approached George at the wheel, a jug in his hand.

'Why do we dump the broad?' he asked.

George took the jug from him, had a long drink. He smacked his lips. 'I been wonderin' myself.'

'We could keep her around for awhile, anyway.'

'Sure.'

Frankie's gold teeth gleamed. 'I might even smuggle her into Miami. I know a place . . .'

'No, by God!' George's voice was ugly. 'We'll draw lots for her.'

Frankie took the jug from him. 'I'm tha boss here, see?'

'Like hell you are.'

Up the angling stairs Crane could see a portion of the rail, a rectangle of French blue sky. Heat from the throbbing engines burned his back, made his skin tight. He didn't dare look at Camelia.

'We'll draw lots,' said George.

'Like hell,' said Frankie.

'Like *hell*, like hell,' said George.

Toad moved into Crane's field of vision. His small eyes peeped between creases of flesh the colour of lard. 'Why not kill her?' he asked in his high voice. 'Why bother with her?'

'You wouldn't understand,' George said.

Heat from the engine was almost unbearable. The exhaust pipe was red half-way to the point where it went through the *Kate's* side. Crane tried to shove his back up the side of Captain Luther's bunk so the captain could reach his bonds, but he couldn't move off the floor. His legs were tied too tightly.

Dopey had joined the conversation on deck. His face was ghastly in the sunlight. It was the colour of a fish's belly. 'Let's get going,' he said.

Fingering his pistol Toad said: 'We're almost in the Gulf Stream.'

'What d'you want with the girl, anyway?' asked Dopey. His hands were fluttering again.

'Ha, ha, ha.' Frankie slapped his thigh. 'He wants t'know what we want wit' her. Tha's a good one. Ha, ha, ha.'

'There's plenty of dames in Miami,' said Dopey.

'Not like this one.'

In his reedy voice, Toad said: 'This one's too hot to take into Miami.'

'We gotta kill her,' said Dopey.

'Like hell.'

'Be reasonable,' said Toad.

'Like hell.'

George, alarmed, suddenly said: 'Holy smoke! Look!'

'What is it?'

'A boat.'

It was a large one, Crane gathered from their remarks, and it was coming their way. They decided it was faster than the *Kate* and therefore dangerous to run away from. Dopey came down into the cabin and put cloth gags on Camelia, Lamphier and Crane. He ignored Captain Luther.

'Just in case,' he said.

On deck the other three men watched the boat approach. 'He's going to hail us,' said George.

'Dopey, you and Toad start fishin',' commanded Frankie. 'Keep your hats over your eyes.' He came to the cabin entrance and got a Panama hat, put it on. 'George, you talk to 'em.'

The gag in Crane's mouth tasted of oil. He lay on his back, on his hands on the cabin floor, put his feet on Captain Luther's bunk. The captain got the idea, fumbled with the ropes around Crane's ankle. He had difficulty with the first knot, but the others came off easily. Crane rubbed his legs for an instant, then hooked his arm over the bunk and stood up. He found his legs would hold him. Captain Luther was untying the cord round his wrists.

The other boat had approached within hailing distance of the *Kate*. A voice called: 'Hello.'

'Hello,' replied George.

'We're looking for Captain Luther Binton's boat, the *Spray*,' called the voice. 'Seen any sign of her?'

'No,' said George. 'We been down to Tortugas all night. Is she lost?'

'We're supposed to meet her.'

'Well, we haven't seen her.'

The captain pulled the last turn of rope off Crane's wrists, then tried to yell for help. His voice was hoarse, feeble. Crane fell to the floor, rolled in a corner, holding his hands behind him as if they were still bound. Dopey came down into the cabin and hit Captain Luther over the head with a pistol butt.

'Try t'make trouble, damn you,' he said.

He went out on deck again.

The man on the other boat had heard nothing. He called: 'If you see the *Spray*, tell Captain Luther we're around, will you?'

'Sure,' said George.

The stutter of the other boat's idling exhaust changed to a steady roar. George gave the *Kate's* engines gas.

Crane got to his feet, pulled off his gag, looked out the port hole. His heart sank. The other boat was pulling away fast, already beyond reach of a shout.

Frankie was saying to George: 'We better scram out to sea. We're liable to run into somebody else.'

'That's what I'm doin',' said George.

Crane scooped up a handful of oily waste from the pile in the corner of the cabin. He dropped it on the glowing exhaust pipe. It burst into flame. He picked it up again, regardless of the blaze, and tossed it into the pile of waste. Orange light filled the cabin, billows of black smoke rose from the pile. He found a large monkey wrench and hid himself beside the cabin stairs. Camelia and Tony watched him through alarmed eyes. The heavy smoke began to pour through the port holes.

Dopey came to the cabin entrance, started to come down the stairs, suddenly thrust his hands in front of him. His voice yelped in terror:

'Fire! Fire! Heavens, a fire!'

George leaped to his side, jerked him off the cabin stairs, sent him sprawling to the deck. 'For Christ's sake, shut up.' He peered down at the smoky interior of the cabin.

Dopey got to his feet, yelled: 'Fire! Help!' Frankie knocked him down.

George shut off the engine and Frankie asked him: 'Where's tha extinguisher?'

'In the cabin.'

The bunk nearest to the pile of flaming waste had caught fire and the wood crackled loudly. Streams of smoke came from the port-holes and billows of it shot up the stairs. The fire was beginning to roar. It was terribly hot in the cabin.

George said: 'Take the wheel. I'll get the extinguisher.'

Slowly, stooping over slightly, he came down the cabin stairs. Crane waited until he reached the floor, then hit him on the head with the wrench. George's skull cracked like a dropped cantaloup. He pitched forward on to the port engine.

On deck Dopey was screaming again. 'Help! Fire! Help!' He was frantic with terror.

Smoke whirled about the interior of the cabin. It was terribly hot. The entire bunk was on fire, was covered with pale yellow flame. It was hard to breathe.

Frankie shouted down the stairs: 'How're you comin'', George?'

Behind him Dopey screamed: 'Help!   Help!'

Frankie shouted: 'George!   *George!*'

The smoke hurt Crane's lungs, choked his throat. He could taste oil in his mouth.   The fire roared.   His eyes smarted.

Dopey screamed: 'Help!   Help!'

Frankie tried to see into the cabin.

A voice from the sea shouted: 'Stand by, *Kate*. We'll help you.'

'Like hell.'   Toad's voice was shrill.   'Stay away.' He fired his pistol over the starboard rail.   'Damn you, stay away.'   He fired again.

Dopey screamed: 'Help!   Help!'

Frankie came part-way down the cabin stairs.

'George!'   Crane got ready to hit him.

The other boat had a Tommy-gun.   Over the roar of the flames it made the noise of long strips of canvas being torn.   Frankie said: 'Hell!' and went back up the stairs.   Toad was firing his pistol over the starboard rail.   Frankie got the *Kate's* Tommy-gun from the shelf above the wheel.   He was pointing it over the starboard rail when he suddenly began to cough.   The gun slipped from his hands, glanced from the rail, clattered on the deck.   He doubled over and pressed both arms against his stomach as though he were hugging a small child.   He coughed again and blood gushed from his mouth.   He fell against the rail. . . .

Crane went back into the cabin and picked up Camelia Essex and carried her up the stairs.   She was unconscious.   He laid her on the deck.   He went back and got Captain Luther.   He weighed less than the girl. He put him on the deck.

Dopey was lying curled up against the stern of the boat and Crane was unable to tell whether or not he was dead.   Toad had been shot in the right arm and he was trying to hold his automatic in his mouth and put a clip in with his left hand. His eyes were beady, like a chicken's eyes. Blood had turned his right sleeve maroon.

Crane went back to the cabin. Smoke choked his lungs. Tony Lamphier was unconscious, too. Crane tried to lift him, but he was too heavy. He dragged him to the stairs, tried to push him up them, but he couldn't get him off the cabin floor. George's body had slid from the port engine to the red-hot exhaust pipe, and the air was filled with an odour of cooking flesh. Crane got above Lamphier and tried to pull him up the stairs. He got him as far as the second step. His lungs hurt; he did not seem to be able to get air to them. He tried again to lift Lamphier.

Some one said: 'I got him, Bill.'

It was O'Rourke. Crane let him have Lamphier and followed them up the cabin stairs. A man with an extinguisher pushed by him, began to spray the cabin. The sunlight, the blue ocean, hurt his eyes; he felt very tired. The deck rose toward him. . . .

He felt sick when he regained consciousness. Smoke was still in his lungs, in his stomach. Captain Enright and a strange man with grey hair were working over Camelia Essex. Tony Lamphier was seated on the deck, conscious. His face was green under oil soot. The fire was practically out. Dopey was handcuffed to a fishing-chair in the stern and beside him sat Toad, holding his wounded arm on his lap. His eyes were closed; his face was calm. Frankie's Tommy-gun was lying where he had been shot, by the starboard rail, in a pool of blood. Crane felt sick again and for a moment he clung to the rail.

O'Rourke and Williams carried up George's body from the cabin. The exhaust pipe had seared the entire

left side of his face, and his blond hair was dark with
blood.

Williams had his feet. 'What'll we do with him?'
he asked O'Rourke.

'Throw him in the stern.'

'You're sure he's dead?' Captain Enright asked.

'Sure,' said O'Rourke.

They threw him in the stern.

O'Rourke said: '"Whoso sheddeth man's blood, by
man shall his blood be shed."'

'Oh, my God!' said Crane. His head was beginning
to clear. He no longer felt sick. 'Oh, my God,
O'Rourke!'

'Our hero's coming to life,' said O'Rourke.

Camelia Essex regained consciousness. 'Tony,' she
said. 'Tony.'

'Here I am.'

'What happened?'

Tony Lamphier got off the deck and took her hand.
We're safe, darling.'

Camelia Essex began to cry. She kissed him, crying
at the same time.

Captain Enright and the grey-haired man were
bending over Captain Luther. 'He'll live, all right,'
said the grey-haired man.

Williams picked up the Tommy-gun Frankie had tried
to use. 'A good thing he never let go with this,' he
said.

Abruptly Crane left the rail, ran toward Williams.
'What happened to him?' he shouted. 'What happened
to Frankie?'

'He fell into the water,' O'Rourke said.

'Did you pull him out?'

'He was dead,' O'Rourke said.

'You didn't pull him out?' Crane was frantic.
'Where is he?' He leaned over the rail, profoundly
moved.

O'Rourke pointed. The deep blue water of the Gulf Stream, twenty-five feet from the boat, was alive with sharks.

They swam close to the surface, showing soap-coloured bellies when they turned. Crane left the rail, slumped down on the deck.

'Why didn't you pull him out?' he asked.

The others looked at his disconsolate face.

'Why should we?' asked O'Rourke. 'What was he to you?'

'Nothing more than my right arm.' Crane's face was tragic. 'He just had my nine grand on him. That's all.' He gazed mournfully at O'Rourke. 'You let nine grand go to the sharks.'

'That's terrible,' said Tony Lamphier, 'but . . .'

'Here,' said O'Rourke. 'Here. I got the nine grand. I got it out of the pocket of that coat on the deck. . . . Frankie's coat. Here.'

'Why, you thieving rat,' said Crane. 'Picking a dead man's pocket. . . .'

VINTAGE CRIME titles available from No Exit Press

Fast One – Paul Cain
0 948353 03 1 (hb) £9.95, 04 X (pb) £3.95

Possibly the toughest tough-guy story ever written. Set in Depression
Los Angeles, it has a surreal quality that is positively hypnotic. It is
the saga of gunman-gambler Gerry Kells and his dipsomaniacal lover
S. Grandquist (she has no first name), who rearrange the Los Angeles
underworld and 'disappear' in an explosive climax that matches their
first appearance. The pace is incredible and the complex plot, with its
twists and turns, defies summary.

The Dead Don't Care – Jonathan Latimer
0 948353 07 4 (hb) £9.95, 08 2 (pb) £3.95

Meet Bill Crane, the hardboiled P.I., and his two sidekicks O'Malley
and Doc Williams. The locale of the cyclonic action is a large Florida
estate near Miami. A varied cast includes a former tragic actress
turned dipso, a gigolo, a 'Babe' from Minsky's, a broken-down
welterweight and an exotic Mayan dancer. Kidnapping and murder
give the final shake to the cocktail and provide an explosive and
shocking climax.

Green Ice – Raoul Whitfield (available January 1988)
0 948353 13 9 (hb) £9.95, 14 7 (pb) £3.95

Watch out for Mal Ourney: where Mal goes, murder follows. It is on
his heels as he walks out of Sing Sing after taking a manslaughter rap
for a dubious dame and follows him all the way on the trail of some
sizzling hot emeralds – 'green ice'. 'Here are 280 pages of naked
action, pounded into tough compactness by staccato, hammer-like
writing.' – Dashiell Hammett.

Death in a Bowl – Raoul Whitfield (available January 1988)
0 948353 23 6 (hb) £9.95, 24 4 (pb) £3.95

Maestro Hans Reiner is on the podium, taking the fiddle players
through a big crescendo. Then something goes off with a bang and it is
not the timpani. Reiner finds himself with a load of lead in the back –
and a new tune: The Funeral March.

The Virgin Kills – Raoul Whitfield (available January 1988)
0 948353 25 2 (hb) £9.95, 26 0 (pb) £3.95

More of the sharpest, toughest writing you will ever read – fast, lean,
without an ounce of sentimentality. 'Raoul Whitfield holds up better
than Ernest Hemingway.' – Pete Hamill.

If you want to obtain any of these titles, please send a cheque for the
appropriate amount, plus 10% for p&p, to: **Oldcastle Books Ltd,
18 Coleswood Road, Harpenden, Herts AL5 1EQ.**